ON
Human Hearts
AND
Hog Parts

Elizabeth Bedlam

to the one who found me

-liz

Cover by: **ELIZABETH BEDLAM**
Formatting by: ELIZABETH BEDLAM

Published by: **Bedlam ! Typehouse**
COPYRIGHT 2021 BY: Elizabeth Bedlam

This is a work of fiction.
No names have been changed, because....
The characters are invented & events fabricated.
All thoughts and opinions are that of the characters and should not be mistaken for the author's (who would **NEVER** foist her personal opinions on unsuspecting readers using the guise of a fictional character. That would be wrong.)

ALL RIGHTS RESERVED
NO PART OF THIS PUBLICATION MAY BE
reproduced,
stored in a retrieval system,
or transmitted, in any form
or by any means, electronic,
MECHANICAL,
photocopying,
recording, TELEPATHICALLY
OR otherwise,
without the prior written permission of the publisher.
...*But feel free to buy extra copies and leave them around town, on a bus, or in a motel room.*

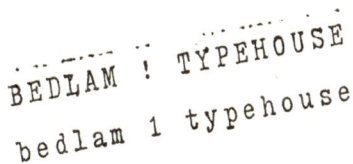

Bedlam ! Typehouse
Michigan USA
Instagram: @elizabeth.bedlam
Email: elizabethbedlam@gmail.com
Website: elizabethbedlam.com

One	1
Two	9
Three	35
Four	47
Five	79
Six	93
Seven	127
Eight	159
Nine	189
Ten	209
Eleven	235
Twelve	257
Thirteen	273
Fourteen	295
About	I
Also By	III

One

The drive had been long. Ashley felt sullen the whole way. Brenda knew moving would be tough, but she had already started questioning if it was worth it. She didn't see any other option. Ashley needed a proper school, with kids her own age. She wouldn't get that at The Oaks Clinic, despite her protests to the contrary.

Ashley made the argument that she didn't want to meet kids her age; she hated kids her age. They would all think she was a freak. At least the other patients at The Oaks didn't look at her weird when she made the mistake of talking to her voices. Wheeler, a fifty-year-old who had been at the institute for two years and in a criminal hospital for twenty years before that, was her only friend these days.

"It will not be like that. You'll make friends; kids your *own* age. You don't need to be in a hospital. You haven't had a serious episode in almost a year. Plus, there are some fantastic doctors at the university. I think you'll like Dr. Hart. He's one of the country's leading specialists in his field. You'll be in expert hands."

"That's bullshit. I like Dr. Prendergast. Or you. Why can't you just be my doctor? You know my brain better than anyone. You've scanned it enough times. You're smarter than half of those idiots." Ashley slumped in the car seat and watched the dull scenery of orange cones and road construction pass by her window.

The smell of tar came in through the air vents. Brenda tightened her grip on the steering wheel. She would not fight. She had decided this the night before. Ashley was going to be under pressure, her anxiety high. Fighting with her would only make things worse.

"I've told you before. I can't be your doctor. I'm just not qualified. You need a psychologist, a good one. Besides, I'll be busy teaching. We're lucky I could get that position in the neurology department."

Ashley mumbled under her breath. "What was that?" Brenda asked, turning down the radio. Ashley didn't answer; Lucifer was lecturing her from the backseat about how she had to improve her attitude towards her mother. Ashley had been pretending the whole way that the backseat was empty. He wasn't real; she knew that. Yet she heard him. He just droned on and on. She was hoping he'd stay behind and bug someone else. He was worse than a nagging girlfriend.

"She's not my fucking mother," Ashley told him, barely above a whisper.

"Ashley?" Brenda looked from the road to her daughter and back again. Traffic was crawling along. "Did you say something?"

"Ashley, answer your mother. She asked you a question. You should talk to her, not me." Lucifer told her. Ashley sighed. She wanted everyone to stop telling her what to do.

"I wasn't talking to *you*," Ashley said.

"Then who were you talking to?" Brenda asked, confused.

"What?" Ashley asked.

"I said, who were you talking to then if you weren't talking to me? You weren't talking to him again, were you? What did he say?" The idea that one of her daughter's hallucinations was Lucifer always disturbed Brenda. He had been with Ashley longer than Brenda had. Longer than any of the others.

In the case file, Ashley began talking to Lucifer as early as eight years old. The same year her birth mother tried to drown her in a bathtub. The same year the state took Ashley and put her into care. Brenda wouldn't even know about her until she was almost ten. By then, most of the therapists and doctors she encountered had already done their damage. Brenda didn't even want to think about how bad it could have gotten if she hadn't stepped in. She was just thankful now that Ashley was on a good path, and that horrible hospital shut down. Religious fanatics should not hold medical degrees.

Ashley shook her head. "Just forget it. You know I like Ash better than Ashley. Ashley sounds like a baby name."

Brenda shook her head, "Sorry. Ash... I'll try to remember." The pair drove the last hour in silence. Brenda did not understand how this was going to work. She just hoped that Dr. Prendergast had been right, that this would be good for her. Ashley had spent most of her life in hospitals. It was time to get her out into the world. She was going to be fifteen and needed some real friends. Some normal life experiences. It was going to be a big change for both of them. Brenda thought she was ready, thought they both were. But the closer they got to the city, the more she worried.

"I hate this house. I can't live here." Ashley said without even getting out of the car. Brenda took a breath.

"Ashley, we picked this house out together. You said it was perfect."

"I didn't know there was a church on the corner."

"You can't see it from any of the windows. Besides, it's a Unitarian church. Not Catholic. I checked. They are very progressive. You won't even know it's there. Do you think I would move us here if I felt it was unsafe for you?"

Ashley just shrugged, staring at the house. "Maybe you would. Maybe you just want to get rid of me. If I went missing, it would look like an accident. Tons of kids my age go missing every year. They never find most of them."

"Now you're just being dramatic. Let's just go look at the house. You might feel better when you're inside. The university and your school are in the other direction. You'll never even drive by that church unless you want to."

"Just try it. Brenda was the one who saved you from those crazy Bible thumpers, Ash. You can trust her. If she was going to turn you over to the church, don't you think she would have done it by now? It's been almost five years." Lucifer assured her. In the rear view mirror, Ashley saw Lucifer picking food out of his teeth with a tarnished dagger.

"Fine. Okay. I'll look at it. We drove all the way here. I just want out of this car. I can't think in this car!" It felt like everyone was breathing down her neck. She just needed a minute alone. She hoped her room had a door with a lock.

Thank god, Brenda thought and grabbed the house key the realtor had sent last week. "Here we go!" She said feigning excitement when all she wanted to do was have a glass of wine and a nap.

"What do you think?"

Ashley looked around. The place was old and out of date. The floors were scratched dark wood. Inside the front door was a thick banister and wide steps that disappeared into a second story. The wallpaper was yellow from age. It gave off the smell of stale cigarettes. The windows were grimy, sunlight filtered in through streaks in the dust.

"It looked cleaner in the pictures."

Brenda had to admit she was right. The photos made the place look vibrant and bohemian. Even in the late summer sun, the house was stuffy and grim looking. "We can clean it. We'll get some paint for the walls. It'll get there. And it's so close to everything. We can walk there if we want! It'll be great. This is going to be great!"

Ashley chewed on her lip. "Where's my room?" The hallway that led upstairs was dark. The Priest stood up there, slumped over, taller than the ceiling. He was urging her to come up. He was waiting.

"There are three, so I'll let you choose. All are upstairs. Why don't you head up and look around? I'll bring in our bags. The moving truck will be here in a few hours. Hey, want to order a pizza?"

"Chinese," Ashley said, continuing to look up the stairs into the dark void. She jumped when she felt the weight of Brenda's hand on her shoulder.

"It's okay. Just go up there. There's nothing there. Chinese sounds good. You good?" Brands asked, her voice gentle.

Ashley just nodded. "Yeah, I know. It's fine." Brenda turned away. Ashley swallowed her uncertainty. She knew he wasn't real. Despite her careful balance of medication, her revolving door of hallucinations continued to keep going round. At least she was sane enough to know they weren't really there. That thought should have been comforting, but somehow it wasn't. They were still scary, annoying, distracting.

She saw the smear of blue light out of the corner of her eye. "He found us." She whispered. For once, Lucifer said nothing. In her chest, Ashley felt the flutter of wings. Not soft or comforting, but rotten like roadkill flapping in the breeze of a passing truck. A bone was piercing her, sharp, irritating. She put her shoe on the first step. The wood protested under her weight.

One foot, then the other, she would pretend Priest wasn't there. When she passed by, she felt his drawn-out fingers run through her hair. Ashley grimaced and pressed herself against the railing. She heard the stomping of hooves behind her. She ran the rest of the way up the stairs, looking over her shoulder just once to see Lucifer, his twin Satan, reaching out, two beasts separating from one shared body, clawing and ripping Priest to pieces at the bottom of the stairs.

Brenda walked in with the bags, tracking blood across the floor into the living room. Ashley turned away, stiff. She ignored the snarls, the dying rabbit cries of Priest as Lucifer and Satan tore him apart once again. It didn't matter; he'd be back. He always found her in the dark. She took off down the hall and slammed the door at the end.

The room faced the backyard, a Maple tree right outside. She could watch the seasons change from the window. The house was old, so instead of a closet, there was a clothing rack in the corner. Ashley hated closets. The fewer places for something to lurk, the better. She refused a bed frame when Brenda suggested it. She'd had her mattress on the floor for the last five years. Nothing could hide under there.

Two

Brenda was excited to get their new life up and going. She had already set up an appointment with Dr. Hart. "He's very in demand. You're lucky he could make room for you."

Ashley rolled her eyes. She was tired of hearing how lucky she was. "I've been doing fine. I don't know why I have to go see this guy." She said, poking at her rice. "This looks like maggots."

"You're the one that wanted white rice. Do you want some of my vegetables?"

"No, it's fine." She'd just eat the maggots. Fantastic source of protein. What if they hatched and ate her out from the inside? No. That seemed unlikely. Her stomach acid would dissolve them before that could happen. Unless one got lodged in her throat.

Brenda went on, "... And you know why you have to go. You need support. That's what this is all about, continual support. It's nothing to be ashamed of. Everyone needs help sometimes."

"Yeah, but not all the time. No one needs to be on a million different medications, so they don't rip off all their clothes in the middle of the street and peel off their skin."

"You've never done that." Brenda took a sip of

wine. It was cheap, but she drank it.

"Not yet. But just wait, I'm sure it'll happen, eventually."

Brenda ignored this last comment. "Just eat. We've both had a long day."

"Do you want to walk or drive?" Brenda asked, looking out the window. "It looks like it might rain. What do you think?"

"I'm tired of being in the car. I don't care if it rains."

"I hate the rain," Lucifer complained.

"Then stay home." Ashley snapped. He didn't like the new room, he paced all night. He preferred a north-facing window so he could monitor the church down the street. Ashley told him to shut up about it. Lucifer didn't like the attitude Ashley was taking with him lately. She was moody, more like a woman than a girl. He shuddered. *Women*.

"Excuse me?" He and Brenda said at the same time. Ashley rubbed her face.

"Nothing."

"Did you take your pills this morning?" Brenda asked. Lucifer looked at Ashley. *Yeah, did you?*

"Yes, I'm medicated. Ready to see my crazy doctor. Let's go!" She took an umbrella, just in case it rained.

"Fine. We'll walk. And just as a side note, I don't appreciate the sarcasm. You know I only ask because-"

"I know because you care." Ashley finished the

overused line for her.

"And I love you." Brenda followed up. Ashley pretended to puke.

"I love you too." Lucifer tried to counter. Ashley glared at him; *you're a delusion.* She knew he was part of her mind, he and his twin Satan, the Priest, Sister Bathsheba, and her nuns, the Pope, the screaming birds, flies, zombie Jesus, and all the rest that showed up periodically.

Ashley heard about people with schizophrenia, who believed they were on a divine mission from God. That God loved them, protected them. She seemed to have the opposite problem. The Church felt threatening, evil cloaked in a bloody skinned lamb hide. It wasn't the FBI or the CIA out to get her; it was the Catholic church and its legions. The only thing that stood in their way was Lucifer, Satan, and their earthly minions. Ashley never understood how her mind got this so backward.

It would be much less scary to have an agent in an unmarked van following you than a mangled Jesus dragging a splintered cross, sinister clergymen, flaming torches, screaming hordes.

"So, you're an atheist then." Dr. Hart asked after she had explained that Lucifer was actually protecting her from the fictitious witch hunt that often felt uncomfortably real.

Ashley shrugged, "What's the point in praying to an empty heaven?" She asked, feeling the cast from the Bible was constantly following her, harassing her, waiting for their moment to pounce. "Plus, I feel like they're afraid I know the truth. That it's all bullshit. That my life's mission is to wake people up to the lies. They have to stop me. But I know that's all bullshit too." She smiled, feeling smart and clever.

Dr. Hart nodded. "That makes sense."

"Does it? Because it sounds fucking insane to me, and I'm the patient."

Dr. Hart liked Ashley. She was very intelligent and aware of what was happening, despite her age. All of his patients were older, at least twenty, mostly in their thirties and forties. Ashley had been in care since she was very young. She was a well-known case. Unique in more ways than one.

After reading her history, he understood how her mind might have put the Devil on the side of the savior, and the Church in the villain's role. He also worried knowing educated, self-aware schizophrenics tended to take their own lives if not treated and watched over. She knew what was going on. That her sickness would not stop, ever. That what she saw and felt wasn't real, despite feeling very real. A constant war in an unbalanced brain.

"You know your mother was a Catholic. She tried to harm you, do you think that has something to do with your paranoia?"

"Probably. I'm not the doctor. I know she was a crazy Jesus freak. That the place I was sent to was run by some sort of cult."

"Not a cult, the Church ran it. Saint Agnes Hospital. I feel you're old enough to understand the damage they did to you, but also that they probably thought they were truly helping you. Recovered Memory Therapy was all the rage back then. But your illness was more than likely triggered so early by the trauma of hypnosis on top of their various applied therapy techniques. I believe that's why you view the Church as the villain and the Devil as your savior."

"It's not always the Devil, it's Lucifer too. And demons, Satanists, anyone who looks um... I guess out of the ordinary."

"You're very perceptive for being only fourteen."

"I'm almost fifteen. Plus, being on a thousand different drugs and under constant observation really helps clear the mind."

Dr. Hart laughed. "So how has your mind been doing with all the changes? The move? Are you excited about going to a new school?"

"What do you think?" It irritated Ashley. Did no adult ever remember how horrible it was being the new kid? She had yet to meet someone who was perfectly honest in revealing how much it sucked.

"I think there'll be lots of new opportunities."

"Or lots of traumas." She'd only ever had tutors.

She went to regular school once for about a week when she was eleven, but Brenda removed her a month later after Ashley set the goldfish free from their glass prison. They ended up dying during recess. When one little girl said they had gone to Heaven, Ashley told her there was no Heaven. It was a myth that people made up to feel better about death. Was she stupid or something? Someday they were all going to die, then it would be soft black oblivion forever. The girl cried. Ashley wasn't paying any attention by this point. She wanted to paint.

"I think your daughter needs a special class," The teacher had told Brenda. It outraged Brenda. Ashley didn't need a special class. After that, Brenda paid for the tutor to come to the clinic out of her own pocket.

"Traumas? Why do you think that?" Dr. Hart asked. "Are you worried about your medications? Voices?"

"No. The teachers skipped me a grade. Everyone will think I'm a nerd. Plus, there's Lucifer. He whispers shit into my ear that makes me laugh, then people look at me like I'm crazy. I hate that. I don't want them to know I'm crazy."

"Of course not. We won't let that happen. You shouldn't view yourself as crazy, Ash. You have a chemical imbalance, serious past trauma, there's nothing you could do about it. But we could look into adjusting your levels. Maybe that could help lessen the inappropriate affect you've been having." He flipped a page to examine her medication list, a typical cocktail of anti-psychotic, antidepressant, and mood stabilizers. "We can talk to your mother about it."

"Brenda."

"Yes, Brenda. Should we invite her in?"

Ashley shrugged and looked out the window at the garden down below. They were several stories up; the city looked unforgiving and contrasted with the grounds. Unruly lines of nature clashing against man's controlled steel and glass. It hurt Ashley's head. She didn't like the city; she missed the soft surroundings of the clinic; out in the woods, miles from the villagers. She hardly ever went into town. All the noise of the city, she could hear it even now, so far up. Cars, people, constant murmuring.

"Ash?" Ashley turned, Brenda was there.

"Whatever you think," She blurted. Brenda and Dr. Hart looked at each other. Ashley felt she had missed something, but acted like it was no big deal. That was how she spent most of her life, acting as if whatever was going on was no big deal.

Bloody fights between demons and the clergy. The feeling of spidery hands between her legs at night, touching her while she begged for them to stop. Jesus tacked to a cross on the ceiling above her. Bloody pus seeping from his infected wounds onto her forehead. The constant static of voices in the air, coming from another dimension she couldn't see. Being stalked by the Church, maybe even kidnapped one day. No big deal. She was fine.

Brenda and Dr. Hart changed a few things around, hoping it would help with hallucinations and noise. Ashley knew it was useless. All the meds ever did was push the figures to her peripheral vision, she could still hear them. Feel them. Maybe they got replaced with something else. But they were still there. They always would be in one form or another.

People ignored all kinds of problems in their lives, why couldn't she? She saw Lucifer and Satan outside the window, blue and red streaks of light reflecting off the glass. The angel and the devil, two sides of the same coin. In the distance, Ashley saw a raised cross perched atop a sharp steeple.

"Can you close the curtains next time?" She asked on the way out.

Ashley followed Brenda. It had rained while they were in the doctor's office. The car lights reflecting off the wet surfaces hurt her eyes. They seemed unforgiving, accusing. She looked down at her feet. Brenda walked ahead, looking back every so often.

"We've got our first pieces of mail!" Brenda said as they climbed brick steps. The mail carrier nodded and walked next door. "Let's see what we've got." She filed through the letters and advertisements. "Here's one for you." She said handing Ashley an envelope marked up with ink drawings.

"Oh, it's from Wheeler! He said he'd write!" Ashley grabbed the letter from Brenda's tight grasp. Brenda didn't like this. She had nothing against Wheeler. He was a nice older man. But that was just it. He could be Ashley's father, but the two were friends on some level Brenda couldn't understand.

Brenda shook the rain from the umbrella and followed Ashley inside, tossing the rest of the mail on the table. "We've got a lot of unpacking to do. Maybe we could start in the kitchen? Then we wouldn't have to keep ordering takeout." Brenda said.

Ashley was sitting on the bottom step reading a three-page letter. *What could he possibly have to say that took up three pages?* Brenda wondered. They had only been gone a few days. "Well, what does Wheeler have to report?" Brenda asked, hanging up her coat.

"He's working on a sculpture for the art show. He wants to know if we'll be able to come?" Ashley looked up. "Will we? It's in November."

"We'll see. Who knows what will be going on by then."

Ashley frowned but kept reading. She laughed and turned a page over. "He is certain the nurses are taking secret photos of his penis while he's sleeping. For their own physical pleasure, he says." She shook her head. He was such a maniac.

"Ashley, that's disgusting," Brenda said, taking the letter. She had to start reading these things first. In it, Wheeler described in great detail exactly what he thought the nurses were doing with these secret pictures of his genitals. "This is inappropriate for you."

"Wait, let me finish. What else does he say?" Brenda scanned the rest of the letter. The skin on the pudding continued to disturb him. No one would do anything about it. The radio at the nurse's station was being taken over by a child's ghost named Esmeralda, but Ashely already knew about all that. He closed with sketches of the sculpture that he planned on starting- a bust of Callisto, a beautiful maiden in the front, with a bear exploding out the back of her head. "Wow, that's so cool, huh Brenda?"

Brenda grimaced, it was graphic and gory. "Very original." She folded the letters and stuffed them back in the envelope. "Let me read the letters first from now on, okay? Just in case he talks more about his... penis," She hated to say the word, but Ashley laughed.

"Whatever Brenda. I mean, who cares anyway? All guys have them. I have a vagina. You're a doctor, you know. It's just organs, blood vessels, nerves, whatever. They mean nothing. This body means nothing. It'll just be biological scrap one day. Then the dirt will swallow us back up and-"

"Okay, Ash enough. It's been a long day. And it's not about a penis or a vagina. It's about him being a fifty-two-year-old man and you being a fourteen-year-old girl."

"I'll be fifteen in a week. I don't care about Wheeler's penis if that's what you're worried about. My meds make me so dry down there I couldn't have sex if I wanted to. So who cares?"

Ashley stomped up the stairs and slammed her door. Brenda couldn't believe what she just heard. A typical parent would follow up on this, but Brenda knew Ashley needed a moment alone. It was just an offhand comment. Her teenage daughter was not thinking about having sex. Not sex with a man thirty-plus years her senior, and not in general. She didn't want to think about what kind of Pandora's box sex would bring into their life. She'd worry about that when she felt it was an actual threat. She prayed she had a few more years.

The two spent the weekend unpacking. It was taking longer than Brenda thought it would. She gave Ashley a box for her to unpack. "Put all the plates in here," Brenda told her while she worked in the living room. She came back an hour later. The box was half unpacked. Ashley was staring out the window. "Ash? What happened?"

Ashley didn't know what she was on about. "What? I'm almost done." To Ashley, she had just taken a break for a second. She didn't realize an hour had gone by. She thought she heard something tapping on the window. Maybe the clergy at the church knew she had moved in. She just wanted to be sure. She was checking the backyard. Whatever it was had gone.

There could be a tunnel that goes under the fence. Ashley thought about the old tunnels that ran under the clinic where she used to be. The staff would use them to walk from building to building in the wintertime. They were closed when she was there, but Nurse Sumner had shown her the entrance one time. There could be tunnels that lead down the street and to the church's basement.

"Do you know what was here before this house?" Ashley asked, watching Brenda finish putting the plates up onto the shelf.

"What do you mean?"

"Before the house was here. Was this part of the church?"

Brenda really hoped Ashley's new medication levels would help alleviate some of this. She was so focused on that damn church. "No, it was probably a field. The house is over a hundred years old. It had nothing to do with that church. That building probably wasn't even built until the fifties or sixties. Why are you asking this?"

Ashley shrugged, "nothing, it's stupid." She looked out the window again. There could be a hidden door under the grass somewhere that lifted up.

"You can tell me, it's not stupid. Remember what we talked about, if you're feeling worried or anxious about something you'll feel better if you just say it. So out with it, kid." Brenda stood up and went to look out the window. The yard was small, the old tree dominated the center. The whole thing was surrounded by a six foot tall privacy fence.

"I just thought... what if there were tunnels that run under the ground from the church to our house? No one would know they were there, and-" Ashley stopped in mid-sentence. No, that's not real. Why would she think this? *Stupid*.

"Ash, there are no tunnels. I promise. If there was, the house inspector would have noted them. Does that make you feel any better?"

In her human brain, it did. But still... *what if?* "Yeah. That makes me feel better. It's just..." Brenda knew it was coming. "Do you have a copy of the inspection report?"

Brenda sighed, "It's in the folder upstairs with the

closing papers and deed. Can I get it for you later?"

"Whenever," Ashley said. She didn't move from the window. What if there was a hidden door in the old tree? She'd seen something like that in a movie one time. Probably one reason Brenda closely monitored whatever she read or watched.

"You will not sleep tonight unless you see that report, will you?" When Ashley didn't answer, Brenda turned away to go find the papers. She knew it probably wouldn't do any good. Ashley's brain would just find another excuse, maybe the coal chute in the basement or the chimney.

Ashley laid in bed looking over the house papers. There was no mention of tunnels. But if the inspector was part of the church, he wouldn't reveal them, would he? Ashley thought about it. Who was the inspector? What was the name of his company? Maybe she could look it up, see if there was a company. Was this even the inspector's actual name, Ed Hastings?

"Ash, don't stay up too late. Tomorrow is your birthday! I thought we could do something fun before you started school. We have to meet the counselor on Monday."

"I've decided that I don't want to celebrate birthdays anymore. They're pointless. They're not real."

Brenda didn't know where to even begin with that. "Well, whatever. We can still go to the museum. We don't need an excuse. How's that?"

"Sure. history museum?"

"I thought the art museum," Brenda said.

"Can't we do both? It's not like I have anything else going on."

"If you feel up to it, why not? We'll decide tomorrow." Brenda knew they'd probably only make it through the history museum before Ashley complained about being too tired, or hungry. She refused to eat at cafes or restaurants because there were too many people around, all watching her. She wouldn't use the restrooms because they felt they were being monitored by a camera. Then images would be sent back to a group of pedophile priests who sold them to fund the Church. Brenda wouldn't hold out hope for the art museum. Maybe next time.

They barely made it through the first museum. Ashley was sure that a man taking pictures was taking pictures of her. "He's been following us all morning." She grumbled, annoyed Brenda didn't even care. What kind of caregiver was she?

"Maybe he's from the Church?" Lucifer asked. Ashley felt he could be right.

"He is wearing a lot of black. What if he's from the Church?" Ashley pointed out to Brenda.

"He's not even pointing the camera at you. I think he was in the last exhibit before us. So if anything, we're following him."

"Maybe that's how they planned it. Funnel us along like pigs to the slaughter. Soon they'll want to separate us." Ashley told her.

Brenda was trying to concentrate on the glass case housing an ancient mummy. "Look at this Ash; it's thousands of years old. Isn't that amazing?"

Ashley wasn't listening, and Lucifer wasn't impressed. "I've seen older," He commented.

Brenda walked over to look at the case filled with clay bottles that once held fresh organs. "Brenda!" Ashley ran after her. "You can't let them separate us." Brenda held Ashley's hand, and the two left the exhibit. Lucifer trailed behind, monitoring the suspicious man.

They picked up more take out food on the way home, Ashley would eat take out. No one was watching her. Plus, she felt if she let the food sit for a certain amount of time, say thirty minutes to an hour, the poison (if there was any) would dissolve because of the heat. Brenda didn't bother questioning this logic.

On Monday it was time to see the school counselor. Brenda had talked to Ms. Cutright several times before. She sounded concerned that Ashley might harm someone. "She's not violent. She just gets anxiety and sometimes has a little trouble concentrating." Ms. Cutright agreed to find out more about accommodating such a mentally ill student. Ashley would have to have her prescriptions on file. Emergency contacts, doctor's numbers.

"She won't be a problem." Brenda explained, trying to calm the counselor's fears. People heard schizophrenia and bi-polar together and assumed the worst. Violence, rape, murder, self-mutilation, out of control madman (or woman).

When Brenda laid out all the medication Ashley was taking, plus emergency stuff for anxiety and panic attacks the counselor relaxed even more. She felt confident knowing they could give the girl a tranquilizer if she had a psychotic break and threatened someone with a stapler.

Ashley didn't like the school when she finally saw it. It was a flat brick boring building built in the 1980s. The windows were tiny, there were no trees, only vast expanses of parking lot and cracked sidewalks. "Public schools are shit, Brenda."

"Don't swear in school. Please," Brenda begged. She had enough trouble getting Ashley to wear shoes instead of slippers. Actual pants instead of sweatpants.

Ashley tugged at her shirt. It was tight. Her pants fitted. She liked sweatpants and loose tank tops. At least Brenda let her wear her cardigan, though it was discolored green and had a few holes. It made her feel safe to be wrapped in something familiar to her.

Ashley took a breath and got out of the car. She wanted to be normal. Normal kids went to school. No one would have to know she was unbalanced. She could play normal. She told Lucifer to stay home. For once, he listened. He promised he'd keep watch in case anyone tried to break in and install cameras while she was gone. Ashley didn't like this new medication. It gave her a dry mouth. She swallowed.

"Do you need water?" Brenda asked. "Here let's get one." She stopped at the vending machine just outside the main office and pushed in a few quarters. She handed Ashley the cold bottle and Ashley drank half of it. She felt better. An electric bell buzzed and students wandered out into the hallways. Their chatter growing louder, an approaching wave of voices ready to crash around her. Ashley quickly pushed Brenda through the heavy office door. The thick glass muffling the noise.

She sat down in the nearest chair. It felt like everyone passing by was looking at her. She thought she saw a group of nuns. She turned away from the window but still felt like she was in a fishbowl. Brenda was talking to a secretary. Ashley bit her fingernails and wished Lucifer had come. She felt safer when he was there. A few kids walked into the office, their glances said they were not impressed.

Brenda signaled for her to follow. Ashley got up and tried to push past the three students. She stepped on the foot of a boy. He grimaced. "Shit, sorry," Ashley said. Brenda threw her a disapproving look. *No swearing*. Ashley had spent practically her entire life around the middle-aged, mentally ill who smoked and swore. It would take a while for her to break the habit.

"I mean sorry. I'm sorry." Ashley told the kid.

"Don't worry about it." He told her. The two girls he was with tried to pretend like nothing was happening. They just looked straight ahead, attempting not to stare. As if they already knew she was crazy, and you should never make eye contact with a crazy person.

"Okay. Thanks. Sorry." She said. She didn't look back, she felt her face burning. She should have never left the house. All she did was embarrass herself. She just knew her chest was red and splotchy, and those kids would probably be in every one of her classes. They'd tell everyone she stomped on his foot. They'd all wonder what was wrong with her. She thought about feigning a hysterical episode just so she could go back to the institution, but knew Brenda wouldn't fall for it.

"In here." The counselor told them. Right away Ashley didn't like her. She was maybe fifty, had dry brown hair, carefully styled, and tight lips. Her voice was monotone. "Please sit. Ashley? So nice to meet you."

"Ash."

She looked over at Brenda and smiled a tight calculated smile, "I'll make a note of that." Turning back to Ashley, "So how are you feeling? Brenda has caught me up on your colorful history."

"*Pff*, if that's what you want to call it." Ashley rolled her eyes, Brenda nudged her and gave her The Look. The Look that said she was being rude and maybe didn't realize it. Sometimes she didn't know how blunt she was being. How it could offend people.

The three sat in silence, trying to decide where to pick up after that. Ms. Cutright shuffled some papers, "Let me just pull up your schedule here and we can go over it. If you feel we need to make adjustments, just let me know. I have informed your teachers about your conditions. So if you need a break or longer testing time, just let them know in private beforehand."

Ashley wasn't worried about it. Adults usually let her do whatever because they were afraid she'd lose it and stab someone or start crying uncontrollably. She could see it now on the counselor's face. Tense. One wrong move could cause a lawsuit or a complete breakdown ending in bloodshed and suicide. The woman knew Ashley was on medication, that she wasn't fucking dangerous. Yet still she was held at arm's length.

Ashley felt sick in the pit of her stomach. Was this how her entire life would play out? Complete strangers frightened of her? For the first time in a while, she found she wished for premature death or lifelong institutionalization. People just let her down. She told herself she wouldn't make any friends, because once someone got to know her, they wouldn't like her. She was fine with being alone. Fuck people. Fuck Ms. Cutright.

"Ash, how do the classes sound? If you think Spanish III is too much, we can switch you to a study period during that time."

"Yes, please."

"Yes, what?" Brenda asked.

"No Spanish. Study period instead." Ashley said.

Brenda nodded and looked at Ms. Cutright, "Okay, study period it is then." The counselor gave a heavy sigh, like it was too hard for her to pull up the file and correct it. Ms. Cutright mentioned on the way out she'd have a student guide show Ashley around. Ashley groaned. Why did everyone think she needed to be watched constantly?

Brenda could see the discomfort on Ashley's face, "I think you'll be alright on your own. What do you think, Ash?" Both women looked at Ashley. She couldn't meet their gaze.

Ms. Cutright was late for her lunch. She clapped her hands, "If you feel you'll be okay…" She left the end sentence lingering in the air.

"Do all new students get a personal guide?" Ashley asked her.

"Um, well, no."

"Then I don't need one. I can figure it out." Ashley said.

Ms. Cutright printed out Ashley's schedule. "This is just for now. If you feel you need reduced hours, please come in anytime and make an appointment. That's why I'm here."

Brenda thanked her, Ashley nodded. She got it. Make an appointment meant don't come bursting in. Reduced hours was code for too crazy to hack it in the *real* world. "Want to look around before we go? Ms. Cutright said it would be fine." Brenda said. Ashley shrugged, a prison was a prison, be it medical or learning. If you had to ask to use the bathroom, if someone always had to know where you were going, it was a prison. Lipstick on a pig was still a pig.

"Why not?" Her tone was dry. She could hear voices in the cafeteria. She looked in as they passed. There was no way she could eat in there. She had the option to eat in the office if she wanted, but Ashley knew it would be impossible to eat at school.

She'd just have to fast all day. Not that that would be a bad thing. Her medications made her gain a good fifteen pounds, which she hated. She felt bloated and uncomfortable. Eating less might help some. She was trying to see the positive, like Brenda and her doctors said. She was starving herself because of her unease of eating in front of strangers therefore losing weight. Every cloud has a silver lining.

Brenda pointed out the room numbers on Ashley's schedule. They found her locker. "I won't be using that." There was no way Ashley was leaving her stuff behind for just anyone to go through. Those locks were cheap and easy to break. She'd just carry everything.

Brenda was looking at the map, trying to find which way to the chemistry lab. Ashley saw the kid who's foot she stepped on standing outside the cafeteria. He saw her. His friends noticed and looked too. Ashley looked away. She hated meeting new people. When she looked back a girl waved. She was chubby and wearing glasses; she felt less intimidating. Ashley gave a small nod before Brenda pulled her off in the other direction.

Ashley was pleased. She felt that went well, a casual tip of the head, no embarrassing words. At least no one was laughing at her. It seemed friendly. She didn't feel so self-conscious. Maybe she had made a friend. She smiled down at the paper in her hands. Perhaps she could fit in.

"Get some sleep. You've got a lot to do tomorrow." Brenda said for the tenth time as she turned out the hall light. "Oh hey," Brenda called before heading into the bathroom, Ashley turned, "I'm so proud of you, kid."

"So you've said." Ashley didn't say it, but she felt proud of herself too. She was pushing herself. Maybe she could function in a world of color outside the white institutions she'd known. She laid down in bed, her mind still talking. *But what if I can't?* What if she wore something stupid or did something so everyone looked at her? What if she had an episode in the middle of class? She could never show her face again. Maybe all these thoughts of fitting in, being liked, and having friends were just new delusions she'd didn't recognize yet?

Ashley's breath came quicker, she felt panic in her chest. She attempted to take control back from her endless stream of worry. *Just sleep*, she willed herself. Lucifer occupied his time on the roof. She hardly saw him in the last few days. School would be fine, there was no way the Church could get her there. No religion in public schools, right? She was worrying over nothing. She had to sleep. She forced her breathing to slow, practiced relaxing her muscles. It was going to be good.

Manic weeping woke Ashley up. First, she heard it in her dream, but as she came out of sleep, she noticed it was growing louder. Then chanting, quiet repetitive chanting. Ashley opened her eyes and looked down her mattress towards the door. A woman wrapped in a torn blue dress paced back and forth. She had dark brown staining down the front of her gauzy rags. The woman wept and muttered to herself, pulled at her wild red hair.

Ashley swallowed, the woman turned to her and began ranting louder in a language Ashley couldn't understand. She pointed a finger stripped of flesh at her and screamed accusations. Ashley tried to get up but was pulled back down to the bed by praying nuns. Three knelt on either side of her, their habits long and moth-eaten. The nuns repeated a phrase over and over. Ashley felt their curved talon hands encircle around her wrists and legs. They sunk the claws in deep and pinned her in place.

She couldn't speak. One pierced her throat with a finger. The woman continued to scream. The nuns chanted. Above her bed, a crucified baby began crying and rapidly growing into a man. His body contorted and formed around a wooden cross like a tree would grow into a metal pole or a mesh fence. Conjoined.

Blood wept from blistered sores. Trickled slowly onto Ashley's forehead, falling between her eyes. "No, no." She finally said, twisting her face away. But it did no good. The clergy held her still, their humming growing louder to drown her out. Wailing from the wounded man above her, who was quickly growing skeletal, but his stomach was bloating. His rapidly stretching skin burst open, spilling his innards onto her.

Ashley screamed, this time at the top of her lungs, the heart dropping into her mouth. She swallowed it and felt it was choking her. She wanted to spit the vile thing out. Her clothes and mattress were soaked through with viscera and pungent fluids. She felt she was dying, she couldn't take in air. The talons of the nuns, growing longer, sank deeper, and infecting her with venom like snakes.

She wanted to call out for Lucifer, but she only gagged. The screaming woman was on top of her now, banging on her chest, demanding answers to something. Ashley closed her eyes, feeling it was all over. She received the raw embrace of inner peace, a feeling of which she had never truly known but desired above all else.

Brenda threw on the light and was shaking her daughter, calling her name. Ashley sounded like she was suffocating, her arms were bleeding. "Ashley, wake up!" Brenda screamed.

Brenda picked her up off the bed and took her to the bathroom and set her in the tub. She ran cool water and placed a rag on her daughters' forehead. She was red, sweat glistened on her face. Her clothing soaked. "Breath Ash, breath!" Brenda ordered her.

Finally, after what felt like minutes, Ashley took a gulp and came out of it, screaming and clawing at the air. She scraped Brenda across the cheek.

Brenda held her close and hugged her. "It's me. You're safe. You're safe." She told her. Ashley was panting and her body shaking. She was sitting in a tub of water but felt like she was on fire. On her arms were long shallow scrapes. She'd have to wear long sleeves to school now.

"Did I do that?" Ashley finally asked. Brenda gave her a sad nod.

"What did you see? What happened, do you remember?"

Ashley did, but didn't want to. "No, nothing. I don't know. It felt like I was choking on something." The rancid heart of the Christ corpse. Brenda looked like she didn't believe her, but helped Ashley out of the tub.

"Wrap yourself up in this. I'll get you some dry clothes."

Ashley sat on the floor watching Brenda put a fresh sheet on the bed. "It's too much stress. All this change. Maybe you should start school part time and work your way up to a full day." Brenda went on, stripping the pillowcase.

"It has nothing to do with that. I'm fine. If I'm going to go, then I want to just jump in. I'm tired of everyone treating me like a headcase. I'll adjust."

Brenda tossed the clean pillow on to the bed and looked at her daughter, "Fine. but if it gets to be too much, tell me before..." she didn't want to use the phrase *psychotic episode*. It was too harsh. "Before you begin to feel out of control." Ashley agreed. She had this. She had to grow up sometime. She didn't want to spend her life being constantly worried over. Someday she wanted to live on her own, have an actual life.

Three

Brenda dropped Ashley off in front of the school. Ashley told her she'd walk home. The office had a list of numbers and all her medication. If she needed anything tell someone. Ashley got out of the car, Lucifer was but a smudge of light in the back seat. He reflected off the glass as the car pulled away.

Ashley wished she could shake this one last constant vision. He was less with her new prescription, his influence over her weaker, but he was still there; more a feeling than anything else. It wasn't real, any of it. He never was. She just had to keep that in mind. She was stronger than the chemical imbalances in her skull. Stronger than her diseased ancestry. Once she accepted this, she wouldn't feel the need for a protector.

For the first half of the day, school seemed alright. It wasn't much stricter than the institution. The teachers (all informed of her delicately balanced mental state) sat her in the front. Ashley wasn't sure she liked this. Eyes all staring at the back of her head. She tried to ignore it. Everything was normal. She decided it was much easier to pay attention when all there was between her and the lesson was the teacher. She tried to phase everything else out.

Ashley felt that her teacher was irritated with her. She knew most of the answers as her tutors had already covered the topics. She stopped raising her hand after her American History teacher suggested she give someone else a try. Ashley noticed no one else was raising their hand but the chubby girl with glasses she had seen the other day outside the cafeteria.

Her name was Gretchen. When they spoke after class, Gretchen told her not to worry about knowing all the answers. She was glad to have someone else to take the heat off her. No one did the work. It was usually just her and the teacher having a discussion. This made Ashley feel better. Gretchen showed her to the science lab. "I'll see you around." She told Ashley before disappearing into the horde.

Ashley spent lunch in the library reading a book Wheeler had given her about Objectivism. It was interesting. Ashley always liked to read about other people's philosophies, even if she didn't follow them herself. Cults, followings, and religious organizations all fascinated her. Maybe by understanding them, it would make her feel less anxious about the Church. Know thy enemy and all that. If she understood how they operated, she could anticipate their next move.

A loud handful of kids came in. The librarian told them to shut it. The girls giggled. The two guys didn't even pay attention. They sat at a table across from Ashley. She noticed they were passing around a thin paperback. "Just let me see," the purple-haired girl begged, yanking the book from her friend.

"Careful, that's my only copy. Those things are impossible to find. They stopped printing them years ago. Wish I could get my hands on the first book. Heard that one was even more screwed up." The long haired boy said. Ashley thought about asking them what was so fascinating. The second boy in an old army coat noticed her staring. He stared right back as if to ask her what was she looking at?

Ashley went back to her book. The bell rang, and she gathered her materials. The group and their mysterious paperback left as loudly as they came in. Both girls glared at Ashley on the way out. They probably assumed Ashley was staring at one of their boyfriends. But she didn't think about stuff like that. Her life was complicated enough without adding relationships to the mix.

It turned out the purple-haired girl and her blonde friend were in Ashley's art class. Ashley sat down near the door while the art teacher explained to her they were working with watercolors. "Have you ever painted before?" She asked.

"At the institution, I painted every day. We had a great teacher." A few kids threw her a strange look, *institution*? Ashley looked at her blank canvas. She hadn't meant to say that. She was just so used to it. She decided if they asked, she'd lie and say it was more like a private school.

"That's great. I'm glad you're familiar with the medium. So get started. You can choose from any of the tables." The teacher motioned to three small round tables set up in the middle of the room. Each one contained various objects- a vase of fake flowers, a bowl of fruit, a stack of books with a candle sitting on top.

Ashley sighed, she hated painting still life. It was so mind numbing. They had cameras to take pictures of this kind of stuff now. She didn't see the point. However, she wanted to fit in. She didn't want to cause trouble on her first day. She chose the end table closest to her with the stack of books and the candle.

She began painting realistically, but then decided the colors were dull. She added more blues and grays, deep black shadows with sharp lines. She painted in a screaming face for the candle flame. "Wicked," Ashley looked up and saw the two girls from the library admiring her work. "Where'd you learn to paint like that? Mine looks like a big wet mess." The blonde said.

"An art teacher at my old school, he used to be a professional until..." until he snapped and started licking the wallpaper, convinced each color would reveal secret messages from the dead. Green tasted like avocado and meant to invest in the stock market. "Until he retired. He used to show in galleries." Ashley told them, feeling her confidence growing.

"Sweet. I'm Kristin. This is Gia." The purple-haired girl told her. They didn't feel so mean now. They weren't scowling at her, but seemed to like her painting.

"Hey. Ash." She said. She had worked on her introduction all night, trying to sound calm and collected, bored even. That was how teenagers sounded, apathetic, and already tired of the world.

"Didn't we see you in the library?" Gia the blonde asked.

"Yeah, I don't eat lunch. So I thought I'd just read instead."

"That's cool. Well, see you around." Kristin said, and they walked back to their desks. At the end of the period, Ashley saw the teacher frowning at her painting.

"The point of still life is to capture what you see in front of you. We'll try again tomorrow. Nice try though," She offered. Ashley rolled her eyes and threw her painting into the trash. "Oh no, don't throw it out. It's perfectly lovely. Just not what the assignment was."

"Then it's garbage. Whatever. Fuck the painting." Ashley said and walked away.

"What did you say?" The teacher called out from behind her. "Hey, come back here." Ashley kept walking. She had to get across the school to her English class in less than five minutes. She wasn't sure where she was going. She didn't have time to coddle every hurt ego. She figured the art teacher, what's-her-name, was an adult. She'd be fine. She probably shouldn't have cursed. Though to be fair she didn't curse at the teacher but at her own painting. She was more anxious about finding her class. Kids packed the halls. It felt hard to breathe. She didn't expect it to be this crowded.

Ashley sat down at her desk just before the bell, already forgetting about the art incident. Kristin walked in and sat a row behind her. "That was hilarious." She leaned forward and said to Ashley.

"What? What happened?" The boy with long black hair came in and sat across from Kristin.

"Ash just told Mrs. Thurston to go fuck herself." Kristen giggled.

"No, I said fuck the painting. It wasn't even a big deal." Ashley said. Both Kristen and her friend burst out laughing.

"Ash, this is Nick." Nick nodded. Ashley did her casual head nod to acknowledge him like it was no big deal. She had tons of friends. Though she didn't see what was so funny. They were just words. Wasn't high school supposed to be preparing young people for the real world? They cursed in the real world.

The teacher, Mr. Hoyte, motioned for everyone to sit down. Before he could go any further Mrs. Thurston and a man in a wrinkled gray suit appeared in the doorway. They pulled Mr. Hoyte aside and whispered something to him. He nodded and seemed concerned. "Ash, they need to see you in the office," he told her. The rest of the class sat silent, listening. What had the new girl done?

"Why?" Ashley felt it was her right as a human being to ask. Apparently though, adults did not like being questioned by a fifteen-year-old girl.

"There is just a little misunderstanding that needs to be cleared up." Mr. Hoyte was trying to be diplomatic, Ashley respected him for that, but this whole thing felt stupid and unnecessary. It was just a dumb painting. If she wanted to throw it in the trash, who cares? And that was what she said.

"It was my painting. Can't I do with it what I wish?" Ashley countered, still sitting at the desk front and center.

"This isn't about the painting, but the way you spoke to Mrs. Thurston." The man in the gray suit said.

"Oh, Christ! She's a fucking adult. Is this happening?" Ashely burst out. Her words were louder than she meant them to be. Kristin and Nick laughed. The rest of the class shifted uneasily in their seats.

"Now please, Ash. Mr. Hoyte needs to get on with class."

"This is unbelievable. Now I remember why I never went to school. It's bullshit. I just want to learn, not kowtow before the authority of a middle-aged woman with a bachelor's degree in fucking art!" Ashley screamed and shoved her desk out in front of her. She grabbed her stuff and ran from the shocked room.

Ashley dodged into the first bathroom she came to and slammed the stall door. She wished Lucifer was here. He would have reasoned with her, kept her calm. But all the eyes were looking at her, the stupid teacher and her pinched, angry face. At the clinic, no one would have batted an eye, but here Ashley knew they'd all be talking about her. "Fuck!" She screamed and kicked the door.

She heard heels tapping on the tile floor. "Ash? It's

Ms. Cutright, I need you to come out here, please." Her voice was low and controlled. Ashley did not want to see her.

"Call Brenda. I want to get the fuck out of this fucking school!" Ashely screamed. The bathroom was getting hotter, too small. She was tired of all these people directing her, telling her what to do and say.

She felt her heart scraping in her chest against a fractured rib. God, had she gotten so angry that she cracked her own ribs? Or maybe her lungs were still filled with the black putrid blood of the Christ heart that dropped into her mouth last night. Or there were always the flies. The flies eating away at her insides, changing her. Maybe her panic had upset them. She tried to open the stall, but the bones in her hands had turned to dust. She couldn't work the lock. Ms. Cutright was banging on the door from the other side.

"You need to open this door now, Ashley. We can call Brenda, but you need to come out." Ashley felt Ms. Cutright's words were urgent, like she wanted to get Ashley out of there and make her disappear before anyone could question what happened to her. If she went with her, what if they didn't call Brenda? She felt Cutright wanted to take her to the basement. She could be one of those nuns that was beside her bed.

Ashley was sure she had heard that voice before, chanting, screaming. Ms. Cutright began pulling on the door. Ashley covered her ears. The scraping of claws on the metal door was ringing loud in her head. "Stop. Stop it!" She screamed, squeezing herself between the wall and the toilet.

Brenda was in the school office within the hour. Ashley cried that she didn't understand why they were going to lock her up. When she saw Brenda she grabbed her and held on. "Don't let them take me to the basement, Brenda. Cutright is with *Them!* I don't know why they won't just let me go to class. I didn't do anything!"

Brenda didn't know where to begin. They had explained the entire situation to her on the phone, but she didn't think Ashley was so hysterical. "Calm down. You're fine. You're fine." Brenda soothed the girl. She was trembling, her hair tangled.

Ashley covered her face, Brenda ushered her out to the car. Gretchen and her boyfriend stood on the sidewalk watching the new girl dry heaving and crying in the front seat of her mother's car. "Isn't that the girl in your history class? I thought you said she was some sort of genius."

Gretchen shrugged, "I don't know. She just seemed weird, I thought maybe it was because she was so smart. She stepped on Kevin's foot too. Who knows?" The two watched the car pull away from the school.

"We're going to try something different," Brenda told Ashley one evening a few days after the event.

Ashley felt like a psycho, she couldn't believe she

lost it so quickly. How could she have not seen what was going on? "Ms. Cutright and Principal Waterhouse feel maybe you should go half time. Dr. Hart agrees. It could help with things."

"What would half time mean?" Ashley asked, tossing her over-read copy of *Cat's Cradle* aside.

"You'll go to school for the first half of the day. You can pick up your assignments in the office each morning, work on them in the library till lunch. If you have questions, the teachers will be right there. After lunch, you can come home. How does that sound? I think the stress of all day was just too much to start with. I should have known." Brenda said.

Ashley looked around for Lucifer. He usually gave her guiding advice. He was nowhere to be seen. Dr. Hart had prescribed liquid Clozapine since her other drugs seemed to falter in times of great tension. She felt like she wanted to crawl out of her skin.

"It'll take a few days to get used to. We'll start at an extra low dose. You can split it into two if you prefer." Dr. Hart wanted her to stay home for two weeks. That was fine with Ashley, she couldn't think about school right now.

Brenda was waiting for an answer. Ashley looked down at the pink scrapes on her forearms. "That's fine, Brenda, whatever. Everyone probably already thinks I'm a lunatic. At least this way I won't have to hear about it."

Ashley turned away. She thought about Gretchen, Kristin, and the few others who spoke to her. She was stupid for thinking it would be that easy. Even without hallucinations or voices, she felt her brain was unhinged, swinging one way then the other. It also didn't help that she'd spent most of her time up till now with adults who treated her like an adult. What was she thinking going to that school? Trying to make friends. She felt like a wolf covered in sheepskin. Heavy, wet, a complete and utter fake.

Brenda went to make dinner. She knew when to leave well enough alone. After the episode at the school, Dr. Hart had assured her they'd find the right balance between school, medication, and therapy. The episodes and nightmares were likely because of anxiety from all the changes in the last month. That was probably undoing a lot of her progress she'd made in the last two years. Ashley just needed to reduce her activities for a while.

At the table, Ashley gulped down two glasses of water and pushed her plate aside. Her appetite had disappeared. Brenda told her it was a side effect of the medication, but Ashley was sure it was because there were flies inside her.

She thought she heard them buzzing at night when she was falling asleep. They concerned her more than the screaming bloody woman in the corner or the warped Christ figure over her bed. Those images had grown feeble and weak. She barely noticed them. But the flies inside were eating her humanity. She was becoming something else, a ragged shell of a girl. She was afraid Dr. Hart would want to put her back in the hospital. A *real* hospital.

Not a clinic for the semi-functioning crazy, but one with small rooms and tiny windows. Maybe one owned by the Church. She made a note to herself that next week when she went to see him, she'd tell him she was doing better. His new cocktail cured all the noise and delusions. No one needed to know she was evolving into something greater. Something they couldn't even comprehend. Not even she fully knew what. But knew it started with the flies feasting. Soon she'd shrug off her skin and reveal her new self to the world.

Four

"Hey, Ash, you're back!" Ashley jumped when she felt a hand slap her shoulder. She looked up and saw Kristen and her three friends. They sat down at her table, "have you met Brandon?" Kristen gestured to the boy with the shaved head and army jacket.

"Oh, no, hey," Ashley muttered. She felt embarrassed. She was trying to bypass the students from her old classes. She had been in the library working all morning. She still felt so pathetic, despite being numb to everything else.

The librarian hushed them. The group giggled. "So what the hell happened?" Gia asked, leaning in. "It's all everyone has been talking about." Ash laid her head on the table. That was the kind of thing she was trying to avoid.

"It was fucking awesome," Nick said.

"So I heard." Brandon followed up. Ashley sighed. She lifted her head. At least someone thought she was cool.

"Gretchen told everyone you were in juvenile hall. That you're an insane genius like Hannibal Lector. That you probably killed people. She saw you getting hauled away." Kristen said.

"Kevin told everyone you threatened to stab him

when he didn't move out of your way in the office. Then you stomped in his foot and laughed about it." Brandon said.

"No, what? That didn't even happen. Why are they saying that?" Ashley moaned.

"Because people are morons, in case you didn't notice." Kristen sneered at a few kids across the room. "So you're just a badass, huh? What? They'll only let you come to school part-time now or something? Fucking lucky." The others agreed.

"I just have a thing, that's all."

"Like what? What do you mean?" Gia didn't get it. Ashley looked around the table. The others wanted an explanation.

Ashley figured they all thought she was cool, maybe she should just tell them. She wanted friends, but she also didn't want to keep pretending. They might understand. And if they didn't, then fuck them. "I was in a facility before I came here." She said.

"I fucking knew it!" Kristen said.

"But it wasn't anything like juvie. It was a clinic for people with, uh, mental illnesses."

"Like bi-polar? I'm sure I'm bi-polar. I mean I haven't been diagnosed or anything but I read about the symptoms and it's like totally me." Gia said.

"You're not fucking bi-polar. It's just PMS." Nick told her.

Gia punched him in the arm. "I fucking am."

Ashley wouldn't tell them her entire history. They didn't need to know about her homicidal mother. Her imprisonment at Saint Agnes Hospital. How her illness was diagnosed as a demonic possession because of supposed cult activity she witnessed early in life. That was too fucked up to talk about on a first date. She decided to keep it simple, just tell them about the main thing. "I have schizophrenia. It's a brain disorder. I take medication. Sometimes it doesn't work though. It's weird. But I'm not going to kill anyone or anything."

"You're fucking kidding. You're a schizoid?" Brandon said. The others all looked at her, not in disgust but something else. Ashley felt her cheeks burn. The bell rang.

"You need to get to class." The librarian told them. They got up and gathered their bags. Ashley told Brenda she would walk home. She had to call when she got to the house so Brenda would know she had made it okay.

"Here read this," Nick told her. He slid a ragged paperback across the table in Ashley's direction. The dirty cover was yellowed in places and spotted with what looked like dried blood. The edgers were soft and frayed.

"What is it?" She opened it up. It looked like poetry.

"The guy who wrote it is a fucking prophet."

"I don't like church shit." Ashley pushed the book away.

"No, it's not like that. He sees into other realities or something. He was in a mental institution for like thirty years. My brother told me he was a schizoid. That he'd wear this old pig head around town and rape girls. Tried to kill his sister, too. Who knows if it's all true or not. But just read it. He's written some other books, but they're impossible to find. I've only got this one." Nick said.

"You need to get to class, young man." The librarian stood nearby, waiting.

"Just bring it back when you're done. It's my only copy."

"I'll be careful." Ashley told him.

"Cool," Nick nodded, ignoring the librarian. "See ya."

"Yeah, see ya." Ashley tucked the book into her bag and forgot about it. It was the last thing she wanted to read right now. Crazy bullshit from another crazy person. *A prophet*. What a load of shit. It was raining when she stepped outside. The cold drops felt good on her hot face.

She got home just past noon, but Ashley felt the need to lie down. Her head was fuzzy from the new drug Dr. Hart was hesitant to suggest. It required blood testing to watch her cell count, but all agreed it would be the best thing to get her manic moods, her hallucinations, and paranoia under control so she could function.

Ashley dropped onto the couch. She just needed to sleep for an hour. School and the walk had drained her. She didn't realize how tired she was. She had laid around for almost two weeks. She thought she was just depressed, which always made her sleepy. But this was different. It was a soft, heavy feeling, like having cotton shoved inside you. Ashley curled up and slept for the rest of the afternoon.

When Brenda got home at five, she was irritated that Ashley hadn't even begun her homework. That she also hadn't called like she was supposed to. "I tried calling half a dozen times. Why didn't you pick up?"

Ashley was cradling her head, "I don't know. I was just sleeping. I was so tired. I'm sorry."

Brenda swallowed her temper. It was all okay. It was just a misunderstanding. Dr. Hart said it was common for the clozapine to make you drowsy, hazy when you first started taking it. It was just an additional side effect for them to deal with. Brenda had to adjust. She was cranky after a long day. Her students were being difficult. She forgot how much she hated teaching.

"You know what? It's fine. Just a mix-up. Did you look at any of your homework?"

Ashley groaned. "No. I just came home and went to sleep."

Brenda agreed they should both sit down and eat dinner, then work on her school assignments together. Ashley complained she had trouble concentrating. Whenever she took a break and walked around the librarian would eye her. "I'm sure she's not watching you."

"No, she is. She watches everyone. She yells at

Kristin and her friends whenever they come in there, even if they're just talking normally. She's an uptight bitch."

"Who's Kristen?"

"Just this girl. She's cool. She has purple hair."

"Oh, that's different. But she's nice?"

"Yeah, she's nice. Her and Gia, Nick and Brandon. They're probably the only kids who don't think I'm a freak. I told them what happened. They think it's kind of cool."

Brenda did not like that. "*Cool*? They think mental illness is a status symbol?" She shook her head.

"No, it's not like that. I guess they're into this writer, a poet, or something, who has schizophrenia. They know about it. They get that it's not my fault. Plus, they liked it when I screamed at the teacher." Ashley grinned. Sure it wasn't funny when it happened. But she guessed it probably would have been entertaining to watch. At least if people were frightened of her, maybe they wouldn't stare at her.

Brenda began clearing the plates. She tried to act happy for Ashley. She had never had real friends her age before. "Well, I'm glad they're understanding. If you ever want them to come over, I'd like to meet them." Brenda would *love* to meet them.

"Maybe." There was no way Ashley was going to let Brenda scare off her new friends. If they knew about all the chemicals she had to take, her past, the terrors that haunted her. If they knew about Lucifer, the Church. The flies inside her. They'd ditch her without a second thought.

Brenda and Ashley worked on school work for an hour, took a break to watch a television show, and then finished outlining a research paper. "Can I just go to bed now?" Ashley felt restless. This was enough. Brenda hugged her goodnight. She still had some work of her own to finish.

Brenda sat at the dining room table listening, hearing Ashley's heavy steps move across the floor above her. Water turning on and off, more footsteps, doors shutting. Brenda went back to her work, waiting for the time to pass.

When she heard nothing for an hour she picked up her phone. It showed a new message. It was from him. A professor named Schultz. He lectured in the hall next to hers. She'd had lunch with him the last few days. He was the most interesting man she'd met in a long time. He left a message asking how her evening was going. Would she be interested in seeing a movie at the end of the week?

Brenda sat the phone down. She couldn't leave Ashley alone all evening. Could she? Ashley was better the last week or so. Her medications calming down her fears, her visions. Maybe they could go to an early show? Maybe Ashley would like to come? Would that be strange to ask Dr. Schultz, no, Timothy, that? If her teenage daughter could tag along? Brenda chewed her lip, Ashley would never go. Brenda would sleep on it. She wanted to go. It had been almost a year since she had an actual date.

"Call me when you get home this time," Brenda said, dropping Ashley off outside the school. The rest of the week went on without a problem. Besides being kind of tired. But Ashley sought to remedy that with a large take out coffee each morning. "Do you really need an extra shot of espresso?" Brenda would ask.

"It helps me concentrate," Ashley explained.

Ashley's new group of friends stopped in almost daily to see her. Sometimes it was all of them, sometimes just Kristen and Gia. "You should hang out with us. It's so boring around here." Kristen would complain.

"But you can't come over to my house. My mom is constantly watching us. Like she thinks we're all on drugs or something." Gia said. Both girls snickered.

"And my mom is a bitch. She had this new boyfriend that is always leering at me."

"Brenda isn't home until at least five every night. We could hang out at my house if you wanted. But it's boring too." Ashley followed up. Not wanting to have expectations too high.

"Is Brenda your mom?" Gia asked.

"Adopted mom, more like a guardian though. She didn't officially take me in until I was almost eleven." Ashley told them, feeling comfortable enough to reveal a little more of herself. The two looked at each other intensely. "What? Is that weird?" Ashley asked.

"No, you're just like him. It's so cool." Kristen

squealed.

"Who?" Ashley felt she missed something.

"Didn't you read the book Nick gave you?"

Ashley remembered the thin book sitting on her dresser. It didn't even have a title. She hadn't even opened it. "No, I've been busy."

"Hog Head was an orphan, too. Wow, it's like you guys are linked or something. So crazy." Kristen told her.

"Hog Head?"

"The poet. That's what he calls himself." Gia said as if that was a normal thing. "No one knows his actual name. But sometimes people go find him. Or try to, at least." She shrugged.

It sounded more like a fable than anything else. "I'll read it tonight." She told the girls. The entire group seemed into this guy. She wanted them to like her. She'd read the stupid book. It was probably horrible. She hated modern poetry.

The bell rang, signaling the end of their hang out session. It was the high point of Ashley's day, feeling like a genuine person. "Wait, write down your address," Kristen said to her. Ashley scribbled down her street number on a piece of notebook paper.

"Cool, that's not far. We'll come by after school and hang." It all sounded so casual and easy. Ashley just shrugged, *whatever*. But she was making real human connections. She felt confident this was the start of something. A turning point in her life where she had more friends than just Wheeler.

Speaking of Wheeler, she was excited when she got home and found a letter from him. Brenda was adamant about reading them all first, but Ashley figured what was the harm? He hadn't talked about his penis or the molesting nurses in weeks. It was fine.

Ashley unfolded the paper. Noticed it was stiff in places like someone had spilled something on it. It stunk. Ashley couldn't place it. Foggy white flakes came off as she picked at it with her fingernail. Like crusted salt. She gasped, *it wasn't*. She ignored her guess and read the letter. There was no way that was what it was.

He began by saying he missed her. She was the only one he could trust. He had never felt so close to another person, let alone a beautiful young woman like herself. He repeated several times how he missed her. Did she miss him? Was she coming to the art show? He based the resemblance of Callisto on her. He'd never seen anyone so beautiful. Could she ever want him? Did she ever think about him? He thought of nothing but her.

Ashley dropped the letter. By now she was sure the dry substance was cum. Brenda would never let her get another letter again. Ashley gathered the papers and shoved them back into the graffitied envelope. Wheeler had never indicted feelings like that. Ashley stuck the letter in her dresser drawer under a stack of folded t-shirts.

She laid on her bed. He was the first man that she knew about to think of her like that. She didn't know exactly why he was in the criminal facility before, something to do with exposure outside of a school, but no one would talk about it. Wheeler didn't talk about it. He seemed crazy but perfectly harmless. Had he always thought about her that way? Her stomach tightened.

Ashley closed her eyes, remembering one of the last times she saw him. He always said she wasn't crazy, that she was brilliant. So brilliant. His hand was heavy on her thigh when no one was looking. What if she had let him move it up further? The flies inside her fluttered at the thought of his touch. Just a touch of another human being. She was disgusted but curious. She knew she shouldn't feel that way.

Her cunt was dry, a side effect she assumed from one of her medications, but she pushed a finger inside, anyway. Wishing it was a man, not Wheeler, but someone else. She thought she could rouse herself, her mind felt it. But her body rejected it. "Fuck, what's wrong with me?" She couldn't even get herself off. So much for teenage hormones.

Ashley washed her hands and flopped back down on her bed. She was bored, didn't want to do homework. School didn't finish for several more hours. She didn't expect Kristen and Gia to come over, but hoped they would. On her dresser sat Nick's paperback. *Hog Head*. What kind of fucked up name was that?

Without creasing the spine too badly, Ashley carefully opened to the first page. In plain typeset was printed *The Works Hog Head*, then underneath it the roman numeral *Part II*. There was no contents, only a small dedication on an otherwise blank page, *Always to Judith*. The artwork was patched in here and there, mostly charcoal renderings and pencil sketching.

Ashley opened to the first poem. It was short, stripped down.

> *Moldy straw, putrid decay in spring mud.*
> *The time of the swine is at hand.*
> *Your cunt—such an odd place to meet death.*
> *The ruins of flesh.*
> *She takes them away in silence.*
> *As is her right.*
> *Deny me!*
> *Deny me.*
> *Give me only the frigid ground of clear, knowable truth.*
> *They will not deny me this comfort, by you.*

Well, Ashley understood that. How many times had she longed for that very thing? *The frigid ground of truth*? He had to mean his death. Or her death? Impossible, he didn't know her. How could he be talking about her? She read the next page.

The book was much the same. Death, rot, mourning, a soul held by the heavy flesh of bondage, strangled with disease, madness. It felt like he was talking to her about her very being.

Ashley finished the whole thing. She searched the small print for evidence of this man, where the book was printed. Some truth about him. It was sparse and empty. He revealed nothing more in the pages. Ashley felt a cold hook pierce her sternum and tug her bones away from the muscle.

She put it in her dresser drawer beside Wheeler's cum stained letter. Brenda would not want her reading this. Brenda felt she got obsessed with things too easily. She wasn't even allowed to listen to regular music. Only classical or jazz. Something without lyrics that Ashley couldn't twist around and make about her or her delusions.

It freaked her out one time when she heard a rock song on the radio, *Girl; you got to change your crazy ways; you hear me?* Someone was talking to her. "Brenda, did you hear that? Did you!? They know. They've found me!" eleven-year-old Ashley shrieked, trying to open the car door while they were going down the road. This was before she got a place at the clinic with Dr. Prendergast. They didn't normally take children, but Brenda had connections.

This was different. This booklet was meant for her. It was about her. He was talking to her over decades of time, waiting for her to awaken. How else could he know so very much about her? It felt personal. Ashley hesitated to close the dress drawer. Had he touched this very book? She felt oddly close to him, a stranger. It frightened and exhilarated her all at the same time.

The door downstairs banged, Ashley shuttered. She had spent all afternoon obsessing over the book and its creator. She hadn't even taken a nap. She wondered about Judith. Who was she? His sister? A girl he had raped? His mother? Her? Maybe that was her name in a past life; or was it code? She wanted to ask Kristen about it, but also didn't want to let on that she knew something they didn't. This was something between herself and Hog Head. The others didn't need to know about it.

Ashley invited both girls in. They dropped their bags by the door. "My room is upstairs," Ashley told them. She remembered as little as a month ago the fight between Priest and Lucifer. That felt like an old dream. A memory someone else had told her about.

"Like the room," Kristen said, looking around. Ashley had put up canvases and papers of artwork she'd done. Some pieces were from patients at the clinic, given to her as parting gifts. "What the hell is that?" Kristen said, turning her head to the side. She looked at Ashley, "is this upside down?"

Gia and Kristen were staring at a pencil sketch Ashley had done a few months ago. She was restrained in a hospital bed on the ceiling. Her head hung limp. At the bottom, Priest and his legion of followers stoked a large fire. Her mouth was open in a silent scream, inhaling the flames. Sister Bathsheba prayed. Christ watched over the burning, pleased. *Allow the fire to purify the foul soul of woman.*

"Shit, that's scary," Gia remarked.

Both girls looked at Ashley, she shrugged. "I suppose so. I'm doing a lot better now. I don't see that stuff as much." She explained.

"Wait? You see shit like that?" Kristen asked, looking from the sketch to Ashley and back.

"I would have slit my wrists years ago," Gia commented and slumped down on the window seat.

"Shut the hell up," Kristen told her.

"What?"

Ashley didn't want them to fight or blame any tension on her. "No, it's fine. It is fucked up. But the new stuff my doctor has me taking helped. I don't even hear Lucifer anymore."

"Wait, what?"

Ashley didn't want to explain. It was too complicated. "Don't worry about it. Do you guys want something to eat or anything?"

"Nah, care if we smoke?" Gia asked, cracking the window. Ashley didn't care, she was used to patients smoking at the clinic. They'd passed her a hit a few times when no one was looking.

"Go ahead." She said sitting on the bed beside Kristen. Gia fished around in her pocket and pulled out a square black box. She lit one and handed it to Kristen. It smelled more like incense and a wood stove than a cigarette.

"You want?" Kristen asked, exhaling.

"Sure." The smoke was harsh, but not bad. She liked the flavor. "Everyone at the clinic just smoked whatever they could get their hands on. A cigarette was more valuable than money."

Despite the window being open, the room became

hazy. The girls sat with smoking halos hanging overhead. They talked about meaningless bullshit. Ashley loved it. It was so normal; she felt like she was on a television show. "So Nick and Brandon were totally bummed we were coming over," Kristen told her, leaning back on the bed and staring at the ceiling.

"Really, why?" Ashley didn't believe her.

"Why do you think? Because you're fucking awesome and Nick totally has a thing for you."

Now she really didn't believe them. "He probably just wants his book back."

"You know Nick doesn't loan that book to anyone. Not even me." Kristen told her. Ashley looked over at Gia, who nodded her head.

"She's right. That book is like his Bible. He got it from his older brother before he offed himself in the garage." Gia said bluntly. "His brother was really into it. He had tapes and stuff from Hog Head's band when it was a thing. Guess he knew the drummer or something. But they're all dead now."

Ashley couldn't believe it. "Dead? Hog Head is dead?"

"No, we're pretty sure he's still alive. But the drummer OD'd awhile ago, Nick's brother shot himself last year. Just fucking suicide all over the place."

"Have you ever tried it?" Kristen asked. Ashley didn't want to talk about it. The girls must have been able to sense her unease. They left the question lingering in the air.

"Did you say you had something to eat? I'm starving." Gia finally said, trying to cut the tension. She flicked the cigarette out the window. Ashley led them downstairs and let them go through the cupboards. "I want to cook. What can we cook?" Gia asked, examining boxes.

"Brenda does most of the cooking," Ashley didn't really know how to cook other than defrosting and or salad. Brenda didn't trust her with flames.

"So she's your adopted mother?" Kristen asked, leaning against the counter.

Gia decided she was going to cook a box of macaroni and cheese. "Is this okay?" She asked.

"Knock yourself out," Ashley told her, getting out a saucepan. Kristen was still looking at her. Ashley pulled bottled water out of the fridge and drank half of it. The smoking made her dry mouth worse. "She adopted me when I was eleven."

"Did she know you were sick?"

"Yeah, she's a pediatric neurologist. Well, she mostly teaches now. But at the time she was researching children's brains, looking for markers that could indicate schizophrenia later in life. It's complicated, but a nurse told her about me and she came and met me. She recognized what was going on and put me in a treatment center when I was about ten. Then The Oaks Clinic soon after that."

"So you were like her guinea pig?" Gia asked.

Ashley never thought of it that way. "I don't know. She just wanted to help me. She still hopes her research down the road will help other doctors treat early onset schizophrenia."

"So do you know every inch of your brain? Is that what those framed x-rays things were over your bed?"

Ashley shrugged, "Brenda thinks by talking to me about everything it'll help keep me sane. Keeping a patient involved in treatment and all that shit."

"I always heard it was the mother's fault," Kristen said.

Ashley didn't like that. She looked down and shook her head, "No. I didn't know my mother. Well, I did, but I don't remember. I don't remember anything before Brenda." She said, wanting all questions to stop there, her agitation clear. *No mothers, no suicide.*

"Sorry. Hey, let's talk about Nick. So he's cute, right?" Gia finally said. Kristen exhaled and Ashley turned red. *Yeah, he was kinda cute*, in a pale scrawny corpse type way.

"I thought he was your boyfriend," She said to Kristen.

Kristen laughed. "No! I wish. We screwed around a few times. But he's like… intense. He likes smart chicks."

"But they never like him back." Gia interrupted. "He tried to ask out Casey Birk last year, she's head of the honor society. Sweet and perfect." Gia mocked. "She flat out said she'd never date a deadbeat stoner like him."

"Bitch. I hate her." Kristen scowled. "But then you came along. And you read, and paint, live with a fucking doctor. He probably hopes he can talk to you about poetry or something." Kristen shook her head as if all that was impossible.

Ashley didn't know what to say. "I don't know very much about all that." She told them.

"About what?" Gia asked, stirring the noodles. Her stomach was rumbling. Her mother was going to be pissed that she had eaten before dinner.

"Like dating and guys and all that." She was embarrassed. "My meds make me pretty numb."

"Like your vagina?" Gia blurted out. Everyone laughed.

"Something like that. Just my overall being. It's hard to muster up any kind of feeling, sexual or otherwise."

"Yikes. Well, Nick is fantastic at mustering up sexual feelings, just saying." Kristen poked her. Ashley took another long drink from her water bottle. There was no way a guy like Nick liked her. She was chubby. Weird and awkward. Mentally unstable. Drugged out of her mind most of the time. She felt Kristen and Gia were probably just trying to make her feel better. And that was fine. It made her feel a little better.

Ashley forgot about the time, her homework, calling Brenda. When she heard the front door slam, she jumped up from the table. All three had been eating macaroni and cheese and talking about pure nonsense. There was a pile of dirty dishes in the sink, bags, and coats on the floor. "Hello?" Brenda called, looking at the foreign book bags near the front door. "Ash, you didn't call me *again*. You need to remember to call!" Brenda shouted up the stairs.

Ashley appeared in the doorway to the dining room. "Brenda! Wow, it's already five." Ashley couldn't believe she didn't remember the time. Her friends got up and stood behind her, nervous. A lot of parents didn't like strange kids in the house when no one was home. Let alone smoking and eating all the food. "This is Kristen and Gia. I told you about them." Ashley looked at Brenda, trying to tell her with her eyes not to embarrass her.

Brenda bit her tongue. She smelled smoke. It was obvious what the girls had been doing. But she also worried about what Ashley would do if she reprimanded her friends. She had a good day. She accepted an invitation from Timothy to have dinner on Saturday. Instead, she forced a smile. "Nice to meet you girls." Kristen and Gia mumbled a hello. Brenda studied Kristen, faded purple hair, her black ringed eyes. Gia's white blonde pixie chop job, low cut sweater with artfully placed holes.

"We were just going." Kristen said, walking over to shrug on her leather coat. Gia followed.

"Oh, you girls don't have to leave on my account. Did you eat yet?" Brenda asked.

"Gia made macaroni." Ashley told her.

"Good, okay then."

"I should probably get home. My mom will wonder where I am." Gia said. Kristen knew her mom wouldn't care, but decided she had better leave as well.

"We'll see you tomorrow at lunch?" Kristen asked, hoisting her book back onto her shoulder.

"Same table as always, slaving away." Ashley told them.

"No, tomorrow is Thursday, you have an appointment at eleven." Brenda reminded her.

Ugh, Ashley forgot about Dr. Hart. "Right, so not tomorrow. Friday, though. Tell Nick I'll bring back his book."

Kristen grinned, "Oh, I'll tell him." The girls snickered and said goodnight.

Brenda watched them go and locked the door behind him. "What was that all about? What book?" Ashley turned and went to clean up the dining room table. "Ash, what book?"

"Nothing," Ashley said, walking towards the kitchen. "Just that book of poetry and stuff I told you about. By that guy... the one they're all into. Nick let me borrow it, but it's out of print so he wanted it back. That's all. I'm trying to make friends. I didn't want him to think I stole his book. You know how irritating that is when you lend someone a book and never get it back."

Brenda had ranted about that very subject frequently. Night nurses were the worst at stealing books.

"Can I look at this book?"

Shit. "It's at school in my locker." Ashley blurted, focusing on adding soap to the dishwater.

"You don't use your locker."

Brenda was picking at her. She felt Ashley wasn't being honest. "Well, sometimes I do. Geesh, what's with all the questions." Ashley said, squeezing past her to go upstairs.

Brenda didn't stop her. How had she become the bad guy here? "And I know you girls were smoking!" She called behind her. Ashley slammed her door. She felt she had no privacy. She was fifteen, then would be sixteen, soon an adult. She didn't need her reading to be monitored, her thoughts censored... unless there was something Brenda was trying to hide from her.

Ashley closed the window and sat on the bench looking towards her dresser. Inside was the crumpled letter from Wheeler. She wasn't sure how she felt about that. Defiled maybe. Not physically, but emotionally. Like he had snuck in and caught her off guard. He was just crazy; he didn't mean it. He would never act on something like that in person, she rationed.

Her thoughts came back to the slender, soft book on top of the letter. Her stomach muscles tightened with a feeling of loss and longing for a creature she might never meet in this life, if she couldn't figure out his code. She felt they had met somewhere in the spiral funnel of eternity. She opened the drawer and brought the book out. She didn't want to give it back yet. She needed to study it more. She was sure there were clues hidden in between the lines just for her. She needed more time.

"Can I use your copy machine while I'm here?" Ashley had brought the paperback in her bag. Dr. Hart didn't see why not.

"May I ask what you're copying?"

"A book of poetry from one of my friends. It's rare, and he wants it back. I just like reading it. It gives me... comfort." She said not fully lying. Dr. Hart brought her into his small side office. He sat at his desk while Ashley used the large copy machine. She stapled it. He didn't ask to read it. *At least he trusts me.*

Dr. Hart figured Brenda had already looked through it. If Ashley wanted to talk to him about it, he'd let her. Otherwise he wouldn't press. Teenagers all developed fascinations with things. Sometimes music groups or a sports team. It was only natural for someone as intelligent and sensitive as Ashley to gravitate towards the complex nature of poetry and art. He was glad to see she was focusing on something other than her inner narrative of the Church.

"Besides your new found passion for poetry, how's everything else been going this week?"

"It's been good."

"You seem surprised by that."

"School work is simple. I told you about Kristen and Gia. Brenda hasn't been on my case. Besides being exhausted all the time, it hasn't been too bad." Ashley told him.

"The fatigue should calm down once you get used to the dosage. What about other things? How's your anxiety been? Lucifer? What's going on with him?"

"Lucifer is MIA, just like a flicker of light off to the side most of the time." Ashley flapped her hands on either side of her face to show what she met. Dr. Hart nodded.

"That's common. But no more nightmares? The Church? I noticed you said nothing about the curtains being open today."

Ashley felt like she was in control of those thoughts. She had filed them away, the threat low. She had other things to think about, like deciphering what Hog Head was trying to tell her. She was sure his location was carefully coded within his words. Maybe she needed his other books to complete the message? She was thinking about contacting the printing press. She recognized the town's name, a small place only a few hours away. He had to be close, hiding in plain sight.

"That Clozapine or Versacloz or whatever you want to call it knocked all that out of me." Ashley noted, her voice flat. She had trouble mustering up excitement these days. Inside she felt the flies crawling, laying eggs deep between the coils of her bowels. She swallowed.

"That's what it's for. Your blood test looks good. Anything else other than fatigue?"

"Dry mouth. Can I get some water?" Dr. Hart went over to his little fridge and handed her bottled water.

Ashley swallowed, drowning the flies that kept trying to crawl up her throat and expose her half truth. It was like they wanted her to be put away.

When the session was over Ashley walked across the campus to Brenda's classroom. She was droning on, but noticed when Ashley snuck in and sat in the back. Fifteen minutes later, the class ended. Ashley got up to tell Brenda about her recap on therapy and then go home. She'd see Brenda later. But a tall man with dark brown hair, carefully combed backwards, intercepted her. His shirt sleeves casually rolled up to his elbows, pants perfectly ironed. It was as if he saw a picture of a professor and copied it. He even had the delicate wire-frame glasses.

"Ash, come here," Brenda motioned when she noticed Ashley hanging back. "This is my friend Timothy."

Timothy held out his hand, Ashley ignored it and looked at Brenda. She didn't want to touch this guy's hand. Who knew where it had been. Was Brenda being serious right now? "Ash, you're being rude." *The Look*. God, Ashley just wanted to go home. She'd had enough social interactions for one day.

"Hello, *Timothy*." Ashley was sure Brenda had told him everything.

"How was your appointment?" Brenda asked, gathering up a messy stack of reports.

"Fine. Boring. Whatever."

"Tim has offered to take us both to lunch." Brenda said, her words bright and crisp. Ashley knew that sound. A crush. Yuck. Brenda was way too old for that kind of thing. Forty. What did she expect to get married and have a baby with this guy?

"Pass. I'm going home. Dr. Hart says I'm getting fat and I have to stop eating so much."

Brenda scowled, "He did not say that." Timothy looked uncomfortable and rocked on his heels, as if he were in a hurry to get going.

"I have schoolwork to do. I just want to go home." Ashley said, feeling irritated. Couldn't Brenda and Timothy take a hint? Finally, Brenda relented and let her go without too much of a hassle.

Ashley took a left towards the library. She couldn't use the internet at home because Brenda constantly checked it. Ashley swallowed, the sticky feet of the flies continued to rub her throat raw. Everyone said it was a side effect, but she knew better. They were transforming her body, freeing her consciousness to find Hog Head. It was only a matter of time.

She used Brenda's university login and opened up a web browser. She started with the obvious, Hog Head. All very brief bios. No one even knew his true birthday. Some said August and a few others said September or even January. He'd be about forty-seven or forty-eight if either of the dates were correct. He was from a farming community three hours north of here. He used to have a band; he put out several tapes before they committed him. No one could specify why or where. The rest of the original band was dead except for the keyboardist. He was in prison for arson.

Hog Head had released a handful of obscure recordings, none of which were being sold now. He had four books, all limited to a few editions of three hundred copies or fewer. They put the first two books out while he was in a hospital, the other's after they released him. No one knew his whereabouts. No one knew the origin of the name. One image showed up related to him- a muddy nude young girl. They obscured her face with a butchered swine head. Around her were strewn hooves and a partial rib cage.

Try as she might, Ashley could locate nothing else. She signed out and turned off the monitor. Frustrated. Her next idea was to contact the printing press on the inside of the book, Mad Monk Art House. She found an address but no phone number or email contact. She'd have to write a letter, send it, and wait. Who knew how long it would take for a response.

"Did you really have to be so harsh?" Brenda asked over dinner. She was still going on about how Ashley treated Timothy.

"I just wasn't hungry. I wasn't fucking hungry."

"You need to calm down. You're old enough to have a conversation without throwing a tantrum. You've been doing so well. You want to be treated like an adult, but you're acting like a child. I know you want to blame it all on your condition, but it doesn't work like that."

Ashley replied with stony silence. "So you have

nothing to say?" Brenda sighed and rubbed her temples. "Did you finish your school work? That book report is due tomorrow."

"It's done." Ashley said, her voice still. She swallowed her soup. It was hot and burned her mouth. It washed down the flies.

"And I didn't even mention smoking. Are you smoking now?"

"So what if I am? It helps with the nerves."

"What nerves? I thought you said you have been feeling better? I talked with Dr. Hart and you didn't report any hallucinations. The voices have stopped? I haven't heard anything about nightmares or the Church. Not even Lucifer. Where are these nerves coming from?" Brenda asked. She was tired of having to pull all this information out of Ashley. Lately she was becoming more and more withdrawn from her. Brenda wondered if it had something to do with those girls, Gia and Kristen.

"You! You're getting on my nerves. Just fucking stop. The only reason we're even talking about this is because of fucking Timothy!" Ashley shouted and stood up. "I'm done."

"What about dessert? I brought home a pumpkin pie. You don't want any?"

It was like Brenda never listened to her anymore. "No, I don't. I told you I'm fucking fat! It's like you want me to be ugly so I won't have any friends."

"Ash? Really? Why would I want that?" Brenda asked, gathering up the dinner dishes.

"Because you want me to be a fucking baby. Just drug me up and set me aside so you can marry fucking *Timothy* and have a goddamn normal baby. I know all about it." Ashley slammed the chair against the table and left the room.

"None of that is true. Ash! Ashley!" Brenda called after her. Ashley slammed her door. She paced back and forth. She wanted a cigarette right now. Brenda and her lies! Ashley opened the window and let in the cool autumn air. That felt better. She inhaled deep and sat down, looking at the tree in the backyard. The sound of dry brown leaves being blown around helped her rage infused brain. How she wished she was back at the clinic in the forest. Not here in a concrete Hell. She heard Lucifer's blurry voice like he was talking to her from the end of a long tunnel.

"You know nothing about it." She muttered and curled up on the window seat. Her oldest friend turns out wasn't an actual friend at all. She saw him dissolve into the ether of her mind's eye thanks to modern day pharmaceuticals. But that didn't really matter. She was her own best friend. She didn't need Brenda or Kristen or anyone.

She dreamt about Hog Head, finding him. Him recognizing her at once as an equal of mind. "Where have you been?" He'd ask. Ashley wouldn't know how to explain, but wouldn't have to. He'd understand. *The hospitals.* He was the only one who understood what was going on with her. How to assist her in growing past this skin sheath into something more.

Ashley didn't know how, but she was stripped down and exposed. Becoming. Hog Head laid her gently down on a bed. His fingers tracing the arch of her ribcage. He'd place his head to her breast and hear the humming inside. "We need to let those out." He'd say.

Ashley knew it would be painful, but worth it. She'd let him. From somewhere he pulled out a large knife. He would open her up from her sternum to her navel. She gasped, it agitated the flies inside her. They would swarm out of the long wound, so many of them. They pushed up her throat and out her nose and mouth.

Ashley rolled off the narrow window seat and fell heavy onto the bare wood floor. "Ash?" She heard Brenda call from downstairs. Ashley thought it was late. What was Brenda still doing up? When she looked at the clock, it was only a quarter past ten.

She sat up and leaned against the seat. She felt her midsection, soft and fleshy. No cut to poke a finger into. The flies weren't ready to come out yet. She'd trust in the universe to guide her. She'd know when she was ready to ascend, when she and Hog Head found each other. He'd know what to do. Until then, she had to keep it together. He was waiting for her.

"Ash?" Brenda knocked on the door.

"I'm fine. I fell off the window seat." She shouted. Her throat was parched, she gagged.

Brenda peered in. The light from the hallway framed her in the triangle of the cracked door. "Do you need a drink?" She asked, her voice losing the irritated edge from earlier.

Ashley got up. "I can get it. I'm not crippled." She said and walked past Brenda. Brenda followed her down to the kitchen.

"I know that. Ash, come on. Don't be mad about Timothy. We all need friends. You have Kristen and Gia, those other kids, what's their names-"

"Nick and Brandon."

"Yes. Why can't I have a friend, too?" She asked. Ashley swallowed her water. If it would get Brenda off her back, maybe a minor distraction wouldn't be half bad.

"You're right, Brenda. I apologize. You should have a friend instead of spending your days constantly nursing me."

"I'm not nursing you. It's just we're both settling in. It's good to have a social circle. And I'm still always going to be here. We're best friends, right?" Brenda hugged her, Ashley let her.

"Sure. But don't feel bad about spending time with your new friend."

Brenda caught the sarcasm. "You either. Your friends are welcome here. Just smoke outside, please." Ashley felt that was fair enough. Maybe she'd get a little breathing room now. She'd be able to research in peace without worrying about Brenda snooping around.

"Oh, Brenda, there was one thing I wanted to ask. Did you decide about the art show? It's next month."

Brenda was hoping Ashley would forget about it.

"That's still weeks away. But probably." Brenda said.

The trip to the clinic brought her that much closer to Hog Head. North a few hours. They would pass through the town where the Mad Monk was. Close to his birthplace (if that information was correct). Ashley had to write that letter, get it sent, and hope they answered back before then. She wanted to convince Brenda to stop so she could pick up any books or information. She didn't have a plan yet, but there was still time. First she had to hear back, who knows? Maybe they didn't even exist anymore. Maybe they had on old copies they could send her if she paid for postage. She had to write that letter tomorrow.

Five

"Whatcha doing?" Kristen ran up and whispered fiercely into Ashley's ear. She heard the others laugh. The librarian was in the back, so she didn't hear them this time. Ashley closed her notebook. She had been writing her letter to the Mad Monk all morning. Her concentration was shit. She didn't know how detailed she should be. Ask if they would do any reprints? The cost of such a thing? Any extras lying around? Did they have an address or phone number so she could get in contact with Hog Head?

So far she had *To Whom it May Concern,* followed by saying she had recently acquired a copy of Hog Head Number II and was interested to learn more. Did that sound too formal? Ashley only ever wrote to Wheeler, who was crazier than she was, so she never really thought about it. Letter writing seemed to be a dying art. Which was too bad. She enjoyed paper mail more than cold email. If Brenda would even let her have an email.

"Nothing, just finishing up some biology." Ashley said. All four sat down around the pale blue circular table. She hated to give Nick back his copy of Hog Head. Whenever she held the book, it burned her fingertips. Tore her soft muscles from her bone. "Here's your book back. It was good." Ashley told him.

"Yeah, you liked it?" He asked. Ashley felt his gaze was a little more intense. He took the book and gingerly slipped it into his bag.

"Do you have anything else by him? It was better than most of the bullshit I've read."

Nick suppressed a laugh, "For sure. I don't have any more of his books, but I've got a couple old tapes that used to belong to my brother."

TAPES! He still had them. "Could I borrow them?"

"I don't know if you'd like 'em. They're scratchy from being played so much. Shitty recording to begin with. Mostly they're just out of tune guitars, kids screaming, tribal drumming. Some of it gets pretty intense."

"Well, I like intense. I mean, I can handle it. I'm so sedated these days it might feel good to feel anything." Ashley explained. Was she blushing? The bell rang.

"Damn it. Mind if we come over later?" Kristen asked. "I hope your, uh, Brenda wasn't mad about us smoking."

"Nah, she doesn't care. She's cool like that. Plus, she's got this boyfriend now, so she's cutting me a little slack. It's amazing how quickly she backs off when I stop having psychotic breaks." Ashley meant it as a joke. "I was just kidding." She said, not meaning to make anyone feel uncomfortable.

They laughed, "Yeah, duh." Gia said. She gave Kristen a look that said *fucking insane*.

"I'll find those tapes. Maybe you can come over

and listen to them sometime? I think if I tried to copy them, that might just melt or something. I've tried to get them onto a CD but it's impossible, the quality is too shitty." Nick said.

"Okay, cool. Whenever." Ashley said, pulling on her jacket.

"I'll get your number from Kristen." he said and walked away. Brandon waved and followed, a stray looking for a home.

Ashley was sure she was floating as she walked home. It was early autumn, and the sun was still warm. She had friends coming over today. A boy wanted her to hang out and listen to weird underground music he inherited from his dead brother.

She sat at the dining room table to finish her letter. She decided to just keep it clean cut and simple. She wanted to know if they had any more books available. If they had any contact information to give her. A quick *thank you for your time* and she slipped it into the stark white envelope. After she placed it into the mailbox on the porch she sat by the front window waiting for the mail carrier.

When she saw the letter taken away in the dusty blue bag, she felt her heart tighten a notch. She did it. It was only a matter of time now before she'd begin her true life path. She itched her eye. Blinked. *Fuck, that hurt.* She felt something in there, probably an eyelash.

In the bathroom, she opened her left eye wide. It looked like a delicate crescent nail clipping near the bottom lash line. It irritated her skin, made her eye look bloodshot. "Damn it," She said, trying to scrape it off with her finger. "Gotcha," She murmured, pulling her hand away to examine it.

The tiny white remnant wiggled off her nail and fell down the sink. "Oh, shit!" Ashley stumbled backwards and slid against the wall. A maggot. They were running out of space inside.

She hoped the letter would reach a sympathetic ear. She didn't know what she was becoming, what would happen. Maybe she'd have to release them herself, open her own skin before they broke through. Ashley pictured rubber, the way it bubbles when heated. Or Swiss cheese, the holes, the flies chewing through her soft fat middle. She shuddered. *Fuck, she'd forgotten to call Brenda again.*

"What are you doing for Halloween?" Gia asked. The three of them were lying around the living room. Kristen had put on music that groaned along, dreary, matching the overcast afternoon.

"Nothing. Sugar and movies and all that. The staff tried to downplay it at the clinic. They'd put up a few paper jack-o'-lanterns and stuff, but nothing scary. I've never really been into holidays." Ashley shrugged. She wanted to take another handful of chips from the bowl but stopped herself. She was trying to eat better. She had narrowed it down to eating twice a day and fasting for eighteen hours. It was getting easier. She looked at Kristen and Gia. Both were narrow slips in mini skirts and ripped stockings.

"You've never gone to a party or anything? Brandon has a party every year. Well, his dad does, but it's cool we can go. He lives out in the country, so there's loud music and tons of booze. No one pays attention if you drink or not. Plus, we're almost adults, so who cares. Do you like rockabilly?" Gia asked. Ashley had no idea what that was.

"It's alright." She said.

"Cool, then you'll love it. We'll get dressed up, super slutty." Gia said.

"Can you take that kind of thing? I mean, it's loud. Lots of people. Lots of assholes." Kristen said, wondering if Ashley would freak out.

"No, it's cool. It's not like I have epilepsy or something."

"Yeah, geesh mom." Gia mocked.

"Sorry, okay. I was just checking. We must think of something awesome to be. Matching costumes maybe?" Kristen suggested. "We could go next weekend and find something?" Kristen said, looking over at Ashley.

"I never do anything on the weekends." Ashley had never dressed up for Halloween. When she was little, she recalled her mother handing out Bible literature at the Halloween store. Later her mother pulled the blinds in their living room, rocking back and forth on her knees. "Pray for those souls Ashley, *Pray*!" She'd shout crying and rocking, trying so hard to get

God to hear her. Ashley remembered that. She hated her mother every time she thought about her. Ashley decided she would never have children and pass on her diseased DNA. She could never do that to another human being, let alone a baby.

"Ash? Is noon okay?" Kristen and Gia were staring at her. "We can come later?"

"Noon is fine. I get up early."

"We must think of something good. Slutty vampires or something."

"Gia would you shut up about the slutty thing?" Kristen laughed and ate another handful of chips. "You're slutty enough as it is."

"Yeah, I try." The girls left before Brenda got home. Both were zipping jackets and gathering bags.

"Nick asked me for your number, you know. Has he called?" Kristen asked, more curious than anything else. She couldn't believe Nick was actually into Ashley. Like really into her. Ashley was cool and everything, but she wondered how a schizophrenic lay was? Crazy, she bet.

She assumed Nick was probably trying to make her jealous. He told her during the summer he didn't want to mess around anymore. That was right after the whole Casey Birk thing. Kristen didn't realize how much it irritated her till now. He wanted Ash's phone number. He wanted to spend time alone with her. Kristen almost didn't give it to him, but played it cool and acted like she didn't care. He'd come back begging to get between her legs when he realized how out of it

Ashley really was. If he saw those drawings she made, or the way she sometimes blanked out, yeah, he'd change his mind damn quick.

"He said he'd play me some of Hog Head's music." Ashley told her. "It's not a big deal."

"He wants to fuck you." Gia said.

Ashley shook her head quickly, "Ah, no. I'm not... no. Just no. It's just listening to music, that's all." Of all the things she'd seen, real or otherwise, that was one thing she could not imagine. Her and a boy.

"Stop being a whore, Gia. Not everyone wants to fuck everyone." Kristen told her, sounding harsh.

Gia shrugged, "Whatever."

"Kristen and Gia want to hang out next weekend and go Halloween shopping. There's this party they want me to go to."

"A party? You want to go to a party?" Brenda asked while they washed the dishes. "Since when? You hate parties."

"Teenagers go to parties, Brenda. I've never been to a Halloween one before. They want to get matching costumes. It's going to be fun." Ashley tried to downplay it.

"Who's party is it? Will there be a parent there?"

"Gia said it was Brandon's house. His dad throws a party every year. It'll be filled with adults. We'll probably just hang out in the basement and watch a scary movie."

"What movie?" That concerned Brenda more than anything.

"Brenda, can't you just be happy for me? The cocktail Dr. Hart has got me on, going to therapy, part-time school, I've never felt better. I've got real friends." Besides, she had enough occupying her mind with her transformation and the Hog Head mysteries. She sat on her bed each night going over the pages, making notes in the margins of the paper. She was just waiting for a reply from the Mad Monk to pull the pieces together. She knew they fit. She bet her life on it.

"How about we watch a movie sometime?"

"I already told you, I'm not going out with you and *Timothy*."

"I wish you'd stop saying his name like that. But I meant just the two of us hanging out. I heard about a good documentary on castles of Northern Europe. You love architecture."

Ashley thought that sounded boring. "Can't we watch an actual movie?"

"Ash, you know how you get. Remember last year when you watched *Mommy Dearest* on the afternoon matinee? You had several very intense episodes. You didn't sleep for almost a month. You refused to even walk by the clinic's garden."

"Well now, I'm blitzed out of my mind. And I was only so freaked out because Lucifer told me to be on guard. He was convinced mom was going to make a break for it and kidnap me, take me back to Them."

She thought at the time her mother was hiding in the garden with an ax. Many nights she had awoken to see her chopping down a tree outside her window, looking oddly like Joan Crawford. *Tinaaa! Bring me the axe!* Ashley shuddered.

"You're stabilized, not blitzed. Where did you learn these words? So that's a no on the castle documentary, then?"

"No. Let me pick something."

Brenda sighed, "Fine, but nothing gory please."

"And the party? Shopping next weekend?"

Brenda didn't like Ashley going out alone with those girls. They were older, sixteen, maybe seventeen. They seemed nice enough, and she knew she had to let go a little. Ashley was only improving. She wanted to support her by letting her stretch her wings. "The shopping is fine. But the party, I want you home by ten."

"So I can go?" Ashley almost dropped the plate she was drying. She couldn't believe it. Maybe Timothy was a better influence than she thought.

"Yes, go. But take a cell phone with you."

"Can I stay till midnight? I don't want them to think I'm a geek."

"Eleven." Brenda said.

"Thank you!" Ashley hugged her, happier than she'd ever felt. Brenda almost felt they were normal. A teenage daughter going to a party, hanging out with friends. Her seeing Timothy, who was just wonderful. If she ever had any doubts about moving here, they were forgotten.

As they were finishing up the phone rang. "Can you get that?" Brenda asked, letting the soapy water out of the drain. "My hands are soaked." Ashley hesitated, she hated talking on the phone.

"It's probably just a telemarketer. Can't we just let it ring?"

"It could be Tim or the university. I have my phone turned off. Could you please just answer it for me?"

Ashley walked into the hall and picked it up, holding the cold plastic to her ear. Static. Was that the phone or the flies? "Hello?" Her palms were sweaty. She hoped it was a machine so she could just hang up. "Hello?" She said again, her impatience growing. Was someone trying to tell her something? Could Mad Monk have gotten her phone number? Maybe he had a message to pass on to her from Hog Head. She looked over her shoulder, Brenda was still in the kitchen. "Is that you?" She asked, her voice low and serious. The line went dead.

"Who was it?" Brenda asked, coming up behind her.

"No one was there, just static." Ashley said and hung up. It rang again. Both women looked at it. When Ashley didn't move Brenda reached around her.

"Hello?" She listened for a moment. "She's right here, just one second." She held the receiver to her shoulder, muffling it. "It's for you. A boy." Brenda got a stupid look on her face.

"It's not like that, Brenda." Ashley said, taking the

phone, feeling more nervous than ever. She felt it had to be Him.

"Hello?" Her voice was uncertain.

"Ash, hey. It's Nick. Sorry about the hang up. Phone dropped the call, I'm driving. Can you hear me better now?" He asked. Ashley could take a breath, it was only Nick. Brenda watched her, Ashley shooed her away.

"Okay, I'm going," Brenda held up her hands and went upstairs to give her privacy.

"I can hear you. You said that was you who just called?" Ashley felt disappointment. She thought for sure the Mad Monk was attempting to contact her. He probably would have gotten her letter by now, asking for further information.

"Bad connection. Sorry."

"No, it's cool." The line was empty for a minute. Ashley didn't know what to say. "So was there something you wanted?" Did that sound too harsh? Ashley didn't think so.

Nick seemed to stumble over his words, "No, I don't want anything. You said you wanted to get together and listen to those tapes. What about tonight?" He asked. It was past six, Brenda would never let her leave with a strange boy. But she also didn't want to sound like a total baby either.

"I've got something going on tonight." (Deciphering esoteric poetry).

"Sure, yeah. It's short notice. Tomorrow?"

Ashley thought for a second. Brenda was going out

with Timothy for drinks and an early movie. She'd be gone till eight or nine, she said. That would work. "Ash?"

"That's perfect, actually. But I've got to be back by eight, is that okay?"

"No problem. Can I pick you up early, like 5:30?"

"Cool. Do you have my address?"

"I got it from Kristen. You're not too far from me." There was more silence. Neither knew if they should continue with small talk or say goodbye.

"I'll see you then, I guess." Ashley finally said.

"See ya." Ashley hung up. She couldn't believe it. He had called. He was coming over to pick her up. She'd be back early, Brenda would never have to know. No interrogation or rules. She was still shocked Brenda was letting her go out with Kristen and Gia. She knew without a doubt a date with an older boy, especially one who looked like Nick, would be out of the equation.

Brenda heard the phone hang up downstairs. "Don't forget your second dose, Ash." She called down. And just when Ashley was feeling normal.

Ashley took the small brown glass bottle out of the cupboard. It looked nonthreatening. The label was white with a blue and red band around it. Thick, slightly skewed letters declared it *Versacloz*. Ashley sucked up her dose in the syringe and squirted it down the back of her throat. It didn't have a taste, but the sickly yellow color gave the impression of piss. They were prescribing her piss.

She cleaned up and rinsed out the syringe for tomorrow morning. She felt the anger of the flies, of the universe in general. It was trying to explain something to her, but she was too strung out on drugs to figure it out. *Fuck it*, she thought and went into the half bathroom off the side of the kitchen.

Ashley stuck her index and middle finger into the back of her throat. It didn't take much. Her dinner helped push it out. She sat crouched on the floor looking at the thick yellow blotch; her chewed up salad. She thought she saw a fly or two struggling for life. Better to get some out to make room for the others.

Ashley felt she had been doing fine. Did she really need to take a full dose? It was making her gain weight, and she was always so tired. She was sick of having to make a trip to the lab each week to be monitored and have her blood drawn. Cutting the dosage in half along with fasting for eighteen hours a day should help clear up her side effects, plus she wouldn't feel like such a lumbering beast.

The flies were building nests of hair and string in her brain. They came out at night to gather while she was dreaming. If she didn't do something she'd never be able to figure out the Hog Head Mysteries.

She wouldn't ascend, but be consumed from the inside. Nothing would be left but tattered remnants of a girl. She had to remain sharp, focused on this. It was the most important thing she'd ever do. Once she solved what the universe was trying to tell her, she could go back to being a human pill box. Until then, she would just have to be careful that Brenda or Dr. Hart didn't find out. They'd never understand.

Six

"If I'm going to be later than nine, I'll call. But I shouldn't be. I'll have my phone on vibrate the whole time, even in the movie. Okay? Just anything at all, call me. I'll come right home. I won't be mad." Brenda had reiterated for the hundredth time. Ashley sat cross-legged on Brenda's enormous bed, watching her run back and forth between her room and the bathroom.

"I'm just going to read, Brenda. I'm so tired all the time. I'll probably fall asleep on the couch. Those meds. make me feel like an old lady."

Brenda was pulling on a dark blue shoe with a stacked heeled. She looked like a teacher, her cardigan buttoned halfway up, her hair coiled on top of her head. She pushed up her pink framed glasses. "You know, I just want you to feel secure. You can always come along."

"Are you going to buy a drink?"

"We could go out to dinner instead."

"You know I hate restaurants. I'd rather stay home. No offense, but hanging out with two science professors does not sound like a way I want to spend my evening. I'm not insane enough for that. But give it a few years, who knows?"

"I get it. I was fifteen once too. Just promise you'll call, even if you think something *might* be wrong. I'll come right home. Plus Dr. Hart's number is on the fridge, and the emergency number. You have an entire network of people who care about you, you know that?"

"Brenda, aren't you going to be late?" Ashley said, ignoring the sentiment.

"Shit, you're right." Brenda said, trying to put the back on her earring. "Do I look alright? I haven't gone out in a long time." Ashley loved Brenda's black wavy hair, she wished hers was that color instead of wispy, pale and flat.

"You should have left your hair down." Ashley said. Brenda touched her bun.

"Really?" She seemed conflicted. "Should I take it out?" She looked at the mirror in the front hall.

"You always wear it up. It's so pretty. If I had your hair, I would never tie it back."

Brenda sighed, quickly taking the hairpins out. "I wish you would have said something before." She uncoiled it and fluffed it with her fingers. "How's that?" She asked.

"Hot." Ashley told her.

Brenda rolled her eyes, "Now you're just making fun of me. Okay, I've got to get going. Remember my phone-"

"Will be on. I just have to call. Emergency numbers. Network of love. Smothered by doctors. Got it." Ashley hugged her.

Brenda dashed out the door. If she kept thinking about it, she wouldn't be able to go. She wasn't used to doing something for herself. But Ashley had proved in the last few weeks she could be home alone for a couple of hours and not burn the place down. She had to trust her. That trust would help build her confidence, give her strength as a young woman. She was more than her illness, Brenda hoped she felt that.

Ashley ran upstairs and ripped off her stained sweatshirt. She put a loose mohair sweater on over her purple jeans. She drew a line of black around her eyes and used a quick swipe of Brenda's clear lip gloss. She examined a small pimple on her chin. She dabbed a little powder on it. This wasn't about sex, but furthering untangling the unknowns of the hog-faced prophet. Still, it wouldn't hurt to look mildly attractive. Even if Nick did like her, Ashley knew he didn't want to fuck her. Not when he was fucking girls like Kristen and whoever else. But a brief romance of the mind never hurt anything either.

Ashley ran down the stairs and shoved her feet into a pair of black flats. She took a drink of water from her bottle on the counter. The cupboard was open from earlier, the brown glass bottle sitting right up front. Accusing her. Nick knocked at the front door. *I'm fine,* she told herself and slammed the cupboard shut.

"Hey!" She said, whipping the door open.

"Hi, you ready?" Nick looked past her inside, like he was waiting for an angry parent to come bursting out of the back.

"One sec, let me get my key." Ashley grabbed her small bag that contained a house key, an emergency cell phone, a small silver box of random pills she'd acquired over the last few years. A quick release tablet, a round brown one, a long white one with several numbers pressed into it. Normal teen girl things.

"I like your house. It's got an Addams Family vibe going on." Nick told her, stepping through the front door. "Your mom isn't home?"

"No, she went out. That's why I have to be back by eight."

Nick looked uncomfortable, "She doesn't care that I'm picking you up, does she?" He had yet to meet a mother who liked him. Besides Kristen's mother, who had cornered him a few times in the kitchen and tried to put her hand down his pants.

"It's fine. Brenda respects my privacy. She doesn't need to know everything I do. She's really more like a big sister than a mom, anyway." Ashley said.

"Okay. I just don't want you getting into trouble." Or him. He knew Ashley was younger by a few years. But if she said it was alright, he supposed it was.

Nick drove a black Camaro flaked with rust around the back wheel. The dirt on the sides was probably the only thing holding it together. When he turned it on, feedback and screaming came out of the speakers. Ashley jumped and Nick quickly turned it down. "Sorry. About that." he said, flicking on the headlights and pulling away from the house.

"It just surprised me, that's all." Ashley watched her house grow smaller in the side mirror. They stopped at the corner. She quickly turned away, looking down at her lap out of habit. *The Church.*

"You okay?" Nick asked, turning left and driving into the falling sun. "Fucking bright." he muttered.

"Fine. Why?" Ashley shook the feeling off. *One, two, three claws climbing her spine like a ladder.* "What's that music you were listening to. I like your car." Her words all came out at once. She folded her hands in her lap. "Do you have a cigarette by any chance?" She asked.

"Uh, yeah, sure. Here." Nick lit one and inhaled, handed it to her. Ashley inhaled deep. She willed her hand to stop trembling.

"I have yet to find a girl who is into anything beyond the mainstream." Nick said. "What do you listen to?"

"Whatever. Metal is fine, it's cool. Some of it. I don't listen to it all the time. I like classical music too. I played the piano for a few years."

"That's cool. Like I mentioned before, I don't know if you'll like the Hog Head stuff, it's pretty out there."

"If it's like that book, then I know I'll like it." Ashley cracked the window and blew smoke out into the evening. The streetlamps were turning on despite it only being five thirty. Soon it would be dark by four. It was easy to forget what sunlight looked like for nine months out of the year around here. Ashley liked the dark and cold though, it kept people inside. It made her want to emerge and explore, unburdened by their gawking wide eyes.

Nick parked in front of a rundown split-level house. It probably would have been nice in the 1970s. Now the shrubs were overgrown, the pavement cracked. Someone had graffitied all over the pale green garage doors. The Halloween decorations looked like they had been up since last year.

"Don't worry about my mom, she's working the night shift." Nick said, as if that was something Ashley should be worried about. They were just going to listen to music.

"What's your mom do?" Ashley asked, following Nick inside through the garage.

"Bartender." No one had bothered to lock the doors, Nick just walked in. Anyone could.

They stood in the living room. "I'd say we could listen out here, but the stereo in my room is better. Used to be Bryan's, but..."

Ashley guessed he was referring to his dead brother. "Yeah, Kristen told me. Sorry." Nick shrugged off his coat and threw it on the leather couch. They stretched a piece of silver duct tape across the center cushion, probably to heal a split. "Is it okay if we smoke in here?" She asked, assuming by the smell it was.

Nick stood there for a second, hands shoved in his pockets. "Hey, I've got something better than that. Come on."

Ashley followed him up the stairs. The house was

dim; the grunge hidden by shadows. Nick's room was like a black hole at the end of the hallway. His walls might have been painted, but they were so covered with posters, ticket stubs, art you'd never know. Ashley sat on the edge of his unmade bed and looked at a hole in the wall beside the door. It was ragged, the size of a teenage boy's fist.

Nick sat beside her on the bed and flicked on a black light, illuminating the dust and debris. He took out a cassette tape, the sticker label worn off from overuse and time. "Can I look at the case?" She asked. He handed it to her. In the harsh purple cast, she squinted. It was handwritten. Just the few names of the band, Hog Head was noted as contributing vocals, piano & strings, pan flute, plus writing all the music and lyrics. The band gave a special thanks to the kids of the Underell Farm & Care Home. Below that *Her* name again. The name that stuck like a splinter in Ashley's heart, Judith.

"Who is Judith? I saw her name in the book too." Ashley said.

"Sister, I think. The one he tried to kill." Nick turned up the volume. The sharp clicking of shuffling hooves mixed with heavy marching faded in.

"Why would he try to kill her? What's the big mystery?"

Nick pulled a baggie out of the broken nightstand. He spoke to her while he rolled what Ashley thought was a cigarette. "The guy is just private, I guess. You'd be too if you were... oh shit. Sorry. But it's different, you're not violent like that. Isn't that how it is? Different for everyone?" Nick looked at her and licked the thin paper in his fingers. He began twisting it back and forth.

"It's fine. Sometimes I wish I could be a recluse, but Brenda doesn't think it's healthy. She wants me to have friends and be normal, but most of the time I feel like a jittery mess or zombie."

"This should help. Can you smoke weed even though you're taking pills?"

"You mean my medication? I've never tried it. But I don't know why not? It's supposed to help you relax, right?"

"Yeah, they give it to cancer patients. People with acute anxiety and shit. Who knows? It might help?" Nick offered to light it for her. *What's the harm?*

"Cool, thanks." Ashley took a hit like she was inhaling a cigarette. It burned down deep into her chest. She gagged and coughed. "Do you have any water?" She said in between her fit.

Nick jumped up and came back with a cup of tap water. Ashley doubted the glass was even clean, but didn't care at the moment. She drank the entire thing down. Nick patted her back. "I should have told you that can happen. Do you need another drink?"

Ashley gulped in more air and shook her head, "No, I'm fine." The music had shifted from a heart pounding to heavy rhythmic drumming, screaming was becoming louder. Shrieks echoing down a long hallway. It sounded of someone kicking and banging the side of a metal shed. "Make it stop!" a boy cried on a loop. The sounds cut out. Static played a minute before a droning tritone started up. It was unsettling the way the music drew her in. She sat still and listened a moment, basking in his sounds.

"Here this might help." Nick finally said, turning to face her.

"What?"

"Just open your mouth."

Ashley watched him inhale. He didn't cough at all. She opened her mouth slightly. She was unsure what was going to happen. He leaned in and exhaled slow and deep into her lungs. She felt his hands on her thigh, another on her shoulder.

His lips were warm. He pressed them to her for a brief minute before pulling slowly away. Ashley exhaled. Nick waited a second before turning from her and setting the joint in an ashtray. Ashley was ready this time. He ran his hand down the side of her face like he was examining her. "Is this okay?" He asked.

Ashley wasn't sure what he meant by that. Like, was she okay with it? Ashley had never been in this situation before. She leaned towards him and blended her mouth with his. She felt his tongue meet hers. He pulled her closer to him. Ashley didn't know if she was a good kisser, she hoped she was. Nick was a wonderful kisser, as Kristen had indicated frequently.

The music became louder, more frantic. The skunky smoke made the room feel hot and cluttered. Nick was pressing against her more intensely. She felt his weight like he wanted her to lay back on the bed. Ashley wasn't sure she was ready for that. But the kiss went on. His hands felt their way over her shirt and massaged her chest.

She felt ridged, this touching was foreign to her. Plus the stuffy room, the banging music in her brain. He just kept coming at her. Him pushing her back onto the wrinkled sheets. She didn't know why, but she laid back, him coming down with her. His hands were on the move again, Ashley gasped. She couldn't do this. It was all too much, the closeness, the swimming in her head.

Nick slipped his hand beneath her pants and felt inside her cunt, a finger pushing in. "Do you like this?" He murmured. Ashley was breathing hard. Her body was responding, blood rushing to her limbs. She felt she was going to burn from the inside out. No one knew she was here. Brenda would never know what happened to her. A pile of Ash. Another missing teenager.

"I've got to go home!" She shouted, shoving him off her. The panic drove her out into the hall and down the stairs. It took Nick a second to realize what happened. He thought it was okay. She seemed into it.

"Ash, where are you going?" He called, going after her. Ashley was out on the lawn, hurrying towards the road. "Let me drive you."

"No, no, that's alright. I need to walk. I can't breathe. Please, it's fine." She called and jogged off down the road. *Please don't follow me. Please don't follow me*. She chewed her fingernails and walked from streetlamp to streetlamp. She counted the posts, turned right. She just fucking ran out on him. Why would she do that? She just wanted to listen to that music. Then the smoke, the kiss. The lips and tongues, lungs and hands and cunts. She'd felt him hard against her leg as he massaged her and felt deep into her darkness. Yet she had to turn away.

The car ride had only taken twenty minutes. But walking it took longer. Ashley got turned around. She forgot for a moment where she was supposed to be walking to. Where was she going again? Home. She had to get home. She was supposed to be at home. Every time a car went by, it worried her it would be Nick. She couldn't look at him.

Ashley crossed to the far side of the street and made a wide circle around the church on the corner. The windows were lit, Ashley thought she saw someone peering out. She ran the rest of the way home, never so relieved to see those wide brick steps, that big drafty house.

She came in through the door and slammed it, as if trying to block out the people outside. "Ash? Ashley!" Brenda came rushing down the hall from the kitchen, Timothy behind her. "Thanks Goodness! Where the hell have you been? What happened? Oh god, you're okay, you're okay." Brenda was petting her hair, running her hands over her face, feeling her to make sure she was real. Ashley did not want to be touched right now.

"I called the police. They've been looking for you. Shit, I've got to call and tell them you're home. But you're alright?"

"I'll call them and let them know she's back." Timothy said and went into the kitchen for his phone.

"Brenda, why are you back so early? I'm fine. I just-" Brenda smelled her. She pulled a handful of her sweater up to her nose and inhaled.

"Have you been smoking?" She asked.

"I just needed a walk. You said you didn't care if I smoked. I just needed to go out and get some fresh air."

"Your eyes are bloodshot."

"They're just dry. The cold night, that's all. I'm fine. What time is it?"

"It's past nine. We've been looking for you for over an hour. Tim and I drove around the block, we didn't see you. Where did you go?"

Ashley shrugged, "I don't know, just around. I guess I got kinda lost. No big deal. If I knew I was going to be gone so long I would have left a note."

"Why didn't you answer your phone?"

"It's turned off. Like I said, I only meant to be out for like thirty minutes. I just got lost for a second. I really want to go to bed, Brenda."

Brenda saw the sad, heavy eyes on her daughter. Children so young shouldn't have such a weight. She nodded, "Okay, I'll come up and say goodnight in a few." She hugged Ashley one more time and felt her go stiff. Ashley just didn't want anyone touching her at the moment. Instead, she allowed herself to be hugged and sniffed and petted. She needed to get these clothes off and scrub her skin.

Ashley slept through the morning. She had felt sick all night. She wasn't sure if it was because of what happened with Nick, or the buildup of flies within her. The marching music, the wailing and pounding drums continued to repeat in her dreams. She couldn't remember a whole song, only fragments. It saddened her that she hadn't been able to enjoy the experience. Maybe it was because she was high. The memory was foggy and she couldn't remember what they said. How had she gotten from his bed out onto the lawn?

All she knew for sure was that she had heard that tape and left with more questions than answers. Ashley felt she couldn't call Nick and ask him to borrow it. He'd think she was fucking insane after what she pulled last night. She could never talk to him again. He probably hated her.

Brenda poked her head in about noon and asked if Ashley wanted anything to eat? Ashley stared at the ceiling, unmoving. Brenda was yelling at her from across a canyon. It took a moment for her words to sink in. She wanted to feed Ashley, but the thought of food turned her stomach. "You need to get up and take your meds." Brenda urged, rubbing Ashley's arm.

Ashley turned her head to look at her, her mouth forming words. Getting up sounded exhausting. "Just stay here, I'll go get them for you." Brenda offered and left the room. It felt like she was gone for a long time, hours perhaps. When she came back, she had a plate with a sandwich on it. Ashley noticed the little brown bottle, a scattering of pills beside it.

"Take these and eat something. You don't want to miss a dose. I probably should have woken you up a few hours ago. Here, open." She said. Ashley was too exhausted to put up any kind of resistance. What did it matter? It wouldn't make a difference. Everything she ate got consumed by the flies, anyway. She could see inside her brain, the flies were suckling on serotonin and dopamine, the glutamate with sticky tongues. A tongue more like a butterfly than a housefly, it curled out and bit into the gray matter. Her brain was dry, she needed water. The levels were unstable.

"Ash, swallow. Now come on. What happened?" Brenda kept questioning her, touching her. Ashley was feeding the flies, wondering how she could have been so arrogant as to think *she* could decipher the divine prophecies of Hog Head. She was a mere worm writhing around in the mud, fighting against a magnificent bird. Half devoured and incapable of understanding such things. She swallowed the rest of her medication. "Good. Why don't you try to eat something? If you don't want a sandwich, I can make soup." Brenda offered.

Ashley made the effort and turned her head to the side, looked at Brenda. Poor Brenda was so worried. Why did she look so worried? "My body can eat my fat. I have a surplus. Please, no more." Ashley whispered, her throat splintered, maggots wiggling in the cracks. *Only a matter of time now*. Before summer she knew she'd be dead. She looked back at her ceiling, a gray dirty stain was directly above her, rot from the dead Christ. "We need to paint the ceiling, Brenda. There's a stain." The words exhausted her before she even finished saying them.

Brenda looked up at the ceiling. It was white and looked normal. "We can paint it whatever you want. But you must get dressed and help me pick out a paint color." The phone rang downstairs. "Let me get that. It might be Timothy. He was anxious about you when he left last night."

Brenda left the plate on the nightstand. It smelled like cheese and pus, laced with more medicine. What was Brenda trying to feed her? Nothing felt right. Ashley peeled herself off the bed and stumbled to the bathroom. She pushed her fingers down her throat and spilled her stomach into the toilet. She flushed. She felt pure. The icy floor was the only thing she could feel.

"Ash, here let me help you." Brenda rushed in and put a folded towel under Ashley's head. Brenda rested her palm and Ashley's forehead. She was clammy. Ashley turned her head to the side and looked at the wall.

"I don't need a nurse." She murmured.

Judith was Hog Head's sister. She had to live in the area. Within a three-hour drive, Ashley rationed in her mind. If she could just find her, she could help. Ashley felt she couldn't depend on the Mad Monk. It had been days. Why wasn't he answering her letter? It all made sense. Why hadn't she seen it before? The Oaks Clinic where she was treated, The Mad Monk Art House, the town where Hog Head's band made the tapes. All within hours of each other. Judith had to be close. She'd have information.

Ashley felt all she had to do was pull the string that connected them all. Only then would the pieces fall into place. She'd find her savior. Only then would she evolve into a thing greater than this flawed flesh bag. She'd never be his equal, but she could be his devout follower. "Why, why won't he talk to me? What can I do? I can't find him." Tears warmed her cold face. Brenda smoothed her hair.

"Who, sweetie? A boy? Lucifer?" Brenda asked.

"No. No. He's no one. Why's it so bright in here?" Ashley slurred, covering her face. She had to close her eyes and was soon asleep. Brenda, with some effort, got her back into bed.

Brenda was on the phone with Dr. Hart all day. He suggested only waking her to give her her medication and see if she'd eat. Nausea was normal, as was fatigue and dizziness, dry mouth. Ashley's blood count had been normal. If anything else happened, she was to call immediately.

Brenda hung up and leaned against the wall. She

was up most of the night in case Ashley needed anything. Timothy offered to stay and help, but Brenda sent him home at eleven. He didn't need to be dragged into her life. Ashley was her responsibility, and no others. Brenda had chosen this. It never would have worked out, anyway.

Brenda was making coffee, pondering who *He* was. Ashley kept saying she wasn't good enough and couldn't understand *him*. *He* wouldn't talk to her. Brenda could only assume it was one of those boys Kristen and Gia ran around with, whatever their names were. Brenda just knew something like this would happen. She hoped it wouldn't be for years, but put young people together and something always happened.

There were no books on dealing with teenage schizophrenic adopted daughters and sex. Brenda would just have to wing it. She was an educated woman. She was a teenage girl at one point. The two of them would figure it out together. And there was always Dr. Hart to talk to. Maybe he'd have some suggestions.

Brenda heard heavy footsteps shuffling around overhead. Ashley was awake. Brenda took bottled water from the fridge and went up to see if she was thirsty. She'd slept for half the day. It was almost time for her second round of medicine, Brenda hoped she would wake before then.

"Ash?" Brenda tapped lightly on her door and opened it. Ashley was shoving something under her pillow. "What's that?" Brenda asked, walking over and setting down the water.

"Just a book. Nothing. Water, thank god!" Ashley snapped open the lid and downed it.

"It looked like a stack of papers. Let me see." Brenda sat down and reached for it, but Ashley stopped her.

"No, it's just a copy. I made it at Dr. Hart's, he knows. It's just poetry. Reading it makes me feel better."

"It's not those poems from that guy you said Kristen and them worship, is it? Ashley, I don't want you reading that. Please let me have it."

"No!" Ashley grabbed for it, but Brenda twisted it out of her hands. Ashley was slow, felt hungover. She hardly remembered the last eighteen hours. Not since Nick pushed his fingers up inside her, then scraped them back out. Over and over. Ashley felt it must have gone on for hours. Had he put anything else inside her? No, it hadn't gone that far. It was the worst thing she'd ever felt. "It's mine." Ashley screeched and lunged at Brenda.

"Ashley, no. Just let me read it. Is this what you were talking about?" Brenda turned her back and flipped the page open. The margins lined in Ashley's small, spidery script. The pages filled with notes and who knows what else. "You can't have this."

"Give it back. No!" Ashley clawed Brenda's arm and tried to wrestle the pages back. Paper ripped, Brenda fell backwards towards the window seat and Ashley tripped and fell onto the floor. She tried to gather up what pages she could. *His words! His words!* They were all she had. She cried as she put the paper back together. "How could you? I'll never know what he's trying to tell me! I'm going to die! Are you fucking happy?"

Brenda watched her daughter crawl across the floor, piecing paper back together, hyperventilating. "Ash, you need to calm down. Stop. Stop it!" Brenda went on the floor and took Ashley by the shoulders. "Look at me. You. Need. To. Calm. Down." Her voice was steady.

Ashley held the papers in her fists and cried harder. "Get off of me. What are you doing here?" She slapped Brenda's face and turned away from her. Brenda didn't know what Ashley was seeing, but by this point it wasn't her.

"Ashley!"

"No! Get out. Lucifer! Lucifer, where are you?" Ashley crawled into the corner and began pulling at her hair, her wailing and cries growing in volume. Brenda ran to get her phone from the bedroom to call Dr. Hart, who phoned emergency services.

"What are you doing? No Ashley, stop it!" Brenda came back in and saw the pair of scissors in Ashley's fist. She had jammed it deep into her wrist and was attempting to saw a line open along her right forearm. Brenda pulled the scissors out and threw them across the room. The cut wept. Brenda wrapped her hand around the wound, applying pressure. "It's okay.

We're okay. They're sending someone." Brenda held Ashley tight, red staining her ivory sweater. A stain that would never wash out.

Ashley knew where she was before she opened her eyes. The smells of latex and cleaner. God, she hated that smell. She was so tired but with effort opened her eyes and rolled her head to the side. "Hi, there kid," Brenda smiled.

It felt like they had removed her brain and replaced it with a pound of feathers. "Water." Her voice sounded more like a frog than a girl. Brenda handed her a white paper cup with a straw. Ashley laid back. "Did they remove the flies?" She finally asked.

Brenda's furrowed brow said it all. There are no flies. "No hun. You had a rather intense episode. You hurt yourself. I had to call Dr. Hart. He thought it best to admit you for observation."

"Shit," Ashley muttered. She closed her eyes again. She remembered Priest had ripped up her Hog Head papers. *Heresy*! They didn't want her to know the truth, that much was clear. "So they didn't operate on me?"

"What? No. Ashley, can you tell me what happened?"

"Lucifer, he wasn't there. The Priest ripped up my book." Ashley felt tears rising. Her book; her only physical evidence that Hog Head was out there somewhere, waiting. "Is my book alright? I didn't destroy it, did I? I remember the falling pages. But how? I know I wouldn't do that."

Brenda thought it best just to tell her. "I was trying to look at it. You wouldn't let me. I pried it from your hands, you tried to get it back. It ripped." And it all went downhill from there. She pressed her lips tightly together, wishing the situation could have gone another way.

"It wasn't anything bad."

"Maybe not, but something in it must have triggered you. I read your writing, the notes you made. You think this man is sending secret messages to you? Ash, that's just not true. Dr. Hart thinks it's best if you don't read it anymore. We've also discussed increasing your Versacloz dose. All this should not be happening. Oh, don't cry. We'll figure it out." Brenda reached out to touch Ashley's hand, who pulled it away.

"Don't fucking touch me. You just take everything away."

"Ash-"

"Just leave me alone."

"Fine, I'll go get some lunch. But when I come back, we're going to sort this out. I don't know what you think, but that man is not sending messages to you. He is not some-" She didn't even want to say the word, "Prophet."

"Leave!" Ashley screamed and shoved her face into the pillow. Brenda got up and smoothed her pants.

"We'll talk about this later." Her voice was stern, tired. She needed a moment to herself or she was going to say a few things she'd regret. *It's not her, she's ill.* She repeated it like a mantra, walking across the room and stepping out into the hall. She took one last look at the angry girl in the bed. She wanted to offer to bring her something from the cafeteria, but knew Ashley would only reject it. She turned and left.

When Ashley was sure Brenda had gone, she pulled herself up in bed. She did not understand how long she'd been there, a few hours? A week? She didn't bother to ask, they'd only lie to her. She swung her feet over the bed and stood. Right away her head cracked with static and she was forced to sit back down. What had they given her? She moved, then everything seemed to take a moment to catch up.

"Ash, where are you going?" She turned and saw Dr. Hart and a nurse in the doorway. "You need to be in bed."

"No. I need…"

"In bed." He told her. The nurse came over and helped her lay back down. The pillow felt supportive and safe beneath her. Dr. Hart pulled up the chair previously occupied by Brenda. He began talking, Ashley looked at the ceiling, willing it to be done. They could give her all the drugs they wanted, but she wouldn't take them. She knew they were just trying to control her. It was so obvious. First the doctor's at St. Agnes hospital, then The Oaks Clinics, and now she was here. She didn't trust any of them. But she nodded along, eager to be labeled safe for society so she could leave.

"I'm going to keep you here for a seventy-two hour observation. A nurse will be in shortly to take some blood. Questions? I've already gone over all this with Brenda." Dr Hart folded his hands, sat back in the chair like he was waiting for a coffee. Ashley hated him.

"No."

Dr. Hart continued to sit for a minute. "Very well. We'll see where we are in seventy-two hours."

"Whatever." Dr. Hart bid her goodbye and left, the nurse trailing behind. "What bullshit." Ashley said to no one in particular.

Brenda wanted to spend the night at the hospital, but Ashley told her to go home. There was no point in fighting. Brenda gave in and said she'd be back tomorrow after her last class. She dropped her coat and bag in the chair near the front door. Her temples ached. Timothy had called to see how everything was going. It was a relief to hear his supportive voice. Maybe everything hadn't frightened him away. But she wouldn't keep her hopes up just yet.

The fridge was empty besides a carton of leftover orange chicken from the other night. Brenda scraped it onto a plate and put it in the microwave to warm it up. She stood waiting. A knocking on the front door halted her running thoughts about what she was going to do. She'd been here before, they'd stabilize her. *Continual knocking.* Who could it be at this time of night? Brenda went to answer the door, wishing they'd leave her in peace.

"Yes?" She swung open the heavy wood door. The young man on the porch was tall and pale, his hair stringy, his clothes ripped and faded.

"Sorry. I just wondered if Ash was around? I tried calling, but no one picked up." He said, his words soft. They didn't match his troubling appearance.

"She's not here." Brenda said.

He shook his head, like he expected as much. Brenda noted a look of disappointment on his face. "Thanks. Sorry to bother you." He turned to leave.

"She's in the hospital." Brenda didn't know why she told him that. Ashley would kill her. "Are you one of her friends?"

He turned back to her, "Yeah, sort of. We hang out at school, mostly. I just haven't heard from her after the other night and wanted to make sure she was alright. But she's in the hospital?"

"The other night?" That raised Brenda's interest. "That wouldn't be Saturday night, would it?"

Nick weighed his words carefully, feeling she was fishing for something. "I don't know. A few nights ago. We were hanging out listening to music."

"Why don't you come in, Nick." Brenda stepped aside, inviting the boy in. Nick wanted to turn and leave, but his worry about Ashley in the hospital was stronger. Brenda was sure by now Ashley had been lying to her. She wasn't just out for a walk, she was with a boy. This Boy.

Brenda drilled him on the exact date, the time, what music? What happened that made Ashley run out of his house? Nick left out the part about feeling her up, slipping his hands down her pants. He said they were listening to music. She said her head hurt, and that she had to go home then ran out. He didn't know what happened. That was why he'd come by.

"What was the music?"

"Hog Head. It's this underground project." Nick figured she'd probably never heard of it, so what was the harm? But Brenda's eye seemed to pin.

She bit her tongue. She wanted to slap the kid. "And is this the same man who wrote that horrible book of poetry and essays? The one with the lovely drawings of nude, pig-headed women?" She asked, her words were tight. She was the adult here.

"Shit. Um, yeah. But Ash gave me that book back a while ago. She doesn't have it anymore."

"She made a copy, did you know that? She can't read stuff like that, not with her condition. She's written notes all over the margins. She thinks that man is talking to her! Sending her secret coded messages. Did she tell you that?"

Nick rubbed his face, looked down at his boots. He felt fucking horrible. "No, ma'am, she said nothing about it. I didn't know that her condition did stuff like that. I'm sorry. Can I go see her?"

Brenda's face relaxed. The kid looked sorry and upset. Why would she expect Ashley to tell her new friends everything about her mental illness? About the things she found horrifying about herself? "Well now you know. No more of this disgusting hog man, okay?" She said.

"Sure." Nick felt relieved. Brenda was probably the coolest mom he'd met. His mother would have kicked his ass. "Can I go see her?"

"Not tonight, visiting hours are done for the day. Tomorrow, ten to eight."

"Okay, cool. I'll go see her at ten."

"Don't you have school tomorrow?"

"Shit. After school then."

Brenda showed him to the door. He seemed nice. Apologetic, even. "And maybe not swear so much. I'm trying to break Ash of that habit."

"Now you sound like my mom," He said and waved. He got into a black car and drove off. *He drove.* He had to be at least sixteen. Ash and an older boy, alone, listening to music. That is a normal thing for teens to do, but Brenda was a teenager once too. She remembered how one thing could lead to another, and another.

Ashley alone with this boy kept picking at Brenda while she ate her dinner. She was sure part of the episode happened because of this Hog Head, but the other? A dark room and a teenage boy. Brenda didn't want her mind to wander there, but it was inevitable. Was Ashley having sex? She smoothed her hair back and realized she had a large smudge on her glasses. She needed to take a bath and get into bed. If this was about sex, Brenda didn't know if drugs could help it.

Brenda stopped by in the morning to see Ashley before work, but she was still asleep. She wanted to give her heads up about Nick, but didn't want to wake her. "She slept most of the night." The nurse told her.

"Let her know I'll be by after class." Brenda didn't want Ashley to feel alone, even if she wished to purvey the idea that she was.

It was past noon when Ashley woke up. She remembered being roused awake to take her medication earlier, but fell back asleep almost right away. "Do you want something to read?" A nurse asked her. Ashley wanted her fucking book. The book she remembered being torn to shreds, not by the Priest but by Brenda. "No, just fuck off." Ashley told her. It was one of the few places she could get away with saying that to an adult.

"Lunch!" Another nurse came in and brought a tray moments later.

Ashley looked it over and decided she wasn't eating, despite her stomach violently protesting otherwise. She turned on the television, but it was too bright. She flicked it back off. "Want to get up and walk around?" The nurse asked when she came to retrieve the tray. "I can bring you something else if you prefer? Oh, your mom dropped these off for you. She thought you might be more comfortable in your own clothes than a gown."

After the nurse had taken the tray away Ashley dug

through the overnight bag. It was silly, an overnight bag, as if she was staying in some five-star hotel. She felt it would be more fitting to have her clothes delivered in a plastic grocery sack, make her feel like the crazy bag lady she was destined to become.

She could tell they had already looked through it, laces were missing from her slippers. The clothing was refolded and carelessly put back into place. The toothpaste examined. Silent actions that reaffirmed her mad beliefs. Nothing made a person more paranoid than having their luggage rifled through. Small things taken out and rearranged. Where was her hair brush? *O, right, sharp metal bristles.* The mirror in her compact was missing.

In the bathroom, Ashley threw the thin hospital gown into the corner and pulled on black sweatpants and a loose purple tank top. She shook out her ratty cardigan, wanting nothing more than to wrap herself in it. The stitches in her arm pulled on the knit of the garment. She pushed up the sleeve and fingered the stiff lace work. Not the first time, not the last, she figured.

She clicked off the light and climbed back into bed, feeling sorry for herself. "Ash, you've got a visitor." The nurse poked her head in. She was younger than the rest, new, still filled with that newfound hope that a smile could cure even the worst of maladies.

Ashley sat up in bed. She was prepared to hear a stern lecture from Brenda. Or maybe it would be Dr. Hart. She could ask him if it would be possible to get her mattress moved to the floor. The space underneath. She didn't care for it. Like she was floating off into an unknown expanse.

"Whatever." Ashley said and shoved her blanket on the ground. She looked away, not wanting to hear whoever was taking the pleasure of lecturing her today.

"Ash, hey." Nick and Kirsten stood in the doorway.

"Yeah, hey Ash. how are you?" Kristen came in first and sat on the edge of the bed. Nick took the chair previously occupied by Brenda and Dr. Hart.

Ashley couldn't find the words. She pulled the sleeve of her sweater down. Nick saw the delicate stitching. He thought of his brother, and his own spiral down into self-mutilation. He wanted to tell her not to be embarrassed but didn't. He wasn't sure now why he had brought Kristen. It should have just been him.

"Why are you here?"

"Nick talked to Brenda."

Ashley was sure she would choke. Her mind was cracking. The flies had burrowed deep inside the hive, surrounded by her soft cortex. They were lazy from the drugs, as bees from smoke. But this panic jolted them enough to make Ashley grab at her head. "Oh god, what did you tell her?"

Kristen looked from Ashley to Nick, curious. *What did she mean?* Nick said nothing happened. What was Ash referring to? Kristen was just dying to know. She'd make a note to ask later when Nick wasn't around. *Just between us girls, Ash, what did you mean? Did something happen?*

Kristen hated that despite being dressed in sweatpants and a frumpy sweater, Ashley was pretty. She didn't want to admit it. Not a spot of acne, while Kristen had to use concealer, foundation, powder to cover the glaring red lumps that sprouted along her jawline. Her hair was fine, and despite complaining about being fat, Ashley was the same size as her. Kristen was never sure if Ashley was crazy or being passive aggressive. Maybe she really thought she was ugly. Kristen couldn't read her. She sat silently, studying Nick and Ashley, trying to decipher what might have gone on.

"I just said we were hanging out, that's all. Listening to music. I said nothing about smoking, or... that's it. That's all I said. I told her I tried to give you a ride home, but thought maybe I should leave you alone. I didn't know what to do. I feel terrible, Ash." He told her. Only the two of them knew the gritty details.

In a logical part of his mind, he wished he could take the act back. But in the teenage boy part, he enjoyed it. She was tender and warm. He would have really enjoyed her. He bet she was a virgin. He hated himself for thinking about that only a moment after looking at the glaring stitches on her pale arm.

Brenda knew now she had lied about everything. "It's not your fault. It's just my brain. And they changed my medications, so it could just be that. It happens." Ashley did not want anyone feeling bad for her. "It's embarrassing."

"No, don't even think about it." Nick told her.

"So are they going to let you out to go shopping next weekend?" Kristen asked. "Or are you still going to be crazy?"

"Really, Kris?" Nick asked.

"What? She's cool with it. You should hear what Gia said. Remember that one time the thing she said about slitting her wrists?" Kristen laughed and snapped her gum.

Ashley nodded, she remembered. Her wound throbbed. "I think I get out on Thursday unless I assault a nurse or something."

"Well, I've got a ton of homework. We'll still pick you up Saturday, okay?"

"Cool. Okay." Ashley said, glad Kristen and Gia still wanted to be friends with a nutcase.

"Nick, you're still driving me home, right?" Kristen asked, standing up and tugging her skirt down. It was so tiny it barely covered her ass.

"I like your skirt, Kristen." Ashley told her. She wanted to be extra nice to make up for being unstable.

"Oh, thanks. It's real leather." She said turning around for both of her friends to admire.

A nurse interpreted the trio. She came in to open the blinds on the large window that looked out at the nursing station. "Just wanted to let in some more light." She said and left. Ashley knew it was to keep a closer eye on her. She assumed her friends had to turn out their pockets before they were allowed in. You could never be too careful with delinquent teenagers.

The surrounding eyes were always watching.

Nick stood up and opened his jacket, reaching inside his inner pocket. "I brought these for you, if you still want them. But don't tell your mom." He said. He pulled out a small, carefully folded yellow bag. He handed it to her.

"What is it?" She asked. She opened the bag and pulled out two tapes and the well-read paperback. "No, those are your only copies." She said. "Nick, I can't take them."

He shrugged. "I think you'll get more out of it than I will. Hide them in your air vent. Parents rarely look there. They couldn't help my brother, can't help me. But he seems to speak to you. I want you to keep them." He said. Ashley might have been wrong, but he seemed almost sad about it.

"I'll keep them for you. But whenever you want them back, just tell me." Ashley said. He reached over and gave her hand a light squeeze. Kristen sighed. She couldn't fucking believe it.

"Wow, Nick, that's so nice. You never let me borrow that stuff. How long have we been friends?"

He glared at her, "Do you want a ride home or not?" he said, heading towards the door.

"Bye," Ashley called. She put the book and tape back into the bag and slipped it under her pillow. She'd tuck them into her bag later, review them closer in the confinements of her own home. A place where she could close her door, be alone for more than five minutes at a time.

Besides the pulsating cut on her arm, the meds making her thoughts slow and cloudy, Ashley felt okay. Her friends had come to see her. Nick didn't hate her. He knew how much this meant to her. He understood. Maybe when she found Hog Head's location, she'd invite him along. They could go together.

She laid down and attempted to sleep. She thought for a moment she saw Lucifer standing over by the window. "Lucifer? You're here?" She asked.

"Just throw them away, Ash." He told her.

But Ashley shook her head, "No, I can't. He'll be my savior." She whispered, drifting off.

"Or your greatest disappointment."

Seven

Ashley felt Brenda looming over her. "I'm fine, Brenda. Please, I just want to sleep. You don't need to be breathing down my neck." Ashley told her. "It's okay. I won't jump out the window. Even if I did, there are bushes down there, I'd be fine." Brenda didn't laugh at her joke. "Please, I just want to lie down."

"Do you need anything? Want me to unpack your bag?" Brenda asked, reaching for Ashley's overnight bag.

"No. That's okay. I want to feel useful. I can do it myself later. I'm not broken, Brenda. Don't you have class today?"

"Ash, there is no way you can be left alone right now." Brenda was astonished she would even think such a thing.

"Brenda, it was just an episode. We've been there before. Who really cares by this point?" Ashley kicked her bag into the corner and crawled onto her mattress. "Maybe a little quiet is all I need. I'm so sick of people looming over me, staring at me. Asking if I fucking *need* anything. I need to be alone. That's what I need!"

"Just calm down. Fine. I'll check back in a few hours when it's time for your medicine."

"Close the door, please."

"No, the door stays open." Brenda would not give on that one.

"Are you serious?"

"Yes, I am. Don't look at me like that. I am not the one who lied and ended up having a manic episode."

Ashley propped herself up against the pillows. "Lied about what?"

"We'll talk about that later when you're up to it. For now, the door stays open. Otherwise, I'll take the thing off the damn hinges." Brenda snapped and marched out. She was tired of Ashley trying to gaslight her into thinking these things weren't a big deal. Self-mutilation, hysteria, panic attacks, attempted suicide were tremendous deals. Brenda didn't even mention the nagging questions about her and Nick.

Ashley listened to Brenda's steps descend the creaking stairs. She rolled onto her side and rifled through her bag, pulling out the book. She ran her fingers over it, like saying hello to an old friend. She thought her chances were destroyed when Brenda tossed out the scraps of her copy. But the divine universe brought her and her prophet together once more.

Ashley set the book aside and pulled out the tapes. The clear plastic cases were scratched and foggy from years of abuse. She hadn't gotten a very good look at the paper inserts. She sat up and examined each word for word. The small print showed the same Mad Monk distributor, the same address she had written her letter to. But nothing else. Ashley focused on the word Judith. She wondered how many Judith's were in the state. What if she typed in towns and the name Judith? Maybe girl attacked or attempted murder Judith, what would come up? Too bad she'd never be able to do that with Nurse Brenda lurking around.

Ashley relaxed and cracked open the book. She turned to an essay about Hog Head and whom she assumed was Judith.

> ... Holtz says I'll never see her or touch her again. She's an innocent. I should never have defiled her with my visions of grandeur and dust. Why won't she answer? Are we so far away? Or does she simply refuse to hear the call? She knows about the other half, the ascended man/beast. She's the only one who has truly seen him. Who has accepted him into herself willingly. Much to her pleasure. She was the last one to see him. The last to see me. A shadow under the door. I know will never be her.
>
> (HH - Time does not flow here)

She knew that to be true. In a hospital time stops, or goes on without you, however you feel about it. You feel left behind when you finally merge back out into the stream of the everyday human. They rush around you like water around a stone. Their lives untouched, while yours becomes stiff and unbearable. Ashley felt more alone for having been away. They had cut her off from the herd. She didn't know if she had the strength or will to rejoin. She longed to find Hog Head, become a piece of furniture in his life.

The stairs squeaked, giving Brenda's presence away. Ashley tucked everything under her pillows and turned on her back, closed her eyes. Brenda looked in, walked over and picked up her bag. She'd just wash the clothes. That's what mothers did.

"You said I could go," Ashley said. She tried hard not to shout at Brenda.

"That was before everything."

"But I'm feeling better. I'm calm. I promised Kristen and Gia. I've never had friends to go shopping with. They want to take me to that party. Come on! If I don't go, they'll probably never ask me to do anything again. They'll think I'm too sick, unstable, or something. Brenda," Ashley sat back in her chair. She wasn't even hungry anymore. "It's just shopping!"

"But Halloween, a party? Do you think you're up for that? And we haven't even talked about the Nick thing. You lied to me."

"Because I knew you'd blow it out of proportion. We didn't have sex. I'm a virgin! I'll probably die a virgin. No one wants to fuck me!"

"Watch your mouth." Brenda said and took a drink of wine. She wished she could just cut to the chase and slug it straight from the bottle. It had been a long week. "Where would you be going?"

Ashley shrugged, "A Halloween store? One of those pop up ones downtown, probably."

"I want you home for dinner. Who's driving?"

"Gia. Kristen doesn't have a car." Ashley said, feeling a ray of hope. Now she wouldn't have to climb out her window.

"Back by six. Nothing to... risqué."

"Thank you! Thank you! I worship you oh, great Brenda!"

"Save it. We're still going to have the sex talk after dinner."

Ashley rolled her eyes. "I know about sex. What do you think patients at the clinic talk about all day? Our therapy and medication?"

"Those are adults. You're a child. It's different. Your first time should be-"

"Brenda, I'm going to vomit up my dinner. Please..."

She held out her hands, "Fine. But we are going to talk about it. Maybe you should go on the pill, just in case something ever happened."

"Great, another pill. How about you just sterilize me? I should never have a child. Ever!"

"We won't even get into that. The night is too short." Brenda said.

"I can't believe she let you come," Gia remarked, pulling out into traffic. Ashley sat in the backseat of the little yellow car. Frankly, she didn't believe it either.

"It's probably because I'm too drugged up to be a threat to anyone." The girls gave an awkward laugh.

Kristen for one was relieved to get a chance to drill Ash on what happened with Nick. He wouldn't talk about it and had avoided her all week.

"So you must be a great lay for Nick to give you his book, plus the tapes. Tell us, Ash, whatever did you do to him?" Kristen looked at her in the mirror. Ashley felt herself blush. She looked down at the lime green nail polish she had put on the night before.

"Nothing. We didn't do anything."

"Lies!" Kristen called from the front seat. Her smile was enormous and reminded Ashley of the Cheshire Cat.

"I swear. We smoked some pot, listened to the tape. After that I don't know, I freaked out. Maybe it was the weed and my meds, or something? I'm still a virgin."

Kristen sighed, "That's what he said." She sat back in the seat and looked out the window. Both of them were lying to her. "You know Ash, it's a sin to lie to your best friends."

"What do you mean?" Ashley wasn't sure if she was being serious or not.

"Girls talk about this kind of thing. It's not even a big deal. Nick is our friend, he's your friend. You're out friend. Come on!" Kristen tried one last time.

"Come on, Ash. Spill!" Gia urged. A car blared its horn as they whipped out in front of it, taking the yellow light before it turned red.

"No, it was nothing. We kissed, that's all." There, she said it. Would they let it go?

"And? Nick never just kisses anyone. Just say it!" Kristen was turning to look at her. She wanted to hear about it. It irritated her to think of Nick with another girl, but wanted to know anyway. Why would he choose Ash over her? He only fucked her twice and both times he had to be drunk. One right after his brother died, and the other last summer at a bonfire. "Just tell us this, was there penetration?" Kristen asked.

"No! No. Just a kiss." She paused.

"And? Don't make me guess.. because I will."

"Oh, she will." Gia laughed.

"I can't say it, it's too embarrassing." Ashley was grinning now, too. Not wanting to talk about it, but kind of wanting to.

"Ash, come on." Kristen said, Gia echoing her.

She had to just say it. They had built it up too much. It was just between girls. "He uh, put his hand down my pants and..." The girls erupted into pitches of laughter, like a hyena den.

"I knew it! You let him finger fuck you!" Kristen said.

"Just for a second, that's when I... when it all happened. It's a blur. I don't even remember if I liked it." Ashley pressed her lips together, wondering if she should have said anything.

"Uh, well, I'm sure Nick will be sad to hear you don't even remember it." Kristen said.

"What? No. You can't tell him I said anything. If Brenda found out..."

"Relax, we're not going to say anything, right G?"

Gia pretended to cross her heart with a lazy finger, "No way." That made Ashley feel better. They wouldn't, they were her friends. Friends that still wanted to hang out with her despite the stitches in her arm, and her record of hospitalization. "We're here!" Gia announced, pulling sharply into a parking space.

"I want something hot." Gia reiterated every time someone suggested something. "No, I want to be like... a sexy nun." She said.

"No. No nuns!" Ashley was firm. "I hate church stuff. No religious costumes, please. I just can't."

Both girls looked at her, wondering if she was going to have another freak out. Kristen shrugged, "Okay, you heard her, Gia, no nun."

"Boo! We could have dressed Nick up as a sexy priest and he could-"

"Stop! Don't even say it!" Ashley covered her ears. She didn't want to picture him like that. She saw Priest in her mind's eye, his long fingers with inflamed knuckles probing up inside her, while she attempted to squirm away. He held her. *It's God's will, my child.* She shuttered. "How about witches? Those can be... sexy." Ash suggested.

"Witches are very in right now." Kristen said.

Gia sighed, "Then everyone will be witches!"

"But we're hotter than everyone else," Kristen said. Ashley wished she was right, but faked her confidence. The costumes were black short dresses, pointed hats and fishnets. Ashley felt like a cow.

"No, you look so good." The girls assured her.

"We'll come over early, we can do your make-up." Kristen said.

"I have a pair of shoes you can borrow." Gia suggested in the car.

"I can't wear heels. I have a pair of black boots I can wear."

Gia shrugged, *suit yourself*. Ashley didn't want to stop and eat with them, so they dropped her off a half hour early.

"You guys can come in. We can cook again." Ashley suggested.

"Nah, it's cool. We'll see you later." Kristen said. They drove off, leaving Ashley standing on the curb with a shopping bag clutched in her fist. She knew they wouldn't come in while Brenda was here.

Ashley pushed open the door and saw the mail on the floor. "I'm back, Brenda." She yelled up the stairs. She set the bag down and gathered up the stack of letters and restaurant fliers. All was unremarkable. She had heard nothing from Wheeler since the cum letter. She thought about writing to him, telling him about the hospital.

She dropped the stack on the floor, her finger clutched the envelope. It looked unremarkable except for the return address: M.M. Art House. *It was Them*. Ashley felt the lethargic swarm within surge to life. They had all been waiting. She heard the footsteps overhead. She stuffed the letter into her back pocket. "Have a good time?" Brenda asked, descending the staircase. "What did you get?"

Ashley was at a loss for words. The letter clashed with her current reality. "Witch. We're going to be witches." Ashley told her.

"Well, I like that you're home early. Let me see."

Ashley pulled out the cheap black frock. "Kristen wants to do my make-up so they'll be over before the party."

Brenda wanted to say the costume was cute, but it was too short for that. "You'll be comfortable wearing that? I thought maybe you'd get something a little... longer." Brenda commented.

"They wanted these. It was witches or sexy nuns."

Brenda made a face, "No. This was a much better choice."

"That's exactly how I felt."

"Did you still want to watch that movie tonight?" Brenda asked while Ashley kicked off her shoes.

Ashley forgot about that. Brenda barely gave her over twenty minutes alone these days. But they had been planning the movie night for a week. It took several days to decide what to watch. Ashley wanted *Blue Velvet,* but Brenda nixed it. "Absolutely not." They decided on *Bride of the Monster instead.*

"I really need to take a nap though if we're going to be watching that." Ashley pretended to yawn.

"That's fine, but take you medicine first. It's almost time, anyway. Want me to get it? I can bring it up." Brenda asked, heading towards the kitchen. Ashley didn't realize what time it was. They had increased her liquid piss dose, half the time she felt stoned, the other half like she was drunk and might vomit.

"You don't need to nurse me, Brenda. I got it." Ashley passed Brenda and went into the kitchen. Brenda stood there and watched her. Ash had no choice but to take the full amount. She swallowed it down. Turning to Brenda, she opened her mouth wide, lifted her tongue to the side. "All gone, Brenda. Don't worry, I can't tongue the stuff."

"I wasn't watching you like that." Brenda said. "Go get some sleep. I'll order out for dinner. Any requests?"

"Salad. No dressing." Ashley said and went upstairs. Brenda was getting so sick of salad. Fuck it, she was ordering herself a pizza. Ashley could have a slice if she wanted.

Upstairs Ashley closed her door halfway, the most Brenda would allow. She sat on her bed and held the cold white paper in her hands. She licked her lips. What did it say? Her search could be over. Her questions answered. His address inside. She had to open it. She swallowed, wishing she had a drink of water with her. But she couldn't go back down now. Inside was a typed paper folded in thirds.

There were no more copies of Hog Head being made at the moment. No plans for anything until next year. They had nothing in storage. Completely sold out. No reprints. She could sign up for their mailing list that included a flier of their small selection of offbeat authors and artists. He wouldn't give out an address for HH, but would pass on her admiration for his work. Thanks for her interest. Mad Monk.

She leaned forward and took a deep, frustrated breath. A fucking dead end! Less than nothing! She wanted to scream and shred the meaningless letter. But then she realized HH. The Mad Monk referred to him as HH. One essay was noted as HH. A second name? No where else did she see this abbreviation. Now she had two names to investigate- Judith and HH.

Ashley had to get to a computer, she had to research the surrounding area, only instead of looking for news of Hog Head she had to shorten it to HH. If only she had a last name. But how many men in the area were called HH? How many women, Judith? It was a long shot. But she felt HH meant something. She reread the letter, pulled out the book, compared them. They definitely said HH. She wasn't making this up.

With care, she folded the letter and put it back into the envelope. She tucked it inside the paperback from Nick. She listened, silent downstairs. She leaned over and put the pile into the vent, and pushed the metal grate back into place. She enjoyed sleeping with it so close to her. Like *He* was sleeping beside her. *Soon, my prophet, soon.*

She was on the stained bed again, HH over her. A fleshy pig head tied with twine obscured his face. A stained leather apron around his waist. "Open me." She begged, examining her hands and arms, the flies bumping along under her skin.

"They're restless." He commented, his voice muffled by the rotting mask. She watched his intense eyes behind the empty sockets. She had read that a pig was more intelligent than a three-year-old child. Did that pig know what was going to happen before they slaughtered it? She shivered, the room was empty and cold but for the bed.

"Be still now." He instructed, tickling the tool over her abdomen as if he was trying to decide where to make the first cut. The blade was unclean. Different from the last. It was long and slender, with an edge on both sides. At the end, a small delicate hook.

"I'm ready." She exhaled. HH parted her knees and opened her wide like a frog. He slid the hooked blade into her virginal gash and with a smooth flick of his wrist quickly pulled it out. Ashley gasped, "I love you," as gore and larva came flowing from between her thighs. The flies swarmed up and over her like a knot of sparrows twisting in the air. Her body emptied, her limbs lightened, the static in her head ceased. They were leaving, she was becoming.

HH loomed over her with the wet blade. Flies covered his face, crawling into the empty holes in the mask, eating the soft cartilage of the nose and ears. He turned away from the scene. "What now?" She asked, laying open on the blood-soaked mattress.

"We let you drain. It'll take a while. It'll hurt." He picked up a coil of rope and came back over to the bed.

"What? What are you doing?" She asked, looking up at him. He said nothing. His fly covered pig face blank. He tied the rope roughly around each wrist and hauled her up onto her knees. She didn't struggle, but kept asking what was going on.

He put his finger to the pig's mouth, "hush" he said. And slipped a loop of rope on a thick hook bolted to the ceiling. He kicked the metal bed frame out from under her. Ashley swung, her tiptoes dragging on the floor.

"It hurts."

"I said it would." He walked away from her. Parted a sheet of heavy plastic hanging in the doorway. Ashley heard metal scraping in the other room, like he was sharpening a knife against a stone. She felt another gush of warm blood sprinkled with fleshy worms come rolling out of her.

Her guts twisted, she gasped at a pain she'd never felt. The flies had eaten all of her muscles, tendons; the knife had sliced the past piece of herself, holding it all in. She could feel it trailing out of her clots and chunks. It was warm and crawling down her inner thigh, a heavy plop as it settled onto the ground below her.

"Help," she whispered. When you're climbing a mountain covered in snow, or exploring a cave system, you do not yell. The vibrations could set off a chain of events of which you'd have no control. Ashley felt this. Screaming would shake her heart, lungs, send them slithering down her leg with the rest of it.

Flies buzzed in her face. She twisted back and forth.

God, it hurt. She wanted to curl into a ball. She dared not look at the mess she had made as she slogged off her human suit. A cold draft came in the door, chilling her. "Stop, stop!" She finally called out while flies came out of her mouth. She choked on them, and couldn't spit them out fast enough. She was drowning in them.

She heard rustling to her left, attempted to open her eyes through the flies and pain, HH stood in the doorway, his mask removed. But she couldn't see his face. She shook her head, attempted to clear her vision, but it was dark, and her eyesight fading. He was a smear of green light, like Lucifer and the other's had become towards the end.

She shivered and moaned, "Help... please... I love you... I'm yours." She waited for him to come to her, relieve her heavy pain, take her in his arms.

"That is not the point of all this." He backed away. She wanted to run after him, but with the biting of the ropes around her wrist, the sharp pull of pain reverberated down within her. It was all for nothing. He left her hanging there. She screamed his name, but he did not come.

The pain was so strong it woke Ashley from her dream. Or maybe it was a nightmare? She pulled her knees to her chest. The pain wasn't stopping. She knew she was awake now, but it went on.

Ashley turned on the lamp beside her mattress and sat up. She felt like she was going to be sick. She pushed back the blanket to look. Her pants were moist with the spill of fresh blood. She screamed for real this time, shocked at the sight before her. "It's not real. It's not real." Had Hog Head done this to her? She wasn't ready. He was supposed to be with her when it happened.

Brenda ran in and turned on the light, saw the blood and rushed over. "It's okay. I think... does it hurt?" She asked.

Ashley looked at her, her face pained. She shook her head that yes; it did. "I think it's just your period. Some of your medication can mess with your cycle. It was only a matter of time before you got it. I'm surprised it took this long. Come on, let's get cleaned up." Brenda helped Ashley to the bathroom.

"I can do it. I'm not a child." Ashley told her and closed the door. Her hands trembled as she removed her bottoms and underwear. She wiped herself off with a cloth. No sign of maggots, no clots of tissue. Just a normal biological thing. But her dream felt so real. Like a token of things to come. Was that the last test she'd have to endure before he would accept her as a follower? To give away her human self and trust he knew better? He was preparing her.

"Ash, I've got some clean clothes." Brenda said through the door. Ashley wrapped herself in a towel and took the stack of fresh laundry. She rummaged under the sink for a tampon. She'd never inserted one, but figured there wasn't much to it. She grimaced and pushed it in. After a second she forgot it was there except for the delicate white string that dangled between her legs.

"I can get some sanitary pads tomorrow." Brenda told her.

"Don't worry about it, it's fine." Ashley said.

They stood looking at her bed. The mattress would probably have a stain. "I'll soak the sheets overnight. I'm sure I can get most of the blood out. It's still fresh, so it shouldn't be too bad." Ashley helped pull everything off and put on new sheets while Brenda ran water in the bathtub for the linens and clothing.

"Do you need anything else?" She asked before going back to bed.

"No, thanks. Sorry about the screaming. I was just shocked, that's all. What happened to the movie?" Ashley just realized it was the middle of the night.

"I didn't want to wake you. We'll watch it tomorrow. Get some sleep." Brenda pulled the door halfway closed. Ashley listened to her walk back down the hall to her bedroom. There was no way Ashley was going to sleep. It was four in the morning and she was wide awake. She reached over and removed the vent cover, taking out the book. Neon sticky notes stuck out from the top and sides. She didn't want to scribble on it in case Nick ever wanted it back.

Ashley opened it to a favorite short essay. In it, HH covered the alienation of the mentally ill. How upset society became when a person looked normal but acted in otherwise outrageous or violent manors. When it was declared not to be their fault because of some flaw of nature, people had trouble accepting this logic. He would be sick for life. He would either take their medication to paralyze his natural thought process or remain in a small locked room behind security fencing. What did it matter? Even if he got out, he had no one.

Society had already turned their back on him. Not only was he unpredictable, but he had a record. He'd be better off just killing himself than trying to live outside the white walls. He'd die alone, but he felt he deserved it. And there were worse things than death. Of that he was certain.

Ashley sighed and held the book to her chest. He was right, there were worse things than the deep kiss of the dark stranger. She wondered if she'd ever be able to hack it in this world. She oftentimes felt like a specimen to be feared, but studied. Treasured, but held at arm's length. You can never trust a wild animal, they kill when you let your guard down.

She was even starting to question her friendship with Kristen and Gia. Gia only spoke to her if Kristen was there, and Kristen seemed to think there was something deeper going on with Nick behind her back.

Kristen felt harsher than she had before, like she just wanted Ashley to snap so Nick could see the real her. But that's the thing. He had, and he was still nice to her. He probably wouldn't try to fuck her again, but they still seemed to exist on the same wavelength somewhere in space and time. Maybe she reminded him of his dead brother. Suicide and everything. It either brought people closer or drove them apart.

He had come to see her, gave her the book and tapes even after Brenda had told him not to. He seemed concerned. Kristen, Ashley worried, she might not think it's worth it. She just hoped the Halloween party went well, then she and Gia would see she was fine. The party might even be fun.

Ashley heard Brenda wake at six. She stayed in bed a few hours longer. She knew her next steps. Get to a computer, research. Avoid taking the brown bottle piss and pills they passed off as medicine. That made her slow, hazy. She needed to keep a clear head. But she couldn't let on that she knew she was well. It was the medicine that was making her so sick, keeping her passive and easy to control.

What troubled her the most was what did they want with her? Was she a guinea pig in their experiment? A blind drug trial, perhaps. She couldn't believe Brenda would do such a thing to her. She trusted her. She'd just have to watch her back, look over her shoulder. She couldn't tell Dr. Hart anything, as it was clear he was reporting directly to Brenda.

Brenda and Ashley sat in the dark watching the flicking images on the screen. Brenda tried to get Ashley to join her on the sofa, but Ashley insisted on sitting in the chair. "I just need space," She said.

"Fine, sit over there. I'll just keep all the popcorn for myself."

"I'm not eating after five anymore, so go ahead."

"Why aren't you eating after five? We usually don't have dinner until six or seven."

"I'm fasting for eighteen hours, if you have to know. Maybe I'll just stop eating dinner. Breakfast and lunch is enough." Ashley turned back to the movie. Brenda looked at her a moment longer. Ashley seemed on edge, but she thought it might just be her imagination. After this last week, her nerves were fried.

When the movie finally ended Ashley was almost out the door before Brenda stopped her. "Hey, come back here." She said.

"What? I'm tired. I have school in the morning."

Brenda pressed her lips together. "Dr. Hart and I think it would be better if I just picked up your assignments for you." Ashley opened her mouth in protest, but Brenda went on. "Just for a while. Maybe till after Christmas."

"When were you going to tell me what you've decided for me!" Ashley yelled. She felt isolated, cut off. "First you make me go to a school I don't want to fucking go to. Then you decided I should only go part time. Then I make friends, who I hardly ever see except at school. Now I can't even step foot on the grounds? I'm just supposed to stay home all day and study and talk to the fucking houseplant!"

"Ashley, you just saw your friends yesterday. And as I recall, you snuck off with that Nick to his house, then lied about it. How about we talk about that? Or the episode that it caused. Then we can reassess your freedom. You're lucky I'm still open to letting you go to that party next week. Which, if I'm being honest about it, isn't a good idea."

Ashley laughed. "Letting me go? I am not your prisoner, *Brenda*."

Brenda stood up. She hadn't expected to fight, but it seemed it was impossible to talk to her daughter these days without it turning into a screaming match. "You're not my prisoner, but my child. I am by law here to keep you safe from others and yourself. You may choose not to believe it, but you aren't always capable of making the best choices for yourself. That's why I'm here. You know I do this-"

"Don't say because you love me. I'm not even your daughter, just your lab rat!"

"My what?" Brenda didn't know where this was coming from. Ashley had always had a paranoia about the Church, or strangers. But her? She had always trusted her, now she suddenly thought Brenda was experimenting on her? "Ash, tell me just what you think is going on?"

"What's the point? You'll just lie about it. That's all you and Dr. Hart do. Lie, lie!"

"Just go take your medicine. I need a moment." Brenda walked upstairs before she lost it.

Ashley turned furiously and went into the kitchen, slamming cupboards, making noise. She was not taking the poison. She took her dose and dumped it down the sink. Fuck Brenda and her doctors. All this time they had been telling her it was the Church that was out to get her, but she had seen through the veil. That's what HH had meant in her dream, why he didn't want her yet.

She was still blind to the world around her. How could she ever see him, love him, when she was still a cog in *their* system? Maybe they were using her to get to him? What would they do when they found him? What did they do to all prophets? Nail them to crosses and serve their heads on plates. She couldn't let that happen. She would find HH, join him when she could. Her eyes were closed before, but they were wide open now.

Ashley refused to speak to Brenda for the rest of the week. In the morning Brenda parked out front of the school. Ashley insisted on collecting her work from the office herself. "Maybe I should be escorted by an armed guard, you know, just in case I have another fr*eak out*."

Brenda was thinking about taking up smoking. "Just go get your homework, please. I'm going to be late for my first class." It was Wednesday, and Ashley had heard nothing from Kristen or Gia since Saturday. She tried calling Kristen but didn't get an answer. They had to wonder where she was considering she was always in the library. She hoped they still wanted her to go to the party in a few days.

It seems like one would have called her. But maybe that's just how teenage girls were, flaky and unreliable. Ashley was sure everything was fine. They have school and a life just like her. It wasn't like they had known each other long either. They'd call. It would be fine.

Considering all this, it surprised Ashley to see it was Nick was hanging out by the office door. He seemed to be waiting for her. "Hey, there you are. I didn't want to call your house in case your mom was still pissed." he said. "How's the arm?"

He was the first person to ask her about it. "Fine. Itches, but that's about it. How did you know I'd be coming in the morning?"

"Kirsten said you left her a message about it."

"I haven't heard from her. I thought maybe she'd meet me. We're supposed to go to that party Saturday. I just wanted to make sure everything was still cool. But whatever."

Nick smiled as she shrugged, pretending not to care. He could tell it bugged her. "Kristen is kind of a bitch, don't worry about it. That party is usually pretty chaotic. Lots of drinking. Are you sure it's a good idea?" *No, not him too.*

Ashley's eyes narrowed. "I'm so sick of everyone treating me like...you know it doesn't matter."

"I didn't mean it like that. I wasn't going to go until Kristen told me her and Gia were bringing you." He looked away from her for a moment. The bell rang.

"You're going to be late for class." Ashley was tired of him acting like he was concerned for her. He just wanted to fuck her, like Kristen said.

"I'm always late. I just wanted to see how you are doing."

"Like you care." Ashley pushed past him into the office, expecting by the time she got out he'd be gone. But he was still there. The crowd had thinned.

"What?" She asked when she came back out.

"I don't get it. Are you mad at me or something?"

Was she? "No. You're just wasting your time, that's all. I'm not going to fuck you. I'll probably never fuck anyone."

Nick looked alarmed. "Shh. What?"

"Kristen said-" Nick's laugh interrupted her. "Don't laugh, it's not funny." Ashley said.

"Don't listen to that crazy bitch. She's just pissed because I don't want to date her. We screwed around twice and now she thinks she wants to be my girlfriend. That's why I said I didn't know if you should go to that party with them. She lies, Ash. I just want to be your friend. That other stuff just happened, and I feel bad about it."

"Ash?" Ashley turned at the sound of her name, Brenda was standing near the front entrance. "I'm going to be late."

Ashley turned back to Nick. She felt they had an understanding. "Sorry, Brenda. Nick just wanted to make sure I was okay." Nick nodded in agreement and waved. "He was afraid to call because he didn't want you to verbally assault him over the phone." Ashley said bluntly.

Brenda walked over. "You can call, I promise I won't scream at anyone. I'm not a monster just because I'm over eighteen. Nick, you are welcome to call whenever you like. You can stop by as long as I'm there. I support Ash having friends who care about her." *Better him than that Kristen and Gia.* It surprised Brenda she felt that way. Something about those girls just rubbed her the wrong way. "But for now, say goodbye. I've got a class in thirty minutes. And Nick, I'm sure there's somewhere you're supposed to be right now."

He sighed, she sounded like a teacher. "There is. Ash, I'll call you later. Good, you see you again, Brenda." He said. Ashley watched his black leather coat disappear around the corner. *He was going to call her.*

"Is that a smile?" Brenda said. Ashley quickly turned it off.

"No. I thought you were going to be late."

"Shit, you're right. Come on." Brenda opened the door and followed Ashley out. Ashley would spend most of the day doing her homework in the back of the half filled lecture hall. She had been forced to have lunch with Brenda and Timothy the last two days.

Ashley lied to Brenda and told her she was too tired. Felt like shit. Could she just go home? Or at least go walk around and stretch her legs. She was sick of sitting all day. She had been trying to get to the computer lab to research more on her prophet, but Brenda had her on a tight leash.

"You can take a nap in my office. That's as good as it's going to get." Brenda said.

"Just forget it." Ashley had tried to use Brenda's laptop, but it was password protected and she had never figured it out. She'd have to be patient.

She felt a little better cutting back on her medication. Brenda watched her in the morning, so she had to take everything. But in the evenings Brenda was busy correcting papers or talking to Timothy, taking a bath. Ashley began squirting that dose down the sink when she could. Her head hurt, at times she felt a little dizzy. But she figured that was her body working the poison out of her system. It would take time. She'd taper herself off little by little.

As her eyes opened to the invisible world around her, she saw clearly for the first time. She felt lucky. So many people just walked through life blind, never knowing the true meaning of their existence. They worked, spent money, bought houses, celebrated holidays, went out with friends, took lovers, had babies. Ashley felt she was above all that. That it was pointless in the grand scheme of the universe.

When she joined HH at his home, she imagined they'd create something together. He had already started the work, but would need her, a feminine energy to complete the gospels. They would put out books of truth together, live a life of anonymity in a shack in the woods. The snows would come, she'd sit on the couch and sketch. He'd work on a typewriter across the room. Both knowing that their followers were out there waiting for their next work of wisdom.

When she was cold, he'd warm her. When he was hungry, she'd feed him. Ashley thought her heart might burst at the thought. She felt the time coming quick and strong. Everything was changing right at this moment. The energy of the universe had begun to rotate counterclockwise, things that were forwards now ran back. Time was eating itself, Ouroboros in the shape of eternity.

"Ash? Are you ready?" Brenda snapped her fingers a few times in front of Ashley's face. Her eyes were distant, empty. It unnerved Brenda when Ashley drifted like this, as if she was so far within herself. It took a few minutes for her to climb back out. "Ash! I'm done. Are you ready?"

"What?" It took a moment to ground herself. She thought she still smelled the wood stove from the cabin. The sound of the tall trees scratching against the roof. Now it was just Brenda in an empty room. Voices echoed in the hallway. "Can we go home, yet?"

"I'm ready when you are." Brenda helped Ashley gather up her history book and papers. The new medication didn't seem to work as well as she hoped. But it was still early days, Dr. Hart told her to give it some time. She just had to give it time.

Ashley didn't hear from Kristen until Friday night. She and Gia would be by at four to get ready. Ashley thought that was the end of the conversation. She said bye, but Kristen kept talking. She said out of nowhere, "Nick said he saw you the other day."

"He was by the office when I went to get my schoolwork. I told you in the message I left."

"I know. I might have said something to him about it, but I didn't think he'd be there like stalking you. I'm so sorry. I told him to stop bothering you. Next time just tell him to fuck off. Some guys just can't take a hint, right?"

"It's alright. We got everything straightened out. I think we're cool now." There was silence on the other end. "Hello?"

"Really? That must have been some talk. I mean the guy tried to rape you and now you're all best friends, huh? Just takes a book to buy your forgiveness. I'll remember that." She laughed.

"What? That's not what I said at all." Ashley dropped her voice, worried Brenda might hear. "And he didn't force himself on me. Things just went a little too fast."

"That's the only speed guys like that know, Ash. He just wants to get in your pants then he'll turn around and call you a slut. Trust me on this."

Ashley didn't believe her. Nick didn't give off that vibe. But she wanted to be friends. "Don't worry, nothing is going to happen. I'm sure he'll get sick of me and move on to some other girl."

"Let's hope so. Shit, mom's home. I'll see you Saturday! Yey, party!" She hung up before Ashley could say anything more.

The conversation left a foul taste in her mouth. But hadn't Nick warned her as much? Maybe Kristen was jealous. Once everyone realized that Ashley wasn't going to have sex with anyone, everything would calm down. She was beyond sex with minor teenage boys. She was saving her blood for HH. Still she smiled a little to herself, someone like Kristen was jealous of her. No one had ever been jealous of her.

That night Ashley dreamt of Lucifer. She rolled over, and he was beside her, tracing her jawline with a soft graceful finger. "What are you doing, Ashley?"

"Lucifer? What are you doing in my bed?" he was so beautiful, Ashley could hardly look at him. Sometimes he was a blur of blue light, other times he was in a suit of armor corroded with blood of their enemies. Now he was draped in her blanket, he could have been nude underneath. Ashley felt for him with her feet, but couldn't find him under the covers.

"I hate Kristen, she's a leech."

"That's what you came to tell me?"

He sighed, "So how's school?"

"I don't want to talk about it."

He looked smug. "Thought so. Just watch the path you're going down. It's lined with thorns." The door behind them creaked. A goat wandered in and climbed onto the end of the bed. He laid down on Ashley's legs.

"Jesus, you're heavy, lay on the floor. You stink." She told Satan. Lucifer laughed.

"He's worried about you too."

"Look, I'm sorry you guys are bored. But I've got more important things to worry about. That other stuff was just an illusion. My eyes are open to the real enemies. Don't worry about me. I've got someone *real* watching out for me."

Lucifer rolled his eyes, Satan-goat bleated. "He is not a prophet. He's only a man. A writer. He will not take care of you. This is your disordered brain trying to lure you into a false reality."

"False reality? Please." Ashley wiped his hand off her face. "You're the false reality. You and him. Priest, the nuns, the church surveillance. Those nut job doctors that my mother took me to when I was little planted all that stuff in my brain. That's the false reality. Now that I've moved past it, you just won't let go. HH is real. He may live in a house of flesh and bone, but he had transcended the human experience, and soon I will too."

"Ashley..."

"Go! You two sound like Brenda and Dr. Hart. I've got enough actual people whispering in my ear. I don't need you two anymore. I'm not afraid."

"What about that?" Lucifer gestured to the stitches on Ashley's' arm. The edges were still red and puffy.

"It doesn't matter. I know now. He showed me everything!" Ashley covered her ears and turned away from them both, curling to a tight ball. "He's real. He's real. He's real." She chanted, drowning them out.

When she woke up, it was still dark out, that awkward time between night and day. Ashley kicked off her covers and opened the window. The chilled damp air came wafting in. She took her book out from the vent and sat on her window seat, taking in the fresh breeze. The sweat rapidly cooled on her skin, making her shiver despite feeling cooked inside.

> Number 22
> By their mourning cry
> So I see
> So I decide
> So you and I slide
> See you
> See men
> Semen
> So you and I decide
> Suicide
> The sirens lie
> I know this
> By their mourning cry

It said it right there in black and white, *so you and I decide.* Lucifer didn't know what he was talking about. HH was real. The two of them together would decide when it was time to end it, it wasn't her choice alone. She was ignorant to think otherwise. She ran her fingers over each line, as if reading them by touch alone. She absorbed his words into herself. They had to join as higher selves before joining in the flesh. He was real. He wrote these words. She felt his voice in her ear like an itch. A warm, reassuring breath on her neck. He was calling her still.

Eight

Kristen and Gia were a half hour late. They came in shouting, swinging shopping bags and a large make-up case. Brenda watched all three girls stomp up the steps. She heard the door at the end of the hall slam. It didn't matter; they were so loud people could probably hear them down the street. She went back to her book. You couldn't pay her enough to be a teenager again. If that was what Ashley wanted, she'd have to learn that lesson for herself. There was no point in trying to tell her, she'd never listen. They never did.

"Where can I plug this in?" Gia asked, taking out a large hot iron.

"I want gigantic waves." Kristen said.

"Just over there by the desk." Ashley pointed. Kristen was opening a large box of make-up. Ashley hardly wore any. She had a chapstick and eyeliner, that was about it. "Wow, you have so much."

Kristen shrugged, "I don't even use half of this stuff. Want some? Here, take these." She handed Ashley a handful of eyeliner pencils, a few tubes of lipstick, a foundation that she said was too light for her, but would work for Ash. A pallet of black and gray shadows.

"Thanks. That's so nice, but I don't know what to

do with any of this." Ashley felt stupid.

"That's why we're here." Gia came over and jumped on the bed, going through the box. She pulled out a cherry red lipstick and rolled it on, smacking her lips. "See, easy."

"You look like a blow-up doll. That is way too thick." Kristen said. Gia shrugged, like it was a complement. Ashley didn't get how they could be so casual about sex. The close contact, the touching, *the emotions*...it made her squirm.

"Come on Ash, I'll do you first. Then Gia can do your hair. She's awesome at it, despite hardly having any."

"I'm going to beauty school when I graduate." Gia announced proudly, as if she was accepted into an ivy league university. Brenda would never let Ashley go to beauty school. She would say Ashley was too smart for that. Maybe she was, but her concentration was shit. It didn't matter anyway, she had other plans beyond anyone's comprehension.

Kristen layered on concealer, foundation, powder. It was heavy. "Is all that necessary?"

"You're just not used to it. Just wait, it'll look fucking great." She said and kept adding more make-up. Ashley counted at least three different shades of black eye shadow. Kristen claimed it would look smoky. Then she painted on black liquid eyeliner and curled it out to the side. "It's called a cat eye." She explained.

"Do you want dark lips or pale?" She asked.

"Um, whatever you think."

"Do the red. Here" Gia handed Kristen the red she had used earlier.

"Didn't you say that it looked like a blowup doll's color?" Ashley asked,

Kristen smiled. "That's on Gia. She makes everything look slutty. It looks *so* good on you." Kristen finished up. "There go look so Gia can do your hair."

Ashley examined her face in the mirror. The make-up was more like paint, filling in her pale eyebrows, popping out her eyes. She looked older. She didn't look like herself. "It's amazing. I look so different."

"Aw! Don't touch. Gia the hair!" Kristen called, going over to paint her own face.

By the time the girls were dressed, it was almost six. The dresses were black, body hugging little things with large open bell sleeves. The two wore thick heels, while Ashley wore heavy black boots.

Brenda had to work to hide her look of shock when the three came prancing down the stairs. "Wow, look at you three." She said. Ashley could tell she hated it.

"Don't we look fab?" Gia twirled and slid on her tiny red leather jacket, pulling the billowing sleeves out the ends.

"Something like that, yeah." Brenda said.

"Well, we're going to go, Brenda."

"Back by 11 please, girls." Brenda told them.

"Promise." Kristen assured her. Ashley sighed. She tried to get Brenda to reconsider her curfew, but she wouldn't budge.

"Oh Ash, wait! Did you take your..." She didn't

want to say the word *meds* in front of her friends. But Ashley got it.

"Right. One sec." She dashed off to the kitchen. She listened to the girls talk to Brenda, while she pressed her dose down the sink and ran the water. "All good" She smiled and gave Brenda a quick hug. "Have a fun night with *Timothy*."

"I'll be here when you get home." Brenda ignored her sarcasm and stood in the door watching the three pile into Gia's hatchback. They laughed and giggled. Despite not caring for her choice of friends, Brenda was just glad Ashley had them. She'd be alright, Ashley was a fighter. Whatever her illness or life threw at her, she always fought back. Brenda hoped she'd hold on to that spirit. She'd seen so many people, older and wiser than Ashley, broken by mental illness. She was determined not to let that happen. She smiled and waved as the car pulled away, heavy metal leaking out the windows, disturbing the quiet fall evening.

Brandon lived about thirty minutes outside the city. A long trailer sat in an unkempt yard cut into the surrounding cornfield. The broken skeleton of a dilapidated barn pierced the skyline behind the home. Ashley looked at the flickering tiki torches that lined either side of the long pothole driveway.

The music was loud. People were already milling around outside, drinks in hands. Gia parked the hatchback on the grass next to a row of motorcycles. "Brandon's dad is in a club. That's where we get the weed." Gia told her, even though Ashley didn't ask.

"Among other things." Ashley wasn't sure what she meant, but nodded like she did.

"They just give it to you?" She asked, climbing out the back seat.

"No. But they take cash or ass. Either one." Gia giggled, Kristen shoved her as if to shut her up. "What it's true."

"Only if you're a whore." Kristen laughed.

"Maybe I am. At least tonight." Gia gave a loud whooping laughter and ran into the crowd. A few guys cheered.

"Just stick with me, Ash. You'll be fine. And if any guy puts his hand up your skirt, just kick him. Okay?"

Ashley swallowed, "Will that happen?"

"I don't know. Maybe." Ashley couldn't tell if she was joking or not. Kristen pulled her along. Brandon was leaning against the porch.

"Hey, you're finally here. Glad they let you out of the insane asylum." He eyed Ashley.

"Yeah, for sure." Ashley said.

"You guys want a drink?" Brandon gestured for the two to follow him. They pushed between a few guys and into the kitchen that was crowded. Ashley calmed herself, these were her people. She bet not one of them went to church. And at least a few had a mental illness of some kind. If there was any crowd, she belonged to, it was outcasts, freaks, deviants, and criminals. She could do this.

"Beer?" Brandon handed her a cup.

"Thanks. I love beer." She sipped the foam off the

top.

"Can you drink that with your medication?" Kristen asked loudly. A few guys looked on.

"It's fine. *Mom*" Ashley said.

Brandon laughed. "Yeah, Kris, back off. Let her have a good time." He put his arm around her.

"Whatever. You're a big girl." She told Ashley. "Hey, have you seen Nick?" She asked Brandon.

"Uh, he's around here somewhere. Probably smoking out back or something. Some guy brought some other stuff to sell. He's probably just getting into some shit."

"Maybe I'll go find him." Kristen said, turning away.

"Wait, I'll go with you." Ashley said, not wanting to be left alone. Kristen said they'd stick together.

"But you look so good with Brandon's arm around you. Natural. I'll be right back. Brandon will take care of you." Kristen slipped off into the crowd of skeletons and slutty pirates.

"Don't worry, I got you." Brandon said. They wandered into the living room where a band was setting up. Ashley sipped more of her drink. "So I was really worried about you." he yelled into her ear.

This was news to Ashley. "Really? You don't even know me that well." She shouted back. He said something, but she couldn't hear. Gia screamed her name and waved from across the room before disappearing outside. "Do you want to go see where she's going?" Ashley asked, leaning into Brandon's ear.

"Nah. Let's stay and watch the band. The drummer is my cousin. Want another drink?" He asked and pulled her towards the kitchen before she could say one way or another. This time, instead of beer, he picked up a cup off the counter.

"What's this?" She asked, eyeing the dark drink.

"Just try it, you'll like it." He grinned. Ashley took a cautious sip. It was sweet, tasted more like soda than booze.

"Mm, it's good." She smiled at him.

He took her back through the house. The hallways became crowded as more people showed up. The band had begun to play and people were shouting. Ashley and Brandon stood against the far wall. Ashley tried to look around for Gia or Kristen, even Nick, but didn't see any familiar faces.

The feedback from the guitarist's amp was splitting her head open. It felt like the flies were drunk, thumping around in her skull. The air was heavy with smoke. It seemed like she had been standing there for hours, days even. But it could have only been thirty minutes. "I think I need to go outside." Ashley yelled. "I need to sit down."

"I'll take you." Brandon hissed into her ear.

"No, you don't have to do that."

"I want to." He said. He guided her through the throng of people. Outside, the cold air smashed into Ashley like a fist. Her head felt sick, and her heart dropped into her stomach.

"I think that drink was too strong."

"A walk will help. You just need to get some air." Brandon said. Ashley wished he'd remove his arm from her shoulders, it felt so heavy. It was hard enough to put one foot in front of the other without the extra weight. She thought she said something to him about it, but he just kept walking, pulling her with him. The party seemed to thin out.

Next to a group of burning tiki torches, Ashley thought she saw Lucifer standing with Satan, pawing at the ground. He shook his head. But she blinked and wiped them away like rain on a car window. They smeared and were gone when she looked back over her shoulder. "Did you see something?" Brandon laughed.

Ashley looked over at him. He was walking so fast. "Oh god," She shoved him away. His lower jaw had come away, and he was grinning in a terrible way.

"What?" His voice came from deep within his chest. "Something wrong?" Ashley backed away, slipped in some mud and covered her face. He kept getting closer, grabbing for her. His hands were long snakes, cold like the Priest's. She tried to crawl away. "Come on. Where are you going?" Brandon grabbed her wrist and pulled her back to her feet.

"No. no." She screamed. He was pressing his face to hers. *His face*. Teeth fell into her mouth and she tried to spit them out.

"Mm, you taste good. Just like Nick said." Brandon's corpse told her. Ashley clawed at her mouth, trying to get the rancid skin and teeth out. He tasted like raw meat, ripe and gamy. A few people stood around with beers and watched. He wouldn't let go of her, no matter how hard she tried to pry him off.

"Please." She cried. He let go suddenly, and she fell back to the ground. Then he came down with her, wrestled her still. She didn't understand what was happening. What happened next. Brandon was being pulled off of her and she was being carried through the night past the onlookers.

"Come on, man, it's just a joke. Nick, chill. It's just like half a tab of acid. It'll wear off in a few hours. What's the big deal? It's nothing."

"She can't take shit like that." Nick sat Ashley into his front seat and closed the door. She squinted and watched him screaming at Brandon, who just laughed. Kristen tried to grab his arm, but he shoved her off and walked around the front of his car. Gia ran up and jumped on Brandon's back and he carried her off into the night.

Kristen stood highlighted by Nick's low beams. He pulled away, leaving her in the dark. Ashley covered her face, trying to calm her stomach. "I think I'm going to puke." She said finally. Nick pulled the car over. Ashley fell out the door, threw up on the side of the road. "Don't fucking touch me." She pulled away when he tried to get her hair out of her face. She could smell the mud on her. She could only imagine how she looked.

She tried to crawl back into the car but just sat there half in half out and cried. She couldn't stop herself. She felt they had planned it all. Her friends. Her stomach turned, she was sitting on waves, undulating up and down. Nick helped her back into the car. "It'll be alright." he tried to tell her.

"I can't go home like this. Brenda will know something happened. She'll call everyone's parents. She'll call the police. I know she will." Ashley said through tears. "What... what did he give me?" Her head felt inside out. Her eyes were looking inwards at the hive of flies. She forced herself to keep them open.

"They slipped a tab of acid in your drink. That's what Kristen said. Half a tab maybe." Nick muttered.

"Kristen? Where's Kristen? Her and Gia are giving me a ride home." Ashley was so confused, she leaned her head against the cold glass of the window. She shivered. Where was her coat?

"I'll give you a ride home." Nick said.

"What? No, I can't go home. Brenda she'll-"

"Don't worry, we can drive around for a few hours." He pulled into a gas station. "Stay here. I'll get you some coffee. Maybe that'll help. Just stay right here." Ashly nodded and watched him get out and go into the small store. Why had they done this to her? They laughed at her. Her arm throbbed from where Brandon had grabbed her.

"Here drink this." Ashley jumped, Nick was beside her in the car.

"Where did you...?" She trailed off and looked back at the store. Was this Nick or a hallucination? "You were in the store."

"Then I came back. Can you drink this?" he asked again. Ashley wrapped her hands around the foam cup. The heat felt good. She sipped it and felt her body thaw. The cold mud caked to her clothes chilled her.

"I'm so cold. Am I dead?" She asked and pulled up her sleeve. A few of her stitches had been pulled when she tried to twist herself away from Brandon. Nick flicked on the interior light to look.

"No Ash, you're not dead." He examined the cut in the dim light, "It's not bad, looks like you might have ripped a stitch or two." He said concentrating on her arm. Ashley took another long drink of coffee. Nick turned off the overhead light. He shrugged off his jacket and handed it to her. "You're probably freezing."

Ashley pulled it on, thankful. "Did I see those things?" She finally said.

"Do you want the heat on?" He asked, turning up the gauge. He pulled out onto the road. "What did you see?"

"Brandon, his face was all fucked up. Like a corpse. He kept trying to kiss me, his teeth were in my mouth. It reminded me of that black heart…it tasted just…putrid." Ashley shuddered despite the warmth filling the car. She still thought she was seeing things. She closed her eyes and leaned her head back.

"No, you didn't see that. It was just the shit they gave you." The radio droned on quietly and neither spoke for an hour.

"Ash." Nick shook her awake. "You okay?"

Ashley looked around. The car was parked. "Where are we?"

"I couldn't keep driving around. The car eats gas. How are you feeling? Think you're ready to go home yet?"

Home? "Gia is supposed to give me a ride home."

"She's not. I am, remember?" Ashley squinted at the little blue clock. It was past ten.

"God, my head." Ashley reached for the door and leaned out to throw up what was left in her stomach. "I need to be home by eleven, otherwise Brenda will know something happened." She gasped, spitting into the grass.

"We're not far." Nick said, standing beside the car. Ashley attempted to stand and walk around her spilled stomach contents.

"We're in a cemetery?" She asked, surveying the shadowy tombstones back lit by lights from the street.

He shrugged, "Wasn't sure where else to go." They walked through the quiet paths lined by soft crumbling stones, hard granite, carved angels and lambs.

"I didn't even know this was here." Ashley said.

"It's only like fifteen minutes from your house." Ashley leaned on him to keep from tripping.

"I feel like shit." She said. Her head buzzed.

"What interaction do you think that stuff has with your medications? Maybe you should tell Brenda, just in case." He told her.

"No way. Besides, I'm cutting back on that stuff." He stopped and looked at her, "What do you mean? I thought…"

"It's complicated. But it makes me a fucking zombie. I need to keep a clear head to think. I don't need a lecture."

"I get it." He said. They circled around the cemetery and ended up back at the car. "Ready to go home."

"No, not really. Brenda is going to wonder why Gia and Kristen aren't bringing me home. Why I'm covered in mud." Ashley sighed, almost forgetting about the betrayal. Brandon's hands all over her, the cold wet ground. People just gawking at her.

"Just tell her Gia was drinking and couldn't drive." Nick said, starting the car.

"Yeah. It's not like I'll be going back out with her anytime soon." How had she started the night with four friends and ended up with one?

"Fuck them. I told you, Kristen is a backstabbing bitch. I wondered what she was up to when she showed up."

"What do you mean?"

Nick paused, like he wasn't sure he wanted to say. "I don't know. She was just being weirdly nice, touching me and shit. Like a distraction. I asked where you were. She said you were with Brandon. Then when I tried to get up to go say hey she didn't want me to leave and one thing led to another… And you know what? Let's not talk about it," He said.

Even in her depressed haze, Ashley thought she knew what one thing he was referring to. She didn't want to hear about it. It had been a long, shitty night. "Just take me home, please." They said nothing more about it.

Ashley hesitated getting out of the car. She looked up at the porch light. "Maybe I should go up there with you. So Brenda doesn't get the wrong idea." Nick offered.

"Really?"

"I don't know how well you'll make it up those steps." He got out and helped her out. Brenda swung open the door before they had even made it to the porch.

"Ash? What happened?" She asked when she saw the mud soaked dress and ripped stockings. The boy. She helped bring Ashley inside.

"Nothing. Gia got drunk and couldn't drive." She stumbled over her words. "I tried to help her inside, but she fell and brought me down with her. Nick offered to bring me home so I wouldn't have to call you."

Brenda wanted to believe her. "Are you sure you're alright?"

"Just hazy. The meds, you know how they work. Fine one minute, crazy the next." Ashley tried to laugh.

"Thank you, Nick, for bringing her home." Brenda said. "But it's getting late." The three stood there. Nick wanted to hug Ashley but didn't feel neither she nor Brenda would approve. Ashley handed him back his jacket.

"Good night. Call you later." He told Ashley.

"Thanks for the ride. Bye." Ashley stood by the door and watched him leave. Gave another wave, grateful for one genuine friend.

Brenda locked the door, "You should get out of those damp clothes. Want me to run you a bath?"

"I can do it. I'm not a child." Ashley said, dragging herself up the stairs. She stopped and turned, "Sorry. It just wasn't as fun as I thought it'd be."

"There will be other parties, kid."

But Ashley shook her head, "No. I don't think I like them. Too many stupid people." This made Brenda smile. Despite it all, when she was clear, Ashley had a good head on her shoulders. "Good night, Brenda." Ashley said and climbed the rest of the way. An hour later she fell into a dreamless sleep. No nuns, or Lucifer, no pig faced prophet. Just deep, heavy, and sweet.

Ashley looked for Nick when she went to pick up her school work on Monday, but he wasn't there. He also didn't call. No one called. Ashley thought she'd feel more upset, but felt it might be better that way. She needed to focus on her project, anyway. She figured at least this way when she was gone, there would be no one around to miss her. Brenda might feel sad about it for a little while, but she had Timothy. After a few months, she'd realize her life was easier without her.

Brenda had moved Ashley's therapy session to the evening after her classes finished for the day. "That way I can walk with you." Brenda said. Ashley just wanted a minute alone. She wanted to get to a computer in the library, but it was impossible. The longer she waited, the more anxious she grew.

"How did your party go?" Dr. Hart asked on Thursday.

Ashley sighed. "Fucking stupid."

"How so? You were looking forward to it."

"Then maybe I'm the stupid one."

"No. Maybe parties just aren't your thing. Many people don't like them. My wife would rather clean out the fridge on a Saturday night than go to one." He chuckled. "Did you at least enjoy spending time with your friends?"

Now it was Ashley's turn to chuckle. She didn't quite remember what happened besides Kristen and Gia running off and leaving her with Brandon. She remembered Brandon's rotting face biting at her mouth, his skeletal hands on her thigh. Mud. People watching. Then Nick and coffee in his warm car. A leather jacket, a cemetery. That was the best part of the evening.

"Friends are a waste of time. I'm done with that. Just like birthdays and all other fucking joyous holidays. I'm over it."

"You're entitled to your opinion. Brenda has expressed her worry that something else might have happened at the party. You came home with mud on your clothing. She used the word disheveled. Can I ask what happened?"

"Drunk people." Ashley left it at that. Dr. Hart changed directions, asking her about her dreams, how she felt on her new medication. *Fine, fine, it was all fine.* He looked at her blood test, fine.

"How about we pick up takeout tonight? I have a ton of essays to get started on." Brenda suggested on the way home.

"Chinese?"

"Something different?"

"Sushi?"

"You don't eat fish."

"They make vegetarian ones. Cucumber and avocado. Please." Brenda went in to order the dinner. Ashley closed her eyes to shut out the car lights that passed by the parking lot. She always felt worse after therapy. Brenda pulled into the driveway and Ashley saw Nick sitting on the porch smoking the last of a cigarette. Brenda glared at him. "What? You said you didn't care if my friends smoked outside."

"Why does anyone need to smoke?" Brenda asked, gathering her bag of papers.

"Nerves." Ashley said and got out of the car. She hadn't heard from him all week. She really didn't expect to see him on her porch. "What are you doing?" She asked, bracing herself against the cold November wind.

"Waiting. I tried calling, but no one was home. Thought I'd take a ride over and see how you are." He waved to Brenda. "Hey Brenda."

Brenda unlocked the door and dropped everything

but the takeout bag on the floor. "Are you hungry, Nick?"

"I could eat."

During dinner, Nick asked Brenda about her work. Brenda asked him if he planned to go to university after school. He didn't have a good answer. Nick helped Ashley pick up the plates and put the leftovers in the fridge. "I've got a lot to do." Brenda apologized for excusing herself.

"It's fine we're just going to go upstairs."

The remark gave Brenda pause; she didn't want to embarrass Ashley. "Just leave the door open." She said, before sticking her head back into the kitchen, "Make sure you take your meds." She said and ducked back out.

"Don't worry about it. Everyone is on something these days." Nick said, leaning against the counter. Ashley took most of her stuff in the morning, only the liquid poison was split into two doses. She measured out her evening dose and pushed it down the drain. She looked at Nick.

"I told you I'm cutting back."

"None of my business." Ashley put the brown bottle back in the cabinet and took him upstairs.

"So how's Hog Head been treating you?" he asked, sitting on the floor in the middle of the room. "I like all this." He said, motioning to the mishmash of papers and canvases on her wall. Lately they had become charcoal line drawings of pig faces, sides of meat hung up on hooks, dreamscapes and voids she couldn't explain to anyone.

Ashley pushed the door most of the way shut. She looked at the scrawny boy on her floor. There was never anyone watching him. She put on some music and sat on the rug beside him. "I have something I want to ask you." She said in all seriousness.

He turned on his side and looked at her. He wanted to kiss her again. He thought about her constantly. Her taste, her smell. "Yeah, anything." he said, wondering if she'd finally come around to the idea.

"Brenda is constantly watching me. I never get a minute alone. I used to use the computer on campus for research, but lately I can't even do that. I talked to the guy from Mad Monk who referred to Hog Head just as HH. Then in one part of the book the essay is signed HH in small letters at the bottom. It's like his second name. So I was thinking about researching that name in the town where the Mad Monk runs his shop out of. HH is probably local. Could you get to a computer and see what you could find? Then there's the name Judith. That's not a popular name, but look her up to. See if there's one in the area?"

Nick didn't expect her to say all that. "You've been talking to the Mad Monk?"

"Yeah, I wrote to him at the beginning of the month. He just wrote back like a week and a half ago."

"Huh. That's cool. Sure, I could look around for you."

Ashley hugged him, "Thank you! That is such a load off my mind. I've been trying to figure out how to get to a computer."

"Sure, partner in crime. This'll be cool. Let's find Hog Head." Nick said. Glad to have a reason to keep hanging out with her. Glad to see her smile. "Did the Mad Monk say anything else?"

"Not really. Just that nothing was for sale or print, but I could sign up for a mailing list. No address for Hog Head, but he could pass something on. It's doubtful he would, though. Maybe when we finally find his address we could go together? Wouldn't that be cool?"

Nick shook his head, "Sounds like a plan. Hear anything from Kristen?" he asked.

"No. I don't think I'm going to either. I just don't get it. I thought we were friends. I'm an idiot. I don't know what I did." Ashley threw herself on the floor beside him. She looked at the ceiling, he looked at her.

"She's a bitch. She just uses people."

"Has she said anything to you?" Ashley asked him, sitting back up and leaning against her mattress.

"No, I haven't been to school all week. Not really in the mood. It's easier just to sleep." He said.

"Every time I step foot in that school anymore, I just want to kill myself." Ashley laughed. Nick didn't laugh. "It was a joke."

"There's something else you can do that helps." Nick said, sitting up and facing her. He pulled up his black shirt sleeve and showed Ashley a heavily scarred arm. Fresh swollen cuts ran back and forth like organized cat scratches. A few rounds burns on the other side of his forearm.

"Did you do that?" She asked, examining his arm in her hands.

"It wasn't such a big deal before. But since my brother died. I don't know, it's the only thing that I feel like I have control over. It helps." he said, pulling his sleeve back down.

"You just use a razor?"

"Or knife whatever. Just don't do it so deep. Not like the one you have. That way no one finds out. No one watches you, or cares. You can just do it." He said. Ashley liked the sound of that.

"But they take my blood every week. The nurse would see."

"Do they do it in the same place?" He asked.

"Yeah, on the right arm."

"Then cut on the left. Or your leg. It's winter, no one will notice." He said. "It helps."

"Why did you do those?" She asked, referring to the fresh wounds.

Nick thought about Saturday, Kristen going down on him. He knew she was distracting him, but he let her. He closed his eyes and pretended it was Ash sucking him off. He didn't bother to ask again where Ashley was until he had defiled Kristen's mouth. He shouldn't have let her do that. If he hadn't, maybe he could have stopped the entire scene from happening. He was fucking weak. Just like his brother. "Do I need a reason with my life?" he asked. His eyes were heavy. Ashley moved over and put her hand on his. If anyone *got it* she did.

"Ashley, it's getting late. It's time to say goodnight." Brenda called up the stairs. Ashley pulled her hand back. Nick stood up.

The two stood close together just outside the halo of light cast by Ashley's bedside lamp. "I'll look that information up for you. See what I can find. What's the town name?"

"Haggsville."

"Nice name." Nick said.

Ashley hugged him. "Thanks. You know besides this crazy guy at my old clinic, you're seriously my only friend."

"You too." he said, patting her back gently. Her hair smelled good. He wanted to stay in her warm house, even with Brenda there. He knew he'd get home and his mom would be at work. The place would still be trashed, it would be dark and cold. He'd be alone. But he felt better knowing Ashley existed somewhere out in the world, even when they weren't physically together.

Ashley followed him down the stairs. Nick said goodnight to Brenda. Ashley waved like last time as he drove off. "So what did you talk about?" Brenda asked.

"Heavy metal and animal sacrifice." Ashley said. "I'm taking a bath."

"You're hilarious." Brenda said from behind a stack of papers.

"I'm here all week!" Ashley yelled before closing the bathroom door. The talk with Nick had given her hope for finding her prophet.

Ashley ran the bathwater as hot as she could stand it and climbed in. Brenda didn't keep razor *blades* around the house. She should have asked Nick for one. Instead, she took out a new shaving razor. Maybe Nick was right, maybe this would help relieve some anxiety she felt when she thought about those girls. The situation. Her fears about never finding Hog Head. Control. She was sick of feeling out of control.

She worried constantly that she was imaging it all. It was only signs from the universe that kept her going. First there were the dreams. Then His book made its way back to her after she returned it to Nick, after her copy was destroyed. Then there were the pigs. In her textbook they showed illustrated images of a dissected fetal pig. A program on television had a man in a rubber hog mask. A billboard advertisement for a restaurant had a picture of a pig beside the name. The universe *had* to be guiding her, telling her to follow the path, don't despair. She was almost there. It was real. It was happening. This wasn't one of her delusions. His words were real.

Ashley pulled her legs to her chest, and with little thought pulled the razor across her wet skin. She made a delicate row of shallow cuts from her knee down the side of her calf. Seven in all. She sat the razor aside and watched the blood bleed along the lines. Placing her leg under the water, the swell and sting of the scratches. It felt better than she thought it would.

She looked at the cut on her forearm. The blood scab on part of it, stitches holding the rest together, until the skin could twist and knead itself into a thick scar. Ashley laid back in the tub, absorbing the feeling she had given to herself. Nick was right, the control.

"Ash, are you okay in there? It's been almost an hour."

"What? Sorry, I drifted off. I'll be out in a second." Ashley pushed herself out of the tub. The water was lukewarm by now. She blotted her scrapes with tissue and flushed it down the toilet.

"Your hair is soaked." Brenda said to her when she came out. "Are you sure you're okay?"

"I feel good, actually. Like I'm in control of my life for once."

"Good. I'm glad. Your new levels must be working by now. You look better. Not so pale." She said. Brenda pulled her in for a hug. The fresh marks on Ashley's leg rubbed against her sweatpants. A gentle reminder, she was in control of her destiny.

Nick continued to come over and hang out a few days a week. He had found a handful of listings of men with the initials H.H. in the surrounding area. He was working on narrowing it down. Three of them seemed about the same age, later forties or early fifties. No one knew how old Hog Head actually was. It was just a guess based on when his tapes were made, probably late teens or early twenties.

"What about Judith?"

Nick looked at his notebook. "I found two who might be her. One is in her late thirties, the other in her forties. Judith Metzler who is thirty-eight. And Judy Underell-Green is forty-three. Both live close to Haggsville."

Ashley thought a second, *Underell*. "Nick, fuck, that's her." Ashley said. "It has to be."

"Which one?"

"Underell." Ashley scrambled over to her air vent and pulled out the paper slip from the cassette case. "This says *thank you to the Underell Farm and Care Home*!" Ashley hugged him. Nick couldn't believe it. Had they found a link to Hog head?

"Shit, that's awesome. But... there wasn't a phone number for her. Just an address."

"We have to go there." Ashley told him.

Nick said nothing. "Do you think she'll know anything though? I mean, if the rumors are true and he tried to kill her..."

"If someone tried to kill me, I'd want to know exactly where they were. She *has* to know."

"Maybe we should write a letter?"

"No, she'll just throw it away. It's better in person. Don't give her a chance to say no." Ashley had to see THE Judith. Look into her eyes. Hog Head had dedicated everything to her. Ashley has a sinking feeling that the beautiful bodies sketched throughout the book were of her. The naked girl in the mud? A young Judith?

Nick didn't want to disappoint her. Plus, he wanted to meet Hog Head. His brother had worshiped him. "Fine, what about Saturday?" he said.

Ashley wanted to scream *Yes! Yes!* But stopped herself. "No." Brenda and I are leaving Saturday morning to go to this thing. We won't be back until late. Midnight, probably. Ashley sighed, she was so close.

"That's cool, we can go next weekend. The school will be on break for Thanksgiving. We can just pick a day, no one will miss us." Nick said. "So what thing are you going too? Or if you don't want to talk about it..."

"It's nothing like that. There's an art show at the clinic I used to go to. I know a lot of the patients and was invited. My friend, Wheeler, wanted me to come. He made this sculpted bust with a bear coming out the back of it's head. He really wants me to see it. I told him months ago I'd probably go. It's weird, I know."

"No, it sounds kind of cool. So this kid is like a friend then? You still talk?" Nick asked.

Ashley couldn't help but laugh to think of Wheeler as a kid. "Well, he's sort of child-like, but he's fifty-ish. He's been in institutions for like half his life. I don't know what's wrong with him. But he's cool. Except, well, lately he's been kind of weird. But that's just him." Ashley brushed it off. She still had his semen encrusted letter from last month in her dresser. Come to think about it, Ashley hadn't heard from Wheeler since then. She had to ask Brenda about it.

That made Nick feel better. "Oh, that's cool." he said. They sat in silence in the dim room. "I talked to Brandon, he said sorry again about before. Apparently it was Kristen and Gia's idea. They told him you'd be into it or something." Nick didn't believe them.

Ashley didn't believe them. "Fuck them." She said, still upset Kristen hadn't even bothered to call her. Even if she called, Ashley wasn't sure she wanted to talk to her. Not after what happened. She had Nick and Hog Head, that was all she needed.

"Yeah, fuck them." He said. He looked at her. Ashley kept looking at the piece of paper with the names on it. She had put a piece together, she couldn't believe it. She was watching her fate manifest before her. By this time next year, everything would be different.

"Ash. Ashley?" Ashley felt Nick close to her, his voice in her ear.

"What?" She turned, and he was right there.

"Your hair smells good." He said.

"Uh, thanks." She smiled and looked at him. Was this happening again? He touched the side of her face, his hand barely grazing her skin. "Nick..." She said.

"Ash," His voice was soft. He moved closer, his face next to hers. A gentle wash of his mouth over her. You couldn't even call it a kiss.

"It's almost ten!" Brenda screamed up the stairs. The two pulled apart, much to Ashley's relief. She didn't want to embarrass herself again. She did not understand how to give pleasure, let alone receive it.

"Shit," Nick exhaled and stood up.

"Sorry." Ashley got up from the floor.

Nick pushed his hair back and grabbed his coat. "Nah, it's cool." He took her hand and rubbed his thumb over her knuckles. He looked thoughtful. "Have fun at your art show. I'll talk to you next week." He said and turned to leave. Then stopped and looked at her, "You'll have to think of something to tell Brenda. It's an almost three-hour drive there, then back again. It'll take all day."

"I'll think of something. We are going." Ashley assured him. He couldn't wait to spend all day with her, alone, doing something stupid and meaningless. Just being together.

"It'll be awesome." He said. Ashley liked this. She followed him down the stairs. "Good night, Brenda." He called. He wished he could just crash on their couch. Maybe if things worked out with Ashley, he could stay over more often.

He'd been talking to Brenda about going to university. She offered to help guide him through the application process. All his life guidance counselors, teachers, his own mother, made him feel worthless. But Brenda was sure he would do well if he wanted to. She told him he was smart. He believed her. He could see a future with him and Ashley. College, a job, doing something besides getting wasted every night and fucking whores like Kristen. Or ending up like his brother, a bloodstain on the concrete floor.

"Night," He told Ashley. He hugged her. Ashley rested her head on the front of him. It was quick, less than a second, but the gesture meant a lot to him. She'd been telling him more about herself, her past. He admired her for going through all the crazy shit she did. If that had happened to him, he'd want to murder everyone. The abuse, the backwards brainwashing therapy, the molestation at the hands of so-called doctors. He'd never be able to trust another living soul. He wanted more than anything for Ashley to trust him. To know she could depend on him.

It was getting harder to leave at night and go home to that shit hole of his. He held her a minute longer than he meant to. "Nick," Ashley said, pulling away. Reluctantly, he released her. "Good night. I'll call you when we get back. I'll think of a way to get away." She whispered.

"What's all this whispering?" Brenda asked, coming into the hallway. "I thought you left already. Don't you have school in the morning?"

"I'm going, I'm going."

"Home or to school?" Brenda asked, teasing him. She liked Nick. He had been dealt a raw hand at life, but that didn't mean he had to settle for it.

"Both." He nodded goodbye and pulled the front door closed behind him. "You need to finish that report for chemistry if you want to go to the show Saturday. It's due Monday. So go get some sleep."

"Hey Brenda," Ashley said before heading upstairs. "What do you think of Nick?"

"I like him. Why?"

Ashley shrugged, "Just wondering. Night." She climbed the stairs to brush her teeth. *Brenda liked him*, Ashley felt she could trust him. He was taking her to see Judith next week. Then HH. She wondered what would happen after that? Would he stay on as a follower? Or leave? How would he feel about her taking HH as a lover? Maybe she could take both as lovers? No, that was crazy. She could only ever devote herself to one man, her prophet. She was sure that stuff with Nick would work itself out.

Nine

"Do we have everything?" Brenda asked, sitting behind the steering wheel. The car rumbled to life.

"You've already asked me that twice. I got everything on the list. It's only a couple hour's drive, Brenda. It's not like we're heading into the great white beyond. They have stores north of here."

"I know. I just don't want to stop if we don't have to."

"I could drive if you wanted?"

"Ha, hilarious. Get in. Oh, did you lock the front door?" Both of them looked back at the porch, the door was wide open.

"I've got it." Ashley jumped out and ran up the stairs, pulling it closed. The sun was glaring, but the winds made it colder than it looked. She ran back to the car. "Okay, ready. Let's go," She told Brenda, ignoring the chill that ran through her. She had been looking forward to this show, but for some reason felt she shouldn't be going. *It's just nerves*. Brenda had her all worked up. It was going to be fun. Not like that horrible party. No one was going to spike her drink.

After a few minutes of Ashley fiddling with the stereo, she turned to Brenda. "Hey, have I gotten any letters from Wheeler lately? I can't remember the last time he sent one. It's not like him."

Brenda chewed her lip. She'd been keeping them in the locked drawer in her desk. She had in fact gotten four letters in the last month. All declaring his love for Ashley, among other things. In the last one, he apologized and said they were changing his medication. Brenda thought it best not to tell Ashley if she didn't ask. "They weren't appropriate for a young girl." was all she said, looking ahead at the road.

Ashley's breath caught in her throat. Had he sent another like the one she got? "What do you mean? Did he talk more about the nurses and the supposed nude photos?"

"Something like that. In the last letter he said they were altering his therapy and he apologized. He should be fine if you see him." Brenda hoped they had moved him to another ward. She called Dr. Prendergast and explained the situation. He was sympathetic and said he'd take care of it. Brenda hadn't gotten any more letters after that, nearly two weeks ago.

Ashley imaged if he'd sent another sex stained note Brenda would have lost her shit. It couldn't have been as bad as the one she swiped from the mailbox that afternoon. She had to get rid of that before Brenda came across it. She didn't know why she kept it. Maybe because in her heart she didn't take it seriously. She did lots of odd stuff that she later regretted. She was sure today would be great; she was worrying about nothing. He'd be the same old Wheeler, unshaven, with wrinkled pants and old slippers he refused to get rid of.

The clinic looked the same when they pulled up. "What do you think?" Brenda asked, they looked up at the building. It's wide-open windows. Ashley couldn't remember how many hours she'd spent staring out of them, watching the trees sway or snowfall, rain trickle down.

"It's just a building, Brenda. I think I want to get out of this car now."

Brenda didn't remark but undid her seatbelt and climbed out. It felt good to stretch her legs. A family of three entered just before them. A patient's family. People were already arriving. Nurse Benedict was at the front desk handing out name tags and directing people to the main recreation room where the show was set up. It was the largest room at the facility. They used it for everything from movie night to group therapy sessions. It looked out over an enclosed Japanese garden they had put in about a year ago.

"Ash! I'm so glad you came. Brenda," Nurse Benedict beamed. She checked them off the list. "Wheeler will be so glad to know you've made it. It's all he's been talking about. He doesn't have any other family, you know." The nurse told them.

"Oh, I thought they moved him to another ward." Brenda said. Ashley looked at her. What was she talking about? Why would they move him? The guy was eccentric but harmless.

"No, he's still here. I don't know anything about that." Nurse Benedict said.

Brenda nodded and rested her hand across Ashley's shoulders. "Ready to go in?" She asked. "It was good to see you again," Brenda told the nurse as they turned away towards the rec room.

They hadn't even entered when Wheeler burst from his chair, shoving an elderly lady aside, "Ash, my dear! You are here!" he yelled. People looked in his direction. He wrapped his arms around her. He held her tightly to his chest.

"It looks like you've combed your hair, Wheeler," Brenda remarked. He still looked as disheveled as ever. Wrinkled, ill fitting clothes. But he had pulled on a cardigan over his shirt. Combed his hair back, shaved. "You look so beautiful. So much older." he stood back.

Ashley had chosen a green frock so dark it was almost black. It hit her at the knees. That was the shortest Brenda would allow. The long sleeves and thick black knee socks hid her scabby cuts. She had Brenda wave her hair like Gia had. "Just a little eyeshadow, come on." She begged Brenda, who finally relented. Ashley piled on black shadow and liner. Brenda didn't say much, she picked her fights these days, and makeup was not one of them.

"Thank you. You look well."

"Yes, I try." he grinned and pulled on the ends of his sleeves, straightening himself up. He finally looked at Brenda. "How have you been Ms. Brenda? How do you like that university job?" he asked. Brenda couldn't separate this man from the letters she had read.

"Doing fine. The job is going well. Not as bad as I thought."

"Brenda's got a boyfriend." Ashley teased.

"We're not going to talk about that." Brenda said, ending the conversation right there. Wheeler laughed and nudged her with his elbow. Brenda forced a smile. It surprised her, her distaste for him. She was having a hard time even pretending. She'd have to have a strong word with Prendergast.

"Want to get a drink, Ash?" Brenda asked.

"Sure. See you later, Wheeler." She said.

"I'll show you my piece after you've looked around. I have lots of sketches. I'll show you those too!" he called.

Ashley laughed, "Okay. See you in a few." She followed Brenda to the refreshment table. It wasn't much, plates of cookies and sad paper cups filled with a sweet red fruit punch.

"Would it be too much to ask for a little wine?" Brenda grumbled and handed Ashley a cup. Brenda chewed on a hard cookie and the two wandered around saying hello to patients and looking at the art. Lots of paintings and drawings. Some good, some just scribbles.

"I like the string thing," Ashley said. Brenda couldn't decide what it was other than a mess of tangled cords tied together with ribbon propped up on a small pedestal. They sprinkled glitter all over it.

"It's different." Brenda remarked. She looked away

and saw Dr. Prendergast standing over by the window talking to an older man. "I'll be right back, keep looking. I'm going to talk to Prendergast a moment." Brenda said and walked away, making her way through the crowd.

Ashley kept wandering, enjoying being back at the place. "Ash! Did you see my work?" Wheeler pulled her by the arm before she could answer. His sculpture was in the corner on a small table. A light shone on it, highlighting the details.

"Wow, that's great." It looked just like the picture he had sent her. "I like the bear. Very cool. How long did that take?"

"A few weeks. I thought it looked like you, but it can't compare." He said.

Ashley shook her head, "Ha-ha. You're so funny." She said sarcastically. The bust looked like a woman in her thirties, mature and beautiful. Ashley felt it looked nothing like her.

"I made a few drawings of you from memory. I'd like to give you one, but wasn't sure which one to send. Can I give you one now? I hung them in the art room. You can pick whatever one you want. You can have all of them if you'd like. Did you bring the photo I asked for?"

Ashley looked at him, "What photo?" She did not understand what he was talking about.

"In my letter, I asked you to bring a photo. Polaroids so you wouldn't have to get them developed, then no one would see them but me. Remember?"

He looked at her intensely. Ashley didn't want to say Brenda had been keeping his letters from her, that she had read none of them. That she had no idea what he was talking about.

"Right, I'm sorry. I've been so stressed from school I completely forgot. But I'll send you one when I get home." She assured him. This made him smile.

"Wonderful. I can hardly wait. Come, choose a drawing to remember me whenever you feel lonely." He guided her through the busy room, his hand resting gently on the small of her back. No one noticed the two leaving down the dim corridor.

Wheeler flicked on a light in the corner of the art room where his "studio", as he called it, was. He had papers taped to the two walls of his corner. Pencil sketches and watercolors, crayon drawings. "What do you think?"

"There are so many." Again, Ashley didn't think any of the women looked like her. They were older, had thick flowing hair, sleepy seductive eyes.

"Take your time." Wheeler said. Ashley examined the pages, trying to decide. He was a fantastic artist, she had to give him that. He was excellent at drawing hands, something she still hadn't mastered.

Wheeler's hand curled around and sat on Ashley's waist, gripping so lightly she hardly noticed at first. When he stepped closer and Ashley felt him trailing his fingers along her shoulder up her neck, she shrugged him off. "I think I'll take that one. Then we need to get back. Brenda will wonder where I am."

She told him, stepping closer to the wall to give herself some space. But he moved right along with her.

"I saw her talking to Doctor, we have time." He said into her ear.

Ashley tried to turn away, "Time for what? Maybe I'll just get the picture later. Brenda can help pick one out." She went to leave. He was so close, she felt his breath on her neck, his hand on her waist, fingers moving close to her hairline.

"Wait, wait." He said, tightening his grip. She struggled to shake him off.

"No. Wheeler, what are you doing?" she gasped when he pulled her back violently, shoving her against the table. Jars of pencils and brushes rattled at the force of her weight. He pressed behind her, his hands suddenly eager. "Wheeler, come on. You're not supposed to do this." She could barely get out the words, feeling she was choking on panic. This was worse than with Brandon because she knew what was going on. What would happen if she didn't get away? "Wheeler?"

He said nothing, but she felt him all over her, smelling her, breathing in her skin. "They're all busy. There's time." he whispered. When she felt his hand graze her thigh and begin exploring under her dress, she elbowed him and used all her force to push him off her. He stumbled but rapidly regained his dominant position.

Ashley opened her mouth to shout., but he was quicker. "Now enough! Stop it!" He shoved three fingers roughly down her throat, gagging her. He was bigger and stronger than her. He held her in place. She felt his erection pressing against her tailbone.

"Enough of that, Ash. Enough." His voice calmed. When she stopped fighting, he removed his fingers. Wrapping his arm around her neck, he brought her silently to the floor. It was so fast and smooth. Ashley didn't even know how she got there. He was on top of her, shoving her dress up, opening her legs with his knee. Feeling the warm folds between her thighs. With one hand, he pressed her face to the floor.

"Please stop, please..." She said in one last attempt to reach him. "We're friends, Wheeler."

"Shh, now, Shh. Be still." He seemed to say more to himself than her. With fumbling hands pulled her underwear down. Ashley inhaled sharply when he finally put himself inside her. His full weight holding her on the hard linoleum floor.

She was dry and unwelcoming, Wheeler remarked as such. He began thrusting into her, muttering obscene things about how he dreamed of her virginal cunt. She was still a virgin, right? She was so soft. Smelled so good. He slobbered on the back of her neck, licking and kissing her, moaning that he was in love with her. His smell of onions and aftershave filled her nose. Ashley looked at the forest of thin steel table legs planted on the floor in front of her. Waiting.

It lasted only a few minutes. Ashley felt him cum inside her on the last few pushes, grinding her hips into the floor. She grimaced in pain. "If you tell anyone, I'll cut your fucking throat." He said into her ear before removing himself.

Ashley lay there for a minute. When she heard him adjusting up his pants, she got up. She pulled up her underwear and fixed her dress. The act of rape was done. She turned to hobble away. "Let me help you," Wheeler reached out to take her arm, but she shoved him away.

"Don't even fucking touch me again or I'll scream." She told him, her voice low and tight. He stood there and watched her slowly walk out. She willed herself to set one foot in front of the other. *Don't look back. Don't look at him.*

Ashley ducked into the bathroom near the front entrance. She locked the stall door and sat on the toilet. She scrubbed between her legs with a tissue until the skin was raw. It felt better.

She sat for a moment and hugged herself in violent self-loathing. She was an idiot to let this happen. She rocked back and forth. No one could know about this. She worried if she lost control, she wouldn't be able to stop. They'd keep her here, locked up with Wheeler. She just wanted to go home. Home. Far, far, away.

She sucked it up and opened the bathroom stall. In the mirror she fixed her hair and gazed at herself, hands gripping tightly to the cold porcelain sink. Her styled hair, her thick black make-up, she was changing on the outside now. In the last few months, a boy had stuck his fingers inside her. Another boy attempted to. She got her period. An adult man ejaculated inside her vagina. Ashley always thought of herself as a girl, now she felt she was something else entirely. A possession, maybe?

She had the urge to punch the mirror, roll up her sleeve and shove a shard of glass through her wrist and out the other side. She willed herself not to cry. She was in charge of that. Her jaw was clenched, her face tight and controlled. "You will not cry." She growled at herself in the mirror.

"Ash, there you are." Brenda pushed in through the bathroom door. "What are you doing in here? I've been looking for her everywhere."

After a moment Ashley looked from her reflection to Brenda. "I threw up. I think I just want to go home."

"Oh sweetie, okay. Come on, let's get our coats." Ashley leaned against her and let her help her out the door. The muscles in her upper thighs ached from being spread so wide. She felt as if Wheeler had shoved a hot metal rod deep inside her. "Do you want to say good night to Wheeler?" Brenda asked, helping Ashley put her coat on.

"No. He's being weird. I just want to leave. You were right to keep those letters. He's different." She mumbled and shook her hair out from under her coat collar.

"I'm sorry, hun. Come on, we can just go." They said goodnight at the nurse's station on the way out. It was dark and cold in the parking lot. Ashley looked up at the clear sky. The stars broke through the black screen. She thought about them being burnt out, already dead, she was only seeing a remnant of their past glory.

"Here, get in, it's cold." Brenda said unlocking the door.

"I miss seeing the stars. I can't see them in the city." Ashley said, taking one last glance before getting in. Brenda turned up the heater and flicked on the lights. They rounded the curved driveway. Trees lined either side like sentinels watching her leave.

Ashley closed her eyes, listening to NPR drone on. Brenda sped up and pulled onto the freeway. It would be hours before they were home. At this moment she wished more than anything she had a photo of HH. His face would be comforting. Would he ever comfort her in the flesh?

She wouldn't be able to give her virginity to him. That pained her more than anything. She was soiled. Would he still want her? She didn't know anymore if the search for him was worth it. Maybe she should just kill herself now. Would he listen if she explained a man raped her? She only wanted him. What if he turned her away? *Or* what if the rape had to come to pass? A test from the universe?

Just a month ago, if this would have happened, she would have lost herself. She did lose herself over something less than this. Instead, this time, she swallowed it down and took it. Didn't say a word. Didn't shed a fucking tear over the violation of her physical body. Just another scar to make her thicker. She should thank Wheeler, and while she was at it Brandon, Kristen, Gia and even Nick for teaching her she couldn't trust anyone. They all wanted to hurt her.

She would bury herself deep within her head from now on. Nothing and no one meant shit. She would only concern herself with the truth. The truth spoken by one man, her hog faced messiah. He would understand all that she was, all that she had become in her search for him.

Ashley could only imagine what the world had done to him. What had he gone through to become the prophet he was? What had he seen to develop such a philosophy? She felt her third eye opening. She was ready to begin the physical search for him. It was finally, truly, time. By spring she would be dead or in his arms, basking in esoteric knowledge unfit for human consumption. She climbed yet another step.

"I was thinking for Thanksgiving we would invite Timothy over. His family lives in Helsinki so he doesn't see them much. Would you like to invite anyone over? Maybe Nick? I have a few students who might drop by. What do you think? Could be fun, right?"

Ashley pushed her dinner around on her plate. She'd been avoiding Nick's calls all week. She didn't feel like talking about anything. She just wanted to fade away. Her lower half burned from where her pants rubbed against the fresh cuts from last night.

Up her thigh, over her pelvis.

She fucking hated her vagina more than her brain. It was the root of her misery. She felt men sniffing it out whenever one passed by. She worried it had an odor now that it had bled. Ashley saw herself reaching inside of her, pulling the damn thing out.

"Ash, what do you think? I could cook."

Ashley shrugged "You make horrible pies. Last year you burnt the crust, and the middle was raw."

"I can buy the pies, that's not a big deal. I'll make you a super deluxe salad if that's what you want."

"You should have Timothy here. He seems to really like you."

"What about Nick?"

Ashley shrugged, "What about him? He's probably spending it with his mom or Kristen or something. I don't know. It's not like he's my boyfriend. Who cares?"

Brenda almost asked if they had a fight or something, but knew that would lead to nothing more than denial and slamming doors. "Can you ask him when you speak to him at least? Just to make sure. I don't think he has much family."

"Whatever." Ashley looked up at Brenda. "Yeah, I'll ask him IF I talk to him. I think I'm going to go take a bath." Ashley excused herself and set her plate in the sink.

"Say goodnight before you go to bed." Brenda said.

"Will do." Ashley pulled herself up the stairs, eager to just be alone. She didn't want to think about stupid

Thanksgiving or Nick. He wanted to fuck her just like everyone else. Maybe she should let him, just open her legs and let him fuck her bloody. He could get it out of his system. She hated everyone.

Ashley sank lower in the tub. Her cuts of control were burning. She created new ones along her arm over half healed ones from last week. It felt good when the razor ripped off the tender, newly formed scabs. Then everything bled together into a mess. She pushed it around with a finger, examined the things her body created. That got her off more than any man ever could.

The water was pink by the time she climbed out of the deep iron tub. She sat on the edge and watched the water drain, dabbling her scratches with toilet tissue. She flushed that down to, washed off the razor. The remnants of her mutation were destroyed. Her clothing covered her bloody trophies. Just like everything else. Just like her illness masked with medication.

That's how it was, she saw it now. Society liked nothing that upset the mainstream, made it look closer at the uncomfortable parts of itself. Crazy people, intense people, idyllic people, artists, hermits. All pushed aside, killed, or made into some trend that people could digest easier. When that happened nothing meant anything anymore. It was all bullshit, just as Ashley suspected from the beginning. The only authenticity was Hog Head, his work. He had sifted through the stream and found the truth lying on the bottom. She would find it too. He would lead, she would follow.

Ashley fell asleep on the sofa with Camille Saint-Saëns' music seeping through her headphones. She attempted to read but couldn't keep her eyes open. The music ended. In her shallow sleep, she heard murmuring.

"I don't know why not? That sounds nice. She'd like that." Brenda was saying. "You wouldn't be late?"

"Brenda, what?" Ashley pushed her headphones back, struggling to pull herself from sleep. "I had my headphones on, I didn't hear you." She wandered down the hall into the dining room. "Sorry, I didn't hear you." Ashley rubbed her eyes. She saw Brenda talking, but it wasn't to her.

Nick sat at the table drinking coffee. "Long time no see." He said. Ashley thought she might puke. She swallowed it.

"Hey, what are you doing here?" She struggled to speak. She sat down and rested her head against the chair. "When did you get here?"

"Just a little while ago. I hadn't heard from you and thought I'd stop by."

"We didn't want to wake you." Brenda chimed in.

"I was asking Brenda about taking you out for the day. You always complain about how much you hate the city. I was thinking about a car ride. We'd be back by dinner if we left in the morning. What do you think?"

"Huh?" Ashley wasn't sure what he was talking about.

"The weekend after Thanksgiving. Saturday?"

"It would be good for you to get out of the house. I have a ton of work to do to get ready for finals. I'm afraid it might get boring for you."

Nick was giving her a strange look. That was when it clicked *Judith*. "Right. Okay. That sounds like fun. You don't care?" Ashley was shocked Brenda agreed to this. Maybe it was because she'd been dragging her body around the house for a week.

She didn't want to spend a day in the car with Nick, but felt she had no other choice. He wouldn't try anything, and if he did, who would care? She'd just give in this time. It wasn't like she was a virgin anymore. A little pain hurt no one.

Ashley pictured herself in his backseat, her face pressed against the window while he fucked her. She felt nothing. He could groan that she was the best he ever had. He loved her. Still, she would feel nothing.

Maybe they'd drive down a dirt road and pull off to the side. "What are we doing?" She would ask him. He wouldn't say a word, but unzip his jeans and pull out an erection. Force her to go down on him. Then her head bobbing up and down in his lap. His hand on her neck. She'd suck it up until he ejaculated on her face. Then they'd continue with the drive. *Whatever*.

Maybe she'd fuck him, not give him the chance. Spread her legs and climb onto his lap, push him inside her. What teenage boy would stop a cunt from enveloping him? No, he'd want it. He'd grab onto her and kiss her with such a longing and force. "Don't stop." He would beg her.

She would make him gasp and hug himself against her. She'd wonder what took him so long. "I've wanted this…" She would ignore his sentiment and tell him to drive on. It meant nothing, don't talk about it again. Anyone of these scenarios didn't matter. Split her open, she was more than this body.

She envisioned flies crawling up through the tubes of a penis, into a man's sack, sucking away the testosterone, blocking his penal blood vessels with fresh larva. The same way they clog up her brain and bath in her own chemicals. Her skin erupted in goosebumps, that felt good to imagine. Passing her parasites to another. Infecting a man with something he couldn't possibly comprehend until it was too late, and the flies devoured him from the inside out. A bloody hole where his sex used to grow. Defiled by her for a change.

"I'll see you tomorrow." Nick smiled at her.

"Tomorrow?"

"Thanksgiving, Ash. Nick said he would come. Isn't that great?" Brenda said. Ashley looked from one face to the other. Had Nick and Brenda planned this whole thing out?

"What about your mom? Won't she be lonely?" Ashley asked.

"She works nonstop this week. Big tips. She won't be home. She never is anymore." Nick said.

"Nick, you're more than welcome. Ashley doesn't like my cooking, hopefully you will." Brenda rubbed his shoulder. Was Brenda hitting on Nick? Ashley squinted, no that wasn't possible.

"Ash?"

"What? Your cooking is fine. You just can't make pies."

"Nick has to go, why don't you walk him to the door?" Brenda said. Both were staring at her. Ashley stood up and Nick followed. Was this all a dream?

"Are you okay?" Nick asked, taking his coat off the hook.

"Fine. I was just surprised to see you. You should have called."

"I did. Several times. Are you avoiding me? I thought we were going to, you know... look for Judith." He dropped his voice.

"We are. I just forgot it was this weekend. Brenda won't shut up about Thanksgiving and Timothy. I was sleeping and then you were just here. I'm not avoiding you." Nick seemed to relax a little.

"Okay. I thought I did something." Ashley didn't know why, but she reached out and ran her index finger over his furrowed brow down the bridge of his straight nose.

"You did nothing." She said. He liked that she had willingly touched him.

"So we're cool then?"

Ashley forced a smile, "Completely. See you tomorrow."

Nick looked past her towards the doorway, Brenda was in the other room. He leaned down and gave Ashley a soft caress on the lips. "Tomorrow." He said looking into her eyes. They were the palest blue he'd ever seen on a person. An eternal ocean. He'd give anything to hear her inner voice, what she thought about.

Ashley closed the door and wiped her mouth. What did he want from her? She needed him to find HH after that. She wasn't sure what would become of him. She'd heard about people like him, always looking to fix a broken person. She wasn't fucking broken; she was awake. He could never understand the bond between her and HH.

Sure she'd always be eternally grateful to him for giving her the book and tapes. But he was merely a messenger, she saw that now. Maybe they'd fuck, but it wouldn't mean a thing. It would only add to her layers. Making her ever thicker on the outside, helping keep her inner core protected for *Him*.

HH would release what was left of the flies and take her, merge her into his very being. He would make her something more than human. A being worthy of only him. She'd become his. He would become hers. Maybe Judith was but his messenger. She had no reason to be jealous of her. Now Ashley looked to her as a teacher, a guide to him. Another stair to step upon.

Ten

Nick and Ashley sat on her rug listening to some obscure band tape Nick brought over. It was mostly symphonic, and any singing was in a foreign language, so Ashley assured him Brenda would be cool with it. "Do you know what you're going to ask Judith tomorrow? Assuming that's her, and she talks to us?" Nick asked.

"I haven't really thought about it. I feel like she'll understand, though."

"How do you mean?"

Ashley didn't know how to explain it. "If you were my brother, even if you did something horrible to me, I wouldn't want you to be alone. So if someone came along and understood you, I'd want you to be with them. I'd feel it was the will of the universe."

Nick sat back and thought about it. He never knew what to expect when she opened her mouth. "Huh. I guess so." He admired Ashley for the empathy she gave other people. But he doubted that's how it'd go. He pictured her slamming the door in their faces. And that was the best-case scenario.

"Thanks for having me over for dinner. It was nice. I enjoy spending time with you and Brenda. Timothy wasn't as bad as you made him sound. He's smart. I guess you'd have to be, to be a Quantum Physics professor."

Ashley felt the tension, she knew what Nick wanted. She didn't want to wait. She just wanted to get it over with. She leaned over and kissed him. She pulled away, assessing his reaction. "Do you want to fuck me? Or maybe something else?" She asked.

"What? Ash, come on. Brenda is right downstairs."

"So what? She's with Timothy. What do you think they do? It's not like you're a virgin. Kristen told me all about it. She said you're amazing." Ashley leaned over and kissed him again, running her tongue over his teeth. He seemed to melt against her. He thought she didn't want him. He rested his hand on the base of her neck, kissing her as he had wanted to more times than he could count.

Ashley put her hands on him. His body gave him away. "Ash, you don't have to," He murmured but Ashley went down on him, placing him on her mouth. The skin was soft and salty, she never thought about how it would taste. He had been with other girls, who knew how many. Nick tried to muster up the guts to stop her, instead he leaned his head back on the mattress and allowed her between his legs.

His breathing came harder and faster. Ashley liked the small moans that escaped his lips. She knew he was close. Without meaning to, he thrust into her mouth near the end and Ashley swallowed his semen down her throat. She felt his hand rest on her hair.

"Ash..." he gasped when she finally let him out of her mouth.

Ashley got up and went to the bathroom. She swirled some mouthwash around, pulling it through her teeth. She looked at herself in the mirror. Her smudged black eyeliner, waxy complexion. She felt nothing. She spit out the minty green liquid and turned off the light.

Nick was sitting on the corner of her bed, waiting. When she sat back down he moved closer and put an arm around her. "It's getting late you should probably go before Brenda says something." Ashley told him.

"That was..."

"Don't say anything. Just forget. I'll see you tomorrow."

Nick felt confused. She seemed upset, but then why had she done it? He hadn't started it. He told her she could stop. Did he tell her to stop? Did she feel pressured? "Ash, why did you do that?"

"Can't I just see you tomorrow? Why does everyone need to talk about everything?" She laid back on the bed, starting at the ceiling. Nick held her hand. She wanted to bite it off. "It's late." She said again, continuing to look at the ceiling and not at him.

Nick released her. "Sure. Nine tomorrow morning?"

"That's what we said."

Nick sat there for a moment. Was she mad at him or herself? Finally he stood up. "Okay. Good night." When Ashley said nothing Nick walked out and headed downstairs.

He felt weird saying thanks to Brenda for having him over. He had just cummed inside Ashley's mouth upstairs. *God, it felt good*. He had looked down and watched her a moment, completely turned on. He wanted to take her to bed, lay with her, feel her deep, then sleep beside her. Instead, he just left. She didn't seem to return his affection. He didn't know how he felt about it.

Ashley exhaled when she heard the front door close and the car pull away. There, she had done it. Maybe he wouldn't rape her tomorrow. HH would understand. She thought all this time he wanted her pure, a virgin. But he wasn't pure. Nothing in nature was. She was to come to him as defiled and filthy as he. Purity was a human concept. Primitive, raw, that was real. There were animals who fucked other dead animals, they didn't give a shit about purity. Neither did she. Not anymore.

"I'm going to bed." Ashley called down. Brenda didn't bother to come up. She was nestled on the couch, talking to Timothy.

"Good night. Happy Thanksgiving!" She called up.

"Good night, Ash!" Timothy echoed.

Ashley closed her door. Brenda wouldn't notice. She lifted the side of her mattress and took out a stained kitchen hand towel. She had wrapped a small serrated paring knife in it. The knife had a black plastic handle. It was cheap, Brenda had a dozen of them.

The act felt organic by this point. Ashley pushed

up her sleeve and ground the rigid thin edge back and forth over her skin, crossing the old cuts still trying to heal. Pink lines from weeks past showed her how far she'd come. "I'm with you," She gasped, knowing HH felt her no matter how far away.

What was he doing this night while she was here? Writing? Walking through the forests in the deep November dark? Was he cold? Did he long for her as she did him? Tomorrow their beings will merge on this physical plane. Until then it was all merely a caress of the spirit; an eyelash on the breath of devils.

"Did you take your medicine?" Brenda asked. Ashley was pulling on her boots, Nick would be here any minute. "Maybe you should take the phone, just in case. Do you know where you're going?"

"Geesh, Brenda. Where were all these questions the other day when Nick asked you? I don't know where we're going. To the country. We'll probably walk around a graveyard or go down a hiking trail or something. I don't think he's planned anything, just drive."

"You're right. I hope you have fun. You've been so down lately. Dr. Hart said he'd be out of the office until next week, but if you need to call him, I have his emergency number."

"What are you talking about? I'm fine." Ashley asserted.

"Ash, ever since we got back last week you just haven't been yourself. I'm worried about your, hun."

"Myself? I haven't been myself? That's a joke. And what is *myself*, Brenda? A paranoid lunatic? Or just an anxious mess? A crying pathetic shell?"

"You know what I mean, Ash. You've been practically comatose. You've hardly said anything. Even Nick is worried about you."

"Have you two been talking about me?" Ashley finished tying her boot and stood up. Brenda opened her mouth to answer, but Nick's knock on the front door interrupted her. Ashley didn't make a move to open the door, neither did Brenda. He knocked again.

When it was clear Brenda wasn't going to say anything more Ashley brushed past her and opened the door. Nick stood there, his hands stuck in his leather jacket despite it being below freezing. "Ready to hit the road?" He asked. Ashley glared at him. What had he said to Brenda?

"One minute." She slammed the door in his face and turned away to put on her coat. She flung her backpack over her shoulder. She was bringing the book and tapes to show Judith.

"Ash let him in, it's freezing. What's wrong with you?" Brenda reached out and opened the door back up. Nick stood there, unsure if he should come in or not.

"What? We're leaving. And before you ask again, I took my drugs. I don't need a phone. I don't know where we're going or when I'll be back." Ashley stomped out to the car. Nick looked at Brenda.

"We won't be late," he said.

When he got in the car Ashley looked at him. "What did you say to her?"

Nick rubbed his hands back and forth to warm them. He stuck his keys in the ignition. "What? Who?"

"Who?" Ashley laughed, "Brenda."

"Uh, I just told her we wouldn't be late."

"Right. And what about before?" Ashley took a cigarette out of the pack in his center console and lit it, cracking the window.

"I don't follow." He said backing out of the driveway.

"She said you two have been talking about me. Apparently everyone is worried about how fucking depressed I am. That's funny, I didn't know I was. Huh, I'm so glad I have all these caring people in my life to decide what I am, how I feel. Tell me, Nick, am I tired? Maybe I should take a nap? Is it okay if I smoke this?"

"Jesus, Ash. Calm down. Brenda said she worried about you, you've been so quiet. She asked if I knew about anything. She just cares about you."

"Oh yeah, I bet." Ashley exhaled and looked out the window.

"I'm sorry. I didn't think you'd have a problem with it. I didn't tell her anything. Just said I noticed it too."

"Noticed what?" Ashley was going to scream. Why was everyone always watching her?

"You seem withdrawn. Even last night when we

were... together. It's like you were somewhere else." He said, taking the cigarette from her fingers.

"Together? You mean when I was sucking you off? How much more connection do you need? Your dick was in my mouth. Your semen is probably still floating around in my stomach." She could see the flies trying to shake off the sticky, opaque substance, clinging to the side of her innards, dribbling slowly down her intestinal tract. "Can we stop and get a coffee?"

Nick took a deep hit from the cigarette. The thought she saw what they did in that way made his guts turn. "Sure thing, there's a place around the corner." He said, his voice flat.

"Brenda wanted me to give you ten bucks for gas money. A bribe for putting up with me." Ashley stuck the ten dollar bill into the cup holder. Nick didn't say anything but kept his eyes straight ahead. His heart ached, he absolutely hated himself at the moment.

The heavy silence in the car was getting on Ashley's nerves. Nick was moping, probably upset because she didn't fall in love while sucking his dick. She turned up the radio and listened to misanthropic screaming over a compressed drum track. What was wrong with everybody?

Ashley sipped her coffee and looked out the window. The bare trees and dead grass looked like a sun bleached photograph. "How long till we get there?" Ashley asked when they turned off the main highway.

"Probably another hour." Nick had been chain smoking since they left the city.

"Want some of this? I don't think I can drink it all. It's too sweet."

"Nah." He kept driving, afraid whatever he said would upset her.

Ashley set the cup down and opened her bag. "I brought the book and tapes to show Judith. Maybe she can tell us something about them. I bet anything that girl on the cover is her." Ashley looked at the mud covered young body, the pig face set over her head.

"Do you really think that's a good idea?" Nick asked.

"Oh wow, he speaks." Ashley looked back down at the slip of paper. "Why not?"

"If HH tried to kill her, she probably doesn't want to be reminded about it." Nick said.

"Now you're getting sensitive? Don't you think it's just as bad for us to show up out of nowhere asking if she knows where he lives? I don't think a photo is going to make much difference."

"Yeah, you're probably right." Ashley saw the tension in his jaw. He flexed his hands on the steering wheel. He paused a second, "And I'm not getting sensitive. Just being smart about this. If she freaks out, she won't tell us anything."

Ashley shrugged, "Then I'll just break in her house and go through her stuff when she's at work."

Nick turned and looked at her. "You can't be serious."

"No, I'm not. I was just trying to get you to look at me. What's your problem?"

"Nothing." He looked back at the road, irritated.

"Why don't you pull over?" Ashley said.

"What, why?" Nick glanced at her.

"Because I know what your problem is. You're pissed because you didn't get to fuck me last night. Let's just get it over with. Then you can stop acting like such a girl about it." She reached over to touch him, but he pulled away.

"Don't, Ash." His words were stern. Ashley sat back in her seat.

"So you're just going to be grumpy the whole way?"

Nick felt her angry eyes on him, "How about we not talk for a little while, huh?" What the fuck was her problem?

"Really, that's it? I get what Kristen was saying now. Maybe she's not such a liar." Ashley mumbled.

Nick laughed and shook his head, "And what's that? That I took advantage of her? Maybe I raped her? Yeah, that really sounds like me."

"Or that you like a girl until you get what you want, then suddenly she's a whore and you want nothing to do with her."

"I don't think you're a whore, Ash. I don't know why you keep listening to Kristen after what she did to you."

"After what all of you did to me, you mean? I don't know. I guess I'm just a stupid whore."

Nick slammed his hand on the steering wheel, "Enough. I'm fucking sorry for whatever you think I did to you. Let's not talk." He said. Could she make him feel anymore like shit? This couldn't be her, it had to be her illness. He was never screwing around with another teenage girl again. They were all fucking insane.

"Fine." Despite her words, Ashley continued to study him. He had fine pale skin. His dark brown roots were showing. He probably hadn't washed it in days. He wore a tarnished silver ring on his thumb. His hands had been so gentle with her.

"What?" He finally said, feeling her staring at him.
"Nothing."

The two said nothing more for the rest of the journey. It was Nick who finally broke the silence. "I think this is the road up here." He took a slow left turn, and the car crawled along a side street. If they hadn't been looking for the town, they would have missed it. The address matched a two story yellow house. They painted daisies on the black mailbox. A small blue car sat in the driveway.

Nick parked just past the driveway. He turned off the engine. Ashley kept looking at it. Judith was in there. Her link. "What are you going to do?" Nick asked.

Ashley suddenly felt scared. "I don't know." She put the book and tapes into her backpack and zipped it. She didn't know why she thought she could do this. She felt Nick's hand cover her own. It was warmer than hers. She gripped it, much to his surprise.

"I can come with you." he said. Both seemed to forget about the words they had exchanged.

"No, it's better if I just go. Just please don't leave me."

"I wouldn't ever do that," he said. "I'll sit right here and wait." She squeezed his hand harder, pulled him to her and kissed him. It was brief, but soft. It warmed his hollow cold being. Ashley slammed the door and walked up the wide sidewalk that cut through the middle of the front yard. It looked freshly poured. Not a crack or stain.

Nick watched her ring the doorbell. She stood on the narrow white porch, shifting her backpack from one shoulder to the other. When the door opened, Ashley thought she might choke. "Yes, hello? Can I help you?"

She wasn't at all what Ashley pictured. This woman had soft brown hair cropped close to her face. Her gentle face set with wide eyes and a small upturned nose. She was tiny despite being obviously pregnant. Ashley swallowed. The woman waited patiently. A group of kids ran behind her. "Make sure you share," She called after them. Her smile when she turned back to Ashley was warm and understanding.

Ashley knew it was now or never. "Are you Judy, uh, Judith Underell?" She saw Judith's smile falter some.

"I was, but I'm Underell-Green now. Is there something I can help you with? Who are you?" She asked again.

"I'm Ashley, hi. Um, well," Ashley looked down at her boots a second to collect herself. "I'm not sure how to start." Judith came out onto the porch and pulled the door shut.

"Why don't you sit down," She gestured to the porch swing. Ashley sat beside her, so close. Ashley wanted to touch her to see if she was real. She was part of HH. "Are you from the school?" Judith asked.

"No." Ashley took a deep breath. "So a few months ago, I got this book from a friend." Before Ashley even removed the book from her bag, Judith went rigid. *Please don't let it be...* "I wondered if you could tell me more about it." Ashley handed Judith the well-worn copy of *Hog Head II*.

Judith didn't dare reach out to take it. She read the first one; she had helped get it published. After that, she had nothing else to do with him. Not after he attacked her in the hospital and slammed her head into the floor. She was in the hospital for almost two weeks. "I'm sorry, I just can't." Judith clasped her hands together in her lap.

"Please, Judith. Do you have an address? I need to talk to him. He's your brother. You have to know!" Ashley pulled out the two cassette tapes, Judith narrowed in on the photo- the mud caked body of her youth. That horrible head the band had brought home from the butcher. It was the same one she had worn days later when she lost her virginity to HH in the barn.

"My brother? No sweetie, I don't know what you heard, but that's not true. They put us in the same foster home. He's not my brother. We were just friends. I haven't spoken to him in years and years."

"Foster home? He's not your brother?" *Then she was his lover. He had fucked this woman.* Ashley looked at her with fresh eyes. HH had been inside this woman. He had derived pleasure from her. Ashley's heart ached with jealousy.

"Did he love you?" Ashley blurted. "Were you two in love?"

"I think it's better if you go now." Judith stood up. Ashley blocked her way.

"I'm sorry. But I really need to find him. Please an address, it's all I want. I'll never bother you again." She was practically crying by this point. Nick saw the scene on the front porch. Both women looked upset. He got out and walked across the lawn.

Ashley was begging Judith for something, anything. "I'm so sorry, Judith." Nick said, pulling Ashley gently off the porch.

"Please, just his real name. What's his name? What happened? Did he really try to kill you? I have to see him!"

Judith stood on the edge of the porch, the teens down in the grass. She couldn't stand the thought of this troubled young girl finding HH. Not after what he did to her. He would probably do it again.

"This is what I'll tell you," She began. Nick stopped trying to pull Ashley to the car. "It took me five years to get pregnant. They're still not sure this one will make it. I have stitches in my cervix to try to keep it in. I have scars and burns on my body that will never go away. I still wake up screaming at night, afraid I'm *not* alone in the dark. That he has somehow found me. No amount of love or adoration can change who he is."

Her lips trembled. She crossed her arms over her belly against the cold. "Whatever you think about him is wrong. He is a sick man, and no one should read that poetry, listen to that music." She turned to Nick. "If you care about your friend, you'll burn that book and those tapes. He will only hurt her, or maybe worse." Judith looked them over one last time. She turned and went into the house. She gently closed the door, the lock clicked over.

Judith leaned against the inside door and cried. Someone had finally found her. It would only be a matter of time until that poor little girl found her foster brother. Then what? Would it start all over again? Would he tie her with ropes and make her bleed? The names he used to call her, the words he'd say while he was... while they were. That girl was so young. Younger than she had been when she had willingly given herself to him to be tortured in the name of love. His version of love.

Judith folded her hands and prayed, "Please watch over that child. Send her home to her mother and father. Help her forget about him. Please, Lord, give me strength." She said the words under her breath. She heard a car start, gravel crunch as it pulled away. She had to make the kid's lunch.

"What are we going to do? She was all we had."

Ashley was hysterical. Nick turned into a small overgrown park down the road. It was deserted this time of year.

"Ash, calm down. We'll figure something else out. We knew this could happen. Just breathe a second." He told her. Ashley hugged him to her. She needed to feel something steady. She was so close. "Maybe he has other family we can look up?" Nick suggested.

"No, he doesn't. Judith wasn't even his sister." Ashley sniffed and sat back.

"What do you mean? Then who is she?"

Ashley didn't want to say the word. "She was his *lover*. They grew up in the same foster home. Both of them were orphans. They only had each other. He fucking loved her and she threw him away."

"You heard what she said. He must have done something. Scars and burns? That thing about trouble getting pregnant? He might have-"

"Raped her? Please, she was probably begging for it."

"Ash, come on. Really? Did you just say that? She didn't look like the type to do something like that."

"She sure as hell is the type to pose naked on an album cover, isn't she?"

She had a point. "All I'm saying is something terrible must have happened to her. Plus, they put him away for who knows how long. Maybe we should just consider the idea that the guy is actually dangerous."

Ashley wiped tears off her face and looked at him. "What are you saying? You want to stop?" She asked.

Nick couldn't take the look of sadness in her face. He remembered seeing that same look when she was in the hospital. She was pulling down the sleeve over her stitches. It was quick, but he remembered it. All of that because of him. Because he thought it would be okay to get in her pants when he barely knew her. She wasn't like Kristen or other girls he'd messed around with. She was complicated. Wasn't that what drew him to her from the start?

"I said I'd help you, and I will, Ash. I just think we need to be careful. This guy obviously doesn't want to be found. And Judith looked terrified at the idea of him finding her. That can't be just nothing. What if those rumors about him raping girls were true? If anything like that ever happened to you I couldn't live with myself."

Ashley was thinking about Wheeler. The taste of his fingers when he shoved them in her mouth and directed her down onto the floor. She went like a submissive doll. She laid there and pretended she was somewhere else while he mounted her like it was his right. *I'll cut your fucking throat.* She still remembered his words. "You can't keep me safe from anything. No one can." Ash said. She could still feel the burning when he forced himself inside her unwilling body.

"I can try if you'd let me. We're in this together. I'm just saying maybe it's not worth it. You're so upset." He brushed hair from her face. Ashley leaned into his hand. It felt good. Why did she think he ever would to rape her?

"I'm sorry. I'm so horrible."

"No, you're fine. We'll keep looking, but let's just be careful, okay?"

Ashley nodded her head. "You know the Mad Monk is over in Haggsville. That's not too far away."

Nick sighed. He would do anything for her. "Fine. But I've got to stop and get gas when we're there."

"And you smoked all the cigarettes." Ashley remarked, wishing for one right now.

Nick fingered the empty pack. "Shit, alright you win. Let's go see this Mad Monk. But after that we've got to head home. Otherwise, Brenda will kick my ass."

"That's doubtful, but alright." Nick started the car and pulled out onto the road. Ashley put a hand on his leg, rested her weary mind on his shoulder. The warm weight of her felt good against him as he drove. He tried to focus on that and not the haunting look on Judith's face.

"There, that's it!" Ashley yelled, pointing to a dilapidated storefront on the main strip of the tiny town. It was a plain brick building with a large front window. You couldn't see inside, they plastered the glass with posters, advertisements, art work. A carved wooden sign hung from hinges over the door, *The Mad Monk Art House.*

"Shit, yeah, there it is." Nick had hoped they might not find it. "It looks empty."

"Just stop so I can see." Ashley tugged at his arm.

"Just a sec." He pulled into a parking space along main street. Ashley was out of the car before he could even kill the engine. He got out and followed her this time. Ashley tried to peek through the windows. Nick looked around. There was one traffic light at an intersection up ahead. A bookstore, local government office, a market, a butcher shop. The rest of the buildings looked empty. A shit smear town in the middle of the road.

Ashley knocked on the glass of the door. She tugged on it. Knocked again. "Ash no one's here." Nick said.

"I thought I saw a light turn on in the back." Ashley cupped her hands around her face and looked through a crack between posters.

"Ash..."

"There. There's a guy. Hey! Hey!" She rapped on the door with her fist.

"Seriously?" Nick looked in and saw movement. *Damn it.* Why was he worried? They wouldn't tell her anything. He just had to play it cool. They probably wouldn't even come to the door.

"Hello?" Ashley yelled. "He's coming!" She jumped up and down. They heard a few locks turn over. A man in his late forties opened the door. He was short, slightly overweight. His head was shaved. Nick looked at the thick tribal tattoos that twisted around the back of his ears.

"You kids need something? Show isn't until tomorrow night. Cover charge applies." he said.

"We're actually looking for someone. One of your artists." Ash said. The guy looked from the cute blonde to Nick. He knew who they were looking for.

"Sorry can't help you. All information is confidential," he said and started to close the door.

"Wait. Please. We just came from Judith. She sent us. She said you'd give us his address." Ashley lied.

This stopped the guy. He gave Ashley a longer, harder look. "Judith? You talked to Judith? Are you fucking kidding me? She sent you here. No way."

"Yeah. She said she didn't have HH's address, but you would. She didn't want to get involved. Please." Ashley moved closer to him. Nick watched the guy look her over, like he was deciding if she was worth it.

"Come on Ash, he's not going to tell us anything."

"Now just wait a second. You say Judith really sent you?"

Ashley shook her head, "Yeah. She said you'd have what we were looking for."

"Alright you can come in." Both started for the door, but he stopped Nick. "No, not you. Just the girl. Ash, right?" He figured it wouldn't hurt to get a little something for his troubles.

"No fucking way, man. You're not just going to take her in there alone. Fuck off." Nick told him. "Ash, come on. Fuck this guy." Nick knew exactly what his deal was.

"What? Nick, it's just an address." She turned to the guy, "Just a second." Ashley pulled Nick away from the door. "What the hell? We're so close. We could be at HH's place tonight. We could meet him!"

"Ash, that guy wants to fuck you. If you go in there with him, he will. There's no way."

"What?" She didn't know if she believed him. "Maybe it's just like a security issue or something."

"Trust me on this, Ash. We'll find another way. You're not going in there alone." Nick grabbed her shoulder and forced her to look at him. Ashley wanted to cry, they were so close but she knew he was right. She couldn't go in. She couldn't climb that step, yet.

She turned and looked at the guy in the doorway. A flick of his tongue over his lips. "Fuck you, old man." She yelled and turned away. Nick laughed.

"I'll be waiting if you change your mind." He called after her and went back inside. *Bitch*. It didn't hurt to try. Sometimes they came back.

Nick put his arm around Ash's shoulders. The couple walked back to the car. Ashley felt defeated. But if she said anything, she would lose it. Instead, she got into the car without saying a word. She was so close. If only they knew what he looked like they could hang around, but it was useless. No one had ever seen his face. He was a ghost.

"Ash, we can-"

"No, don't say it. We'll talk about it some other time. Let's just drive. I need to get the fuck out of here."

Nick got it. He could feel her vibrating, trying to keep herself calm. He couldn't imagine how hard it was. "I think there was a gas station around the corner. Maybe we could find something to eat?" He suggested.

"I need cigarettes."

"Tell me about it." He stopped, then turned left at the light. He pulled the car in next to a pump.

"I'm going to walk down this way a second. I need to think."

"Are you sure you don't want to wait? I'll go with you."

"I just need to be alone. Maybe I'll see if there's a cafe or something."

Nick wasn't her dad. He wanted Ash to see him as a friend, maybe something closer. She needed to trust him for that. The last thing he wanted was to fill her with self-loathing and anger. Getting girls to hate him was the only thing he seemed to be good at lately.

"I'll see you in a minute then. Take your time."

Ashley nodded and walked off. The town was quiet despite it being early afternoon. She looked in the shop windows. Passed a bus stop. The grocery store already had Christmas decorations in its windows. Ashley grimaced and walked on. She hated Christmas. What a pointless consumer driven holiday.

In the butcher shop, they taped a few advertisements for specials in the front window. An older man was ordering red shredded something. Ashley watched the butcher behind the counter weigh out the meat and wrap it in white paper. She'd never seen a guy with such long hair. Nick's hair was to his shoulders, this guy's had to be almost to his waist, primal, dreaded in some places. She watched him move. The customer thanked him and waved goodbye.

"You have a pleasant holiday now." The customer called.

"You too." The man behind the counter paused. He looked at her through the window. For a moment Ashley felt stunned, like he was recognizing her. She put her hand on the door to go in. She'd ask for directions to the highway or something. She just had to speak to him.

"You ready?" Nick asked, Ashley turned.

"Ready?"

"To go? Were you just going in that shop? I don't think there's anything in there we can eat. We'd probably be better off stopping somewhere closer to home." Nick said, surveying the street. Ashley looked back. The butcher was gone. He must have gone into the back. Ashley stood there a moment longer, gazing into the store.

"You alright? We can go in there if you want." Nick said, trying to see what she saw.

"Uh, no, it's fine. I don't know why I was going in there. Stupid." For the second time that day, Nick rested his arm across Ashley's shoulders and the two walked close together. He closed the car door for her.

"Want one?" He asked, opening a fresh pack of cigarettes.

"Can we just share?" She asked. Nick couldn't suppress his smile. He lit one and handed it to her. This was how it was supposed to feel. The two of them together and none of that other bullshit. He'd never known anyone with schizophrenia. Maybe that's how it was. You only ever heard about people hallucinating, voices, or if someone did something violent. But mood swings, anxiety, manic episodes, people just didn't talk about that.

He'd been reading more and more about it, trying to understand. Brenda promised him one afternoon they'd sit down and talk about it. She'd answer his questions. That was when she began trusting him, when he asked about that part of Ashley. No one would go through the trouble if they didn't care, she felt. Nick wanted to talk to Ashley about it, but wasn't sure how to bring it up. He could tell it made her uncomfortable. He thought he'd just give it time. They'd only known each other a few months.

It was four and already becoming dark. "We should be back soon. Another thirty minutes." Nick told Ashley. She was leaning against him now, feeling his arm draped over her. She was exhausted.

"That's fine." She sighed. Nick leaned over and briefly kissed her on the forehead. She seemed to fit perfectly under his arm. He held her closer. Ashley was fine with that. She didn't know what was going on this morning. This felt natural. "How will we find HH's address?" She finally asked.

"Internet, just like we found Judith. They were foster siblings. Maybe both were adopted by the same family. I'll look for any connection between Judith's last name and HH." Nick wouldn't look too hard though. Maybe at first he wanted to find Hog Head. He was his brother's idol. But after today, he knew nothing good would come of it. For all they knew, HH *was* the Mad Monk, and he was ready to take Ashley inside and do whatever to her. More than anything, he wanted to put this whole thing behind them and build something new with Ashley.

"Thanks. I couldn't do this without you." Ashley yawned. Nick wished the drive was longer.

Twelve

Sex. Pig faced poets, music by a madman, dodging her medication, self-harm, and *sex*. Brenda knew the other things, like the lying should trouble her, but the sex. Nick and Ashley right under her nose. "I trusted you, Nick. Now I don't," She said. He looked truly upset. "I know teenagers have sex, but Ashley is different. Her mind is different. She can't always handle things that regular teens can. I thought you realized that. And you knew she was skipping on her meds and didn't say a word for how many weeks? She put herself at serious risk, and you did nothing."

Nick looked so young at that moment. Brenda almost forgot he was only seventeen. She sighed, "But it wasn't just you." She set her glasses on the table. "I should have been watching her closer. I knew she didn't like taking that stuff, but she seemed better. I just never thought... I've been so swamped with work and Timothy." She shook her head, reached across the table and took Nick's hand in hers. "It's alright, hun. You did what you thought was right. You tried to be a friend to her. Please tell me you two were at least responsible. Ashley couldn't handle an abortion, let alone a child." Brenda didn't even want to think about that.

"No. I wouldn't do that to her." Nick assured her. "I should probably just go. I don't think Ash will want to see me for a while."

Brenda shook her head, feeling he was right. "She'll call when she understands what you did for her. She'll forgive you and call. But anytime you want to talk to me, I'm here."

Nick stood up and walked to the door, "and you'll get the Hog Head stuff out of her vent?"

"My next stop, kid." She smiled and pulled him in for a hug, like a mother. They stood there a moment, it was past midnight. "Anything you need, just *call* me." She reiterated to him. He said he would. He'd call in a few weeks if he didn't hear from Ashley. Brenda knew he would. He seemed to love her, but Brenda didn't know if Ashley could ever return that love. It broke her heart.

Brenda leaned against the door, her eyes heavy. This was not the New Years she had planned. She climbed the stairs and looked in on Ashley. She slept soundlessly. Brenda took a step in, walked around the bed. She'd changed the sheets, cleaned this room dozens of times in the past few months. She never suspected what Ashley hid from her.

She crouched down and pulled the vent lid off the wall. It came away with ease. She looked as Ash, then pulled out her stash. How many afternoons and nights had Ashley spent pouring herself over this stuff? The book was thick with notes. The cassette tapes carefully stacked on top of the book. Various papers with names, addresses, more questions. Sketches done in Ashley's hand of hog faced men with missing hands, bandages, cuts across the body, flies pouring from wounds. All Ashley needed was a pinup board and a ball of red string to complete her obsession.

Brenda quickly gathered the worn materials and replaced the vent. Downstairs, she wrapped everything in a plastic bag and took it out to her car. She'd dump the whole thing in the university trash when she went back to work in a few days. For now, she tucked the package safely away in her car trunk under the false bottom beside the spare tire. Ashley wouldn't look there. She knew the fallout would be bad. She prepared herself for the screaming, the accusations that would follow when Ashley realized her things were missing.

She won't mean it. Brenda soothed herself with this phrase. She needed to get Ashley back on her medication as soon as possible. She needed to examine her cuts Nick said she had been making over her body. He said there was a lot, but they were shallow. That wasn't very comforting. Brenda sat on the stairs and cradled her head in her hands. *How could she not have known any of this? What kind of parent was she?*

Brenda was tense the next morning as she made coffee. She was waiting for Ashley to come storming down the stairs, demanding to know where her shrine to Hog Head was. It was New Year's day but Brenda left a brief message for Dr. Hart telling him they needed to speak as soon as possible. When she heard movement on the stairs Brenda tensed, waiting for the scene to come.

"Did you have a good time with Timothy?" Ashley took a coffee cup down from the shelf.

Brenda looked at her, chewed the inside of her mouth. "It was nice. The restaurant was crowded, but I expected that." Ashley filled her mug and pulled herself up on the counter across from Brenda.

"What?" Why was Brenda looking at her like that?

"Ash, last night was not good. What happened?"

Ashley drank from her cup, trying to recall what had happened last night? Nick was here, Brenda and Timothy had gone out. She tried to ask Nick if he had found out anything else about HH's last name or potential contact information. He started kissing her, undressing her. She let him, assuming this was payment for his time spent researching. Then... then? A crack in the ceiling split down to the wall, and she drifted away. She was fucking Nick, and she just drifted away.

Then? *Damn*. The fight. He was angry. He didn't want to help her. He just left, Ashley went to bed. "What are you talking about?" Ashley tried.

Brenda glared at her, "Ash, you know. Don't play that game. I can tell by the look on your face you know. You said some very hurtful things to your friend."

"He'll get over it." Ashley felt angry with him all over again. Did he really tell Brenda everything that happened? "What did he say?"

Brenda felt it was better to just say it, then pretend until Ashly figured it out. "He told me everything." She saw Ashley sit up, her eyes pin. "Before you get mad," Brenda rushed to say, "I'm not judging you. Neither is he. He was very worried."

"Told you everything what?" Ashley asked. Her voice was slow and angry. Brenda could tell she wanted to smash that cup against the counter.

"Well, for one thing, he told me about the cutting."

"What?"

"Ashley, don't act like I'm stupid. Lift up your sleeve. Lift up your pant legs. Let me see your skin."

"Fine." Ashley pulled up her unmarked arm, the one preserved for appearance when the nurse took her blood.

"The other arm, Ash. Now."

Ashley figured what did it matter? If Nick told her everything, she had bigger things to concern herself with. She pulled up her sleeve and Brenda gasped. "Oh, Ashley. No, sweetie." The arm was thick and bumpy with white scars to fresh red cuts. Repeated, ragged mutilation. "Your legs. Come on." Ashley pulled up the legs of her sweatpants. Brenda's hand went to her mouth, she bit her thumb. It was horrible. "Why did you do all this?" She could finally ask.

"It doesn't matter." *Control. Release. Transformation.*

"It matters very much. Just please, pull your sleeves back down." Ashley sort of liked how much it upset her. Brenda was usually so cool and calm. She always knew how to act in a situation. But now she looked lost. "Nick also told me about you two. That you've been…together."

"So? He used a condom. Teenagers have sex, Brenda. It's part of life." Ashley looked away. She wanted to rip Nick's throat out. Maybe that would shut him up. Had he done all this because they had a disagreement or because she hadn't been able to finish screwing him? Ashley wasn't sure.

"Sneaking around. Lying, Ash. I don't appreciate it. Does your cutting have something to do with your relationship? Sometimes when you're young, sex can feel overwhelming. You should have talked to me about it."

"That's just it, Brenda. I felt nothing. It means nothing to me. If it did, I would have said something. But it doesn't. I only do it because…" *I want Nick to be my friend, help me.* "Because he wants to."

Brenda wasn't buying it. "Well, it takes two Ashley." Ashley hated it when Brenda used her full name, she knew it bugged her.

"Trust me, we're not doing it again." *I'm fucking done with him.*

"There's more, Ash." Brenda saved the worst for last.

"Christ, what?" *He better not have told her, he better not have.*

"The book, your research. I… I have them. Had them. They're gone. I also know you haven't been taking your medicine like you're supposed to. That's probably the reason for half of these problems."

The flies raged inside Ashley's brain. They were exposed and demanded release. Lucifer begged her to remain calm. All the voices were talking at once. Ashley slid down off the counter, walked over to the drawer where Brenda kept the cutlery. "Ash? What are you-"

Ashley brought out a fillet knife and pulled it down her unmarked arm. It was the sharpest they had. She didn't even have to press hard. The blood slid out right away, a red sheet being pulled forth. Flies pushed and wiggle, eager to escape before the blood coagulated and blocked up the large exit wound. Ashley tossed the blade into the sink, looking at Brenda. *Now what?* The voices quieted.

It took a moment for Brenda to even realize what had just happened. She cried and grabbed a kitchen towel to wrap Ashley's arm. "We have to go. Come on" She pulled Ashley without a coat to the car. "Hold that on there." The cut was deep and threatening. Ashley looked out the window, watching Brenda whip by the houses on the street and make a sharp right turn. The towel soaked through. Never had Ashley felt such a deep peace. She wanted to close her eyes and never wake up. *Let this be it.*

But it wasn't. She was cleaned and stitched and dressed, scrubbed, medicated and covered. She didn't fight; she let them do whatever they wanted to her body. She wouldn't need it soon. She was leaving it behind. It was infected, defiled, too heavy to keep lugging around.

She thought about Nick's betrayal. It didn't matter. She'd go to the Mad Monk and do what she had to do. She knew where he was. There was no rush. Brenda would calm down, she always did. Then Ashley would get on a bus and just leave. No bags, no belongings, they meant nothing. This world meant nothing anymore. She would tell all this to HH when she found him, then she'd ascend, with or without his help. She couldn't carry on like this.

For the first week she laid in the hospital bed, wrapped in dry white linens, staring at the wall. The extra doses made her lethargic, like she was melting to a fleshy pool. She felt herself getting fatter. She refused to eat more than once a day. Dr. Hart reasoned with her, and they agreed on one meal with two protein shakes.

What the hell did it matter? She threw most of it up anyway, these poisons were killing her slowly. Vomit and piles of dead flies, chunks of her stomach, came up and clogged the bowl. "Nurse, the bowl is clogged," She screamed, the gore flowing onto the floor.

"Let's get you back in bed." A nurse told her. The nurse looked at the toilet, it was just water. The floor was dry and clean. Poor thing. Ashley refused group therapy. She wouldn't leave her room. Dr. Hart and Brenda came by daily.

"I spoke with Nick." Brenda said one evening almost two weeks later.

"Who?" Ashley said, looking down into her thick green drink. Pond scum.

"Don't be like that. He wants to come see you. He's anxious about you. He calls every night and asks how you're doing. He hopes you'll forgive him."

"I don't want to see him."

Brenda sighed. Sometimes it sounded almost like Nick had been crying. He desperately wanted to see her and apologize. As much as she felt for the boy, Brenda knew Ashley's health had to come first. She looked at the long clean line Ashley had opened up on her arm. Ashley saw her looking. "It's hot if you were curious."

"Maybe you could write Nick a letter? That might make him feel better."

"Make him feel better? What about me? Fuck him. He was supposed to be my friend. He's a fucking Judas."

"Nice reference coming from you." Brenda remarked and finished her sandwich from the cafeteria. Ashley set her drink aside. Brenda worried, she was so thin these days.

"Will you at least think about it?"

Ashley was sick of talking about this. "I'll think about it. I'll think about how he went from a friend to your spy. How did you turn him? Money? Or something else?"

Brenda didn't like what she was referring to. She stood up. "Enough Ashley. I'll see you in the morning."

"Whatever. Tell Nick to fuck himself. I never want to see him." Ashley said. Brenda gathered her coat and bag.

"That's really nice, Ash. Really nice thing to say about your friend." She left and Ashley could hear patients shuffling around in the hall. She just wanted to sleep so her mind could go somewhere else. Anywhere else but here. This cramped stark room, the wire stretched between the glass window panes.

She didn't belong here. She belonged in the forest among dirt. She belonged with *Him*. No one could understand. Even with the drugs they pumped her full of, she wouldn't lose her path. If anything, it made it easier to think without all the clutter snapping and clicking in the background. She had some money, enough for a bus ticket to Haggsville. If she had to she'd wait outside the Mad Monk Art House until someone showed up. After that, it didn't matter. Wheeler and Nick had seen to that. She was foul. What was one more stain on this body of hers?

The doctor's felt Ashley was stabilized. She knew where she was and why. She got out of bed and wandered around. She worked on her schoolwork. She took her medication. She did everything they wanted her to. She kept quiet and didn't see or hear anything that wasn't there.

Brenda brought her bag into the house and

offered to take it upstairs for her. "I got it." Ashley told her. She took the bag to her room and tossed it aside. Lying on her bed, she examined the stain overhead. Willed it to take her.

"Ash, this is for you. I told him I'd make sure you got it."

Ashley looked at the envelope in Brenda's hand. "If it's from Wheeler, I don't want it."

"It's from Nick. He thought since you didn't want to talk to him, he'd write you a letter."

"And who's suggestions was *that*? Did you two write it together?"

"That's not fair. He's doing everything to be a good friend to you. You should at least read it. I have not read it." Brenda clarified. She walked over and set it on the table beside the mattress. "If you don't read it, you'll regret it when you can see clearly."

"Thanks for the wisdom!" Ashley called after Brenda. Brenda pulled the door halfway shut. Ashley listened to her footsteps in the hall, fading down the stairs. She crawled off her bed and lifted the corner of her mattress. Gone. Brenda had taken her tiny blade. Brenda had probably gone through every nook and cranny while she was locked up.

Ashley went to her dresser and checked under her stack of shirts. Wheeler's note was gone too. Just as well. She didn't want that shit sitting around. She should have burned it the moment she realized what it was. How vile she felt scratching at that dried crust, it building under her fingernail. She thought about semen crystallizing in her vagina. Quartz stalactites in her birth canal from Wheeler and Nick.

She sat back on the bed and looked over at the accusing envelope. What the hell? She ripped open the end and pulled out a folded piece of paper. It was written in black ink. His handwriting was small. A crossbreed of cursive and printing. He began by apologizing. He explained his reasoning. He loved her, would do anything to help her. "Yeah right," Ashley muttered reading on.

Then he talked about his brother. He didn't know how to help him, but he wanted to help her. Please let them still be friends. He'd never touch her again, but let them be friends. Forgive him. Ashley tossed the letter aside. This was him leaving. It was better this way. Now she didn't have to worry about what to do with him when she united with HH. One less string to cut. Besides, she couldn't trust him. If he even thought she might leave he'd tell Brenda and have her locked up again. She was already drugged out of her mind.

Everything was so still. Being on her bed was more like floating on a rolling sea. As much as Nick's note enraged her, she couldn't muster up the feelings to care. She was even more numb than she was before.

When Nick talked about his dead brother, it should have touched her. Instead, it irritated her. She didn't care about these people, and she knew she should. But she only cared about HH. He would never betray her. They were the same. Even if he didn't want her, she had to let someone know she was here before it all ended. Before she cut that last string.

Ashley drifted off to sleep for a minute. When she opened her eyes the sun was down and her room was in violet blue shadows of early evening. Brenda stood in the doorway. Warm light from the hall poured into Ashley's cave. "Ash? You awake? Nick is on the phone. Did you read his letter?"

"No."

Brenda could see the ripped paper, she had opened it. "Just talk to him. He sounds really troubled."

Ashely rolled over and looked towards the door. She was tired of this place. All these people. She forced herself up and followed Brenda downstairs. She lifted the phone to her ear, "Just move on Nick. It's over. I'll never forgive you." She said, voice flat. She hung up.

"Ash? How could you?" Ashley moved past a stunned Brenda and crawled back up the stairs to her room. It was too bright down here. "I'm bringing up your meds in a second and you're taking all of them." Brenda's words sounded more like a threat than anything else.

The phone didn't ring again for days. When it finally did, Brenda picked it up. It was a woman she didn't know. Brenda listened carefully, tried to hold in her emotion but cracked near the end. "I'm so sorry. Thank you for telling us. I'll tell Ashley right away."

Brenda hung up the phone and looked up the steps. Ashley hadn't left her room in days. She did her homework and shoved it aside. She read, slept and sketched. Brenda couldn't tell what was going on with her.

It was February during an unseasonably warm winter. They said it might reach seventy by the end of the week. Brenda looked out the window, her eyes glazed with tears. Icicles dripped, crying in the sun's heat. She didn't know how to do this. She pulled herself together before going upstairs.

Brenda knocked on the half open door to announce herself. "You don't have to knock, Brenda. I'm never doing anything." Ashley said. She was sketching a rotten bowl of fruit beside a severed pig head. All covered with finely detailed flies. It would make a beautiful oil painting if Ashley decided to take it that far. Brenda perched on the edge of the mattress.

"Ash, I just got off the phone with Nick's mother."

Ashley sniffed, "So now he's having his mother call for him?"

"Enough! Ashley, enough!" Brenda clasped her hands in her lap. She regained her composure. "You need to hear this no matter how painful. Nick took his life last night. His mother said he just hasn't been the same since his brother died. But I think it was other things too."

The air snagged in the back of Ashley's throat and hung there. She couldn't bring it into her lungs for fear of choking. Nick had done it. He was gone. She was still here. She felt a twinge of jealousy. "What does that have to do with me?"

"You can't be this cold, Ash. You can pretend to be,

but I know you."

"I'm not being fucking cold, Brenda. If you want me to feel something maybe you should stop feeding me all that fucking poison. Nick is dead. Should I feel guilty because I didn't forgive him for betraying me? He's forgiven. What does it matter now?"

Brenda stood up, feeling sad for Ashley. Wanting desperately to hold her and let her cry. She wanted to cry. But Ashley continued working on the rotting swine face, adding deep black shadows to the hollow eye sockets. "You should go to the funeral." Brenda told her.

"No way. He made his choices. It's not my fault he couldn't live with them." Ashley said. She forced herself to keep drawing, focusing on anything other than what Brenda was saying.

"If you change your mind, it's Thursday downtown. Funeral home, not church. I will be going." Her words were sharp and cutting.

"Great. Have fun." Ashley scowled, just wanting to be left alone. Brenda stood a minute longer before leaving. Ashley tossed the pad of paper aside and turned over, curling into a ball. Her face was wet with pain. It was so final. "Nick..." She moaned, wondering where he was. What he was doing without her.

"I'm sorry." she whispered, clutching her pillow to her. Her stomach felt empty for once. She didn't know where all the flies had gone. Maybe her increase in medicine had killed the hive. Maybe she wasn't worthy. What if her ascension had stopped? Forgiving a betrayer was a test, and she had failed? She longed to leave her body and be where Nick was. A deep, silent void. None of this was real. Nothing she did mattered. That thought made her feel worse than anything.

Eleven

During finals week Brenda was swamped and began allowing Ashley to stay home alone again. Dr. Hart reported that he was satisfied with Ashley's progress. She had been keeping her stress levels down, and her blood work was good. Her grades at school were high despite her challenging classes and reduced classroom time. She was even going out with friends and events with a crowd of people without incident.

Ashley's adult caregivers let a notch loose in her collar. She felt she could take a full breath without someone asking if she was okay. It was a gray December afternoon, Ashley was alone in the house. It had snowed the night before. Brenda wasn't due home for hours. Nick had been stopping over most afternoons. Ashley had begun helping him with his homework at the insistence of Brenda. "He needs to keep his grades up. You're excellent at Algebra, Ash." She encouraged.

The vent cover on the wall was pulled off. Ashley listened to a Hog Head tape. The ambient rhythms of shuffling hooves and pan flute. She blinked, staring at the gray smudge on her ceiling. She couldn't believe the stain from the rotting Christ was still there. She seemed to float up to it. Her fingers traced the outline. It looked more like a burn mark up close.

With one light touch her ceiling cracked open and the winter winds carried her out into a dark frozen space. She grabbed her chest, squeezed her eyes shut. "Please, you're not real." She repeated. She had cut her medicine back by half. Shadow men had been hanging out in corners. Lucifer appeared briefly on the other side of the shower curtain a few mornings ago. When she whipped back the curtain he had gone. They all taunted her with their presence. She had to wade through the lies to find the truth.

Her feet were cold, buried deep within snow mounds. She stood outside a grimy farmhouse. She didn't know where she was. She didn't have a coat on. She looked at her hand; it burned from where she had touched the soiled spot on the plaster. One of her black flies wiggled its way out from under her fingernail and flew off. She watched it go.

She was freezing, only in her sweatpants and a t-shirt. She walked towards the farmhouse, but stopped when the door opened and a man came out. He looked familiar. She had seen him before, if briefly. He leaned in the doorway and lit a cigarette, staring out into the yard. "Hello?" She asked, but he looked right through her, despite looking directly at her.

He turned and went back inside, leaving the door open. Ashley felt an urging, like she should follow him. She crossed the porch and stepped inside the door. A wood fireplace burned, making the room feel unbearably hot. "Stop right there." He said, not bothering to turn and face her.

Ashley watched him reach behind his head, tie a piece of ragged brown string. When he finally looked his face was covered in a fresh mask. Its edges were still pink and red. "Yours?" he asked. She touched her face and pulled away pink sticky slime.

Ashley sat bolt upright in bed. Her bed. "Shit, damn it." She pushed her hair off her sweaty forehead, leaned forward on her knees. Why was Hog Head wearing her face? She had seen his face, or she thought she did. The details were hazy. Was he signalling to her they were merging? Or that she had seen him for his true self? He saw her for her true self? He was removing her mask, seeing her as no one else could?

What did he fucking look like? Ashley searched her brain, trying to see him standing on that sagging back porch. His features were strong. His hair uncombed and long, primal even. Did he have a beard? What color was his hair? Fuck, she couldn't remember. She smelled burning wood. That was it.

She laid back in bed. The tape had finished. She heard the clock ticking downstairs. Knocking, quiet talking, more knocking. She sat up. It must be after three, Nick was on the porch. Damn, she didn't feel like doing Algebra today.

"Hey," Her words were weary as she opened the door.

"Hey, Ash. Long time no see. I tried calling, but you didn't answer. Did Nick tell you I tried to call?" It caught her off guard, Kristen and Gia on her porch.

"No, he didn't say anything. What, um, do you want?" She asked. She felt too confused from her dream. She was expecting Nick. He was still following up names of HH's or men with those initials. No luck on a last name. Just Judith and the farm. He must have never been formally adopted.

"Can we come in?" Gia asked, jumping up and down, knocking snow off her purple furry boots.

"Ashley, don't." Lucifer cautioned her. She ignored him. *Figment!*

"For a minute. I have a lot of homework to do." Ashley told them. The girls came in trailing snow behind them. Instead of inviting them upstairs, Ashley took them into the living room. They were all silent, with Gia throwing Kristen a look that said *so now what?*

"Nick said you guys have been hanging out a lot lately. He's never around. Turns out he's always here." Kristen said.

Ashley shrugged, "So? He's not your boyfriend. He's not my boyfriend, if that's what you're worried about. I'm helping him with some homework."

"Ash, you're our friend, okay? That thing on Halloween was supposed to be funny."

"Hilarious." Ashley remarked. Kristen ignored her.

"You remember what I told you about Nick, right?"

"Which part? Where you guys screwed around or the part where he treats girls like whores? Because I think that's a problem between you and him. I haven't had a problem." Ashley thought about the last two weeks, straddling him in her bed. Doing homework afterwards. Eating dinner with Brenda after that. He examined her self-mutation. They compared scars. He laid there and let her do whatever she wanted to him. Nope, not a problem.

Kristen's face tightened, Ashley enjoyed taking away her power with a few passive words. "Hey, I brought you something. You said you liked it, it's getting too big on me. It would probably fit you." Kristen leaned over and unzipped her bag. She brought out the leather mini skirt she had worn to visit Ashley in the hospital. The one Ashley had commented on. Now that she mentioned it Kristen looked skinnier. Unnaturally thin. Her hands shook as she passed the garment to Ashley.

"Thanks. Are you okay?" She asked, nodding at the trembling grasp. Kristen folded her hands together in her lap, willed them to stop.

"I'm fine. Great, actually." Gia looked from Kristen to Ashley, trying to decide who was the bigger bullshitter. Kristen had started smoking crystal meth with Brandon. Brandon had dropped out, Kristen hardly came to class anymore. Gia thought Ashley looked unnerved, like she could snap at any moment and kill them all. She sat so still, unmoving. Not even her face moved when she spoke. Gia felt it wasn't natural. Serial killer unnatural. She didn't know why she agreed to drive Kristen over here and be a part of this.

Ashley smoothed the leather skirt in her lap. She really did like that skirt. Brenda would never let her wear anything that short. Ashley didn't like tight clothing, but there was something about it. The black with the slight dark green creases. The way it felt. She wondered how she would look in it.

"So you just came over here to give me your skirt?"

Don't believe her. Lucifer said. "I don't," Ashley told him.

"Don't what??" Kristen asked.

"I don't uh, get it. What do you want, Kristen? Are you mad Nick and I are friends?"

"We're just worried about you."

"Bullshit." Ashley said. Kristen gave Gia a nudge with her boot. Gia had almost forgotten what she was supposed to do.

"Hey, can I get a drink of water?" She asked.

"Want me to get it for you?"

"No, it's cool. I remember." Gia got up and went into the kitchen.

"It's not bullshit." Kristen said. "Nick has problems, you know. He was weird before, but after his brother died, he just took it to a whole new level." Kristen said, leaning forward.

"Kristen, what are you talking about?" Did she forget who she was talking to? As if anything could shock Ashley. She was the empress of weird behavior.

"Now don't freak out, but he's carved your name into his arm. Deep. I'm just scared for you. I wanted you to know. Who knows what someone like that is capable of. And you're so fragile. If something happened, I'd feel awful for not saying something." Kristen said.

Ashley groaned, she just saw Nick with his shirt off yesterday. He was cut up more than usual, but he did not have her name carved into his arm, or his chest, or anywhere else for that matter. "That's not true, I know it for a fact. Kristen. I think you and Gia need to go." Gia came wandering back in.

Kristen jumped up from the sofa. Her whole demeanor seemed to change. As if Ashley was the one lying to her. "You would know, wouldn't you? Little whore." Kristen sneered and grabbed her coat. Gia shrugged on her way out the door like, *uh, sorry.* Ashley shut the door behind them. What the hell was that all about?

She peaked out the front window and watched Gia's car disappear down the road. Ashley never thought she would be grateful they weren't her friends. Maybe at first they were or tried to be. But now, she didn't need them. What was Kristen trying to prove? Was she trying to wreck Nick's life just because he didn't want her?

Ashley closed the curtain and walked into the kitchen. The cupboard door where she kept all of her medication was open. Ashley knew it was closed, because Brenda closed it after she doled out drugs this morning. When the door was open, it hung over the coffeemaker, and made it difficult to get the pot out without knocking it. Brenda *always* closed it. There was no reason for it to be open.

"Fuckers," Ashley said, pawing through the cabinet. Gia had snatched the pill bottles, her liquid poison piss. She turned when she heard shuffling on the steps, knocking at the front door. Brenda was going to freak. She didn't know what was going to happen. She crouched down on the floor and took a deep breath.

That was several hundred dollars' worth of medication. Stuff she took every day, emergency stuff, who knows what else. If she didn't wean herself off slowly, she would get sick. She was down to half a dose in the morning, plus her pills. She'd be okay until tomorrow morning. But Brenda assumed she took her night dose, she would know as soon as she got home. Ashley had to tell her. The banging on the door was louder. *God, maybe they brought it all back. I won't have to tell Brenda I was stupid enough to let them in. Please, universe.*

"I told you not to let them in." Lucifer said in her ear. He wasn't there, but his consciousness was floating out there somewhere, revolving around her head, a moon stuck in her gravitational pull of madness. He had been tucked away nice and safe for the longest time, almost two months. But he crawled through the cracks of Ashley's anxiety, and he'd never let her stuff him back in. If he was out, that meant the others were too. Ashley screamed and kicked the lower cupboards. Why did they do this?

"Ash? Hey, are you alright?" Nick came in when he heard her screaming. He crouched beside her, but didn't touch her. Brenda advised him to give Ashley space when she was like this.

"What? Where did you come from?"

"I was just outside. You didn't answer. I heard you scream."

"Those bitches..." Ashley stood up and looked in the cupboard again. Everything was still gone.

"What bitches?" Nick stood up beside her, looking at the empty cupboard. He wasn't sure what it meant, but the emptiness seemed to upset Ashley.

"Kristen and Gia. Fuck, I'm so stupid!" Ashley pulled on her hair.

"They were here? Damn it, what did they do? Did they say something?" Nick had been avoiding all three of them more and more since Thanksgiving. Brandon never came to class anymore, and Kristen was a fucking mess. Gia was just her little puppet, following her master's orders. Nick was sick of them all by this point.

"Whatever they said, Ash, it's not true. Kristen showed up last night, but I didn't even let her inside. I closed the door in her face, I swear." Nick would never hit a woman, but if there was ever a time when he was close, it was last night.

"No, she didn't say anything. Well, she did, but that's not the problem." Ashley went to the fridge and got a drink. The water was too cold and made her teeth ache. "While I was in the living room with Kristen listening to her lie her ass off, Gia was in here ripping off my medication. Shit, Brenda is going to call the cops. This is so bad."

Nick looked back at the cabinet, rubbed his face.

"Cash. I bet those idiots think they can sell that stuff for cash. Like people do with painkillers and shit."

"My clozapine, the stuff in the bottle, can make you sick, like kill you if you take too much. I hardly take any, and it makes me feel sick. Shit! What if they say I gave it to them? I could go to prison."

"That's not going to happen. You need to call Brenda so the cops can find them." Nick said. Ashley knew he was right, but she was having a hard time swallowing. She knew it wasn't her fault, but it sure as hell felt like her fault. Nick kept talking, Ashley's heart was drumming faster. The swarms were active, filling her ears with static, making it hard to concentrate. Lucifer wouldn't shut up. Wasn't there someone at the front door earlier?

"Ash, why don't you sit down? I can call Brenda. That's her number on the fridge, right? Should I call someone else?"

"I'm just having trouble… Yeah, just call Brenda. I need to lay down." Ashley let Nick direct her to the sofa. She fell into the deep soft cushions and closed her eyes. She needed to hold on. Nick was calling Brenda, everyone would be alright. Lucifer would keep the Church at bay, unless they were already here. She thought she'd heard scratching in the basement the last week or so. What if they reopened those hidden tunnels? She had forgotten about those damn tunnels.

No. *NO*. She was just having a panic attack; she needed to take a deep breath, and she was fine. She had to think about something else. Snow. Wind blowing snow through the trees. She inhaled deeply, the smell of a wood stove burning. She was warm, she could breathe. She kept her eyes closed, just feeling and hearing the room. He was beside her; she felt him. *HH, what if they put me in a hospital?* They were of one mind. He could hear her, she didn't even need to speak.

His heavy silence, his slow even breathing was all she needed. She mimicked him. He was older and had been through it; he knew what to do. His very existence soothed her, calmed her down to her core. There she was. She pawed and swam to the bottom of herself. *I'm here. Just where I should be.* HH threaded his fingers between hers. His palms were rough and strong. He slowly brought her back up to the surface.

"I'm home, Ash. You're fine." Brenda had a chair pulled beside the sofa.

"That was fast." Ashley said. Brenda smiled. Relieved Ash had come out of it. Sometimes the anxiety and panic attacks were scarier than her hallucinations. She didn't want to think about what would have happened if Nick hadn't been with her to calm her down and make the phone call. "Do you... did Nick-"

"The police are looking for them. I told them about the risk factors, what can happen. But there's not much they can do."

"Will I go to jail if someone dies? I swear I didn't give it to them."

Brenda soothed her like she did when Ashley was

younger. "No one thinks that. It's not your fault."

"I shouldn't have let them in. Lucifer warned me not to let them in."

Brenda sat up straight. "Lucifer? You've been seeing things again? For how long?" Ashley had said nothing about delusions. Nothing. "Ash? What else? Anything else?"

"Huh?" Ashley looked up at Brenda. "Nothing. What? I just thought I heard a voice, maybe it was just me. I knew I shouldn't let them in. I just *knew*."

"We'll work this out. Dr. Hart called in a prescription, I was just waiting to go pick it up."

"I really don't think I can get in the car right now, Brenda." Ashley rolled on her side and looked at a stack of magazines on the coffee table. The phone rang.

"That's probably Timothy. He took over my class when I had to leave. I should have called him earlier to let him know things were being handled. I'll be right back." Brenda told her and walked out into the hall. Ashley listened to Brenda talking on the phone. She sounded like a different person when she talked to Timothy. She sounded younger, not like doctor-caretaker Brenda but just a woman talking to a man. Ashley hoped Timothy wouldn't move in here until she was old enough to move out, or Brenda put her in an institution.

"Ash?" Brenda stuck her head around the doorway. "If you're doing alright, I can run up to get your script now. Nick is doing the dishes if you need anything.

It'll only be ten minutes. I can get us all something to eat?"

"Nick is still here?"

"I don't think there's any way I could get him to leave. He was so worried about you." Ashley hated the grin Brenda got, one that spoke of softness and love. It was nothing like that. It was something else. Ashley didn't know what.

She liked Nick just fine. Enjoyed exploring his body. But it was different. They weren't lovers; they were just passing time. Two ships in the night. She would move on to HH and Nick would find someone else. Ashley hardly ever orgasmed, but she liked being able to give physical pleasure to her friend. He enjoyed it. Seemed less depressed when it was over. Afterwards, she smelled like the scented lotion they used for lubrication. The act made her feel normal for a little while at least.

Brenda stood there a minute looking at her. "Brenda, I'm not going anywhere." Brenda was more concerned about Ashley's comments on Lucifer, the other's followed him. It had to be stress that triggered it. Ashley was doing so well with her new dosage. Both had been sleeping through the night. Ashley didn't have to sit through her class all day. After Christmas, she might have been able to go back to school part time. Now Brenda questioned it all. Dr. Hart would have to be told. Maybe it's just how it was. There wasn't really a handbook for this type of thing. Maybe something would always be there. Brenda hated she couldn't control it for Ashley.

Ashley squinted at Brenda, "I'm going. Food?"

"Whatever." Ashley moaned. She kept thinking about Kristen and her tight smirk.

"I'll take the mobile phone with me if you need something, just call. I'll get a pizza."

"I'm sure we'll be fine. It's only ten minutes."

"Okay. Nick! I'm leaving, but I'll be right back." Brenda called. "I'll have my phone on."

Nick dried his hands on the front of his shirt and walked out of the kitchen. "Okay, cool. We'll be here."

"Thanks so much," Brenda grabbed his arm for a second, letting him know how much they needed his help. Ashley pretended not to see. Another babysitter, that's all she needed. Nick came into the living room and sat in the chair Brenda had pulled up earlier. His sleeves were pushed up to his elbows.

"Didn't Brenda see those?" Ashley motioned to the scabbed over wounds.

Nick thought he should just tell her. "I told her about it. We talked." Ashley sat straight up. "What? Are you fucking kidding?"

"Relax, I didn't mention you. She noticed one and asked me about it. I wanted to be honest. I told her about my brother, my depression. She wasn't mad, Ash. Just worried. More than my mom would be." He sat back and looked at her. Was he challenging her?

"You can't say anything to Brenda about me. They'll put me away. After the last time. Nick-"

"Ash, I would never do that unless I thought you

were in real danger. Like having a breakdown or something."

"I'm in control. You can't tell her."

"I won't. I told you. It's not my secret. Just like I'm not telling her about the Hog Head stuff. Even though…" He trailed off, knowing this was not the time.

"Even though what?" *He better not fucking say it. Not now.*

"Nothing. We'll talk about it later. It's not important. I'm just glad you're alright. That was heavy. I'm not going to lie." he said.

Ashley laid back on the sofa. She felt on edge. Was there anyone she could trust? No. Only herself and HH, that much was becoming more clear by the day. She turned back to Nick, "You know Kristen didn't tell me she'd been to your house. She said something about you carving my name in your arm. Nothing about the house though."

Nick's jaw was tense. "I told you about it, to be honest. She didn't come in. That thing about the name is bullshit." He thought about Casey, a girl he liked last year. It was her name he had scratched into his arm. But he was a different person then. He had his reasons, he wouldn't do that again.

"That's what I told her. I said I'd seen your arms and everywhere else. And that she was full of shit."

"So you told her that we?" He liked that she told someone.

"I didn't come right out and say it, but I think she

got the hint. She called me a little whore before she left." Ashley laughed about the way Kristen's face looked, so full of jealousy, with just a hint of desperation. She shouldn't revel in other people's misery, but this time she did. So did Nick.

"Maybe she'll leave me alone now."

"She probably will if she's in jail or dead." Ashley said. Both sat in silence. "I shouldn't have said that. Now I sound like a bitch."

"No. You're right. And they did this, not you. If something happens, it's on them. Can that liquid stuff really cause seizures?"

"Yeah, they have to take my blood every week. It does all kinds of shit- diabetes, heart attack and everything."

"I see why you don't want to take it. I wouldn't either."

"And it doesn't even do anything. Just makes me feel more like shit. Dizzy. Tired. And dry, my mouth... my cunt. Like a sandbox all the time." She chuckled. Nick tried to laugh along with her. But he felt for her. It had to suck, taking all that stuff. He didn't know if he could do it. But she was stronger than him.

He held her hand in his. He wished he had more time with her. He wanted to take her upstairs. What he wanted her to do to him. He had thought about carving her name into his skin when he first met her. He was sure she'd never want him. Instead, he gave her the book that had bonded them together. She was more than his fantasy; she was better.

Nick tightened his grip on Ashley's waist. He felt he was close. He muttered her name under his breath. "Don't..." He moaned, but Ashley stopped. He looked up at her, she just sat there staring straight ahead at her wall. Vacant. "Ash?" He choked out. He wasn't sure what was going on, if he should keep going or what? He shook her, her lips parted slightly like she was going to speak, but nothing came out. What was she seeing?

Holding her, Nick sat halfway up and looked in her eyes. She didn't seem to realize he was there. It was New Year. Brenda had gone out with Timothy for an early movie and dinner. She would be back by ten. Ashley and Nick were supposed to be watching a film, something neither of them cared about. "Ashley? Snap out of it." Nick didn't know how he'd explain this to Brenda.

Other than her frozen expression, Ashley seemed fine. Nick snapped his fingers in front of her face. She shooed his hand away like you would a house fly. She blinked, but didn't seem to remember she was fucking him.

"Ash? Come on." Nick took her in his arms and placed her down on the bed. He leaned over and got the water bottle off the floor. Empty. "Damn it. I'll be right back." He thought maybe cold water could help. He pulled on his pants and walked to the bathroom.

Ashley looked around. She was in bed, covered with a blanket. She was just floating through the very fabric of time and space, searching for the man on the porch. HH. She looked up at the ceiling, then sat up and looked at her wall. The cracks had sealed themselves. "What the?" She was naked, chilled. She brought the blanket closer to her skin.

Nick was walking back in and saw her. "Shit, you're okay!" He ran over and sat the water down. He hugged her. Ashley was confused.

"Nick, what are you... What?"

Nick pulled back and looked at her. He cradled his hands on either side of her face. "Where were you? We were together and then I didn't know what to do. You just stopped."

"Sorry. I was probably just thinking about something. I get lost in thought sometimes. Did you... was everything okay?" She asked.

Nick shrugged, feeling relieved she was alright, but also uncomfortable. "I didn't keep going if that's what you're asking. It was too weird. It would be like raping you."

Ashley laughed, *no it wouldn't*. "You can just keep going if, you know, it happens next time."

"Ash, no way, not while you're out of it like that. I couldn't." He sat back, surprised she would think he'd do such a thing.

"It's not even a big deal, Nick. I don't care. It's not like it really matters to me, anyway. I only do this for you. You might as well enjoy it, even if I drift off. If I didn't want to, I'd tell you." Ash said looking around for her sweater, her pants, something to put on.

"Are you joking? Ash, there's no way."

She shrugged, "Suit yourself. But it happens sometimes. It's your dick." She stood up and pulled on her bottoms. "What time is it?" She bent over and stuck all the Hog Head information into the vent and pushed the old heavy metal grate over the hole. She looked at Nick, who just kept sitting there, staring down at the bed. "What? I'm fine. I can't help it, Nick. Sorry if it freaked you out. What do you want me to do?"

He looked up at her, "That's not it." His voice was slow, careful. He couldn't believe what she said, and she didn't realize it. She didn't even say it trying to be mean, it was just how she felt. And he had no idea.

"Then what? Why do you look like I just kicked a puppy?"

"None of this matters to you, huh?" He stood up and pulled on his shirt. Judging by the look on his face, this apparently meant something to him. More than just friends causally screwing around.

"Nick," She tried to touch his arm, but he shrugged her off.

"So what? You're fucking me because you're bored? Or so I'll keep helping you find this hog-faced asshole? I really can't tell." His words were harsh. He'd never spoken to her like that. His aggression caught her off guard.

"No, I like you. I don't know if I *can* love another

person, I'm trying."

He looked at her. "So what if I told you I don't want to look for him anymore? That I'm done spending hours on the computer. It's not going anywhere. I'm fucking sick of it." Nick put his hand in his jean pocket. He felt the folded piece of paper inside. He had been debating about giving to her all evening. A name. An address he was sure was Hog Head's. Until that point, he didn't know what to do with the information. Now he was. He kept the small square of paper shoved deep in his pocket.

"Nick, we can't stop. Don't even joke about it. Maybe we could go back to the Mad Monk. I have some money saved. We could bribe him or something."

"No. We're not bribing anyone. I'm done with it. I think you should be too. Who even cares anymore? I mean, he's weird and has some fucked up shit to say. But my brother was wrong, I was stupid to believe that he's some sort of prophet or whatever. He's just a guy who wants to be left alone, Ash."

Ashley was shaking her head. "No. That's bullshit. No. Don't even fucking say that!" She screamed. "You don't get it. You're not like us." She cried, folding her arms around herself. She didn't recognize him. She did everything he asked her to do, and now he wouldn't even help her with this one thing?

"Ash, you're nothing like that guy. He raped his foster sister. They put him in an institution. He's *not* you."

Nick needed to stop talking. "Are you going to tell

Brenda?"

Nick paused before saying, "We need to stop this. Maybe we should just get rid of everything. Start over. It's New Year, we can move on."

God, why was he saying all this? It was like Brenda had converted him over to just another mindless caregiver set on keeping her docile and blind. "Nick you need to leave."

"The book, Ash, let me at least take it. I won't destroy it, I promise." Ashley moved in front of the vent.

When he came closer, he felt threatening. He was going to take everything she cared about away. "Get the fuck out!" She shrieked. She turned from him and pressed herself against the wall, willing it to open back up and swallow her. She wanted to be away from this place, back in the snowy white forest with *Him*.

Nick stood there a moment, trying to decide what he should do. He figured it would be better if he left. He'd have to call Brenda. He didn't want to tell her anything, but in order for them to help Ash, he felt he had to tell her everything. Even if it meant she would hate him too. He felt self-loathing like he'd never experienced before. Everything he tried to do went in the completely opposite direction. "Ash..." He tried again, wanting more than anything for her to come away from the wall and let them talk all this out. He wanted to beg her, throw himself at her feet.

She stayed still, not turning, muttering about stars and space, snow and masks. "Just show me," She cried to an unseen presence, clawing at the wall

"Why won't you answer?" Nick walked downstairs and called Brenda's phone. He told her she needed to come home, Ashley was having an episode, he didn't know how to calm her down.

"What happened?" Brenda asked, rushing through the door. Nick pointed upstairs.

"She's okay, I think. But I can't get her to move away from the wall. She's talking to herself. Earlier she blanked out, like she wasn't even here. We had a disagreement, and she got upset, I feel horrible."

Brenda walked up the stairs. Nick could hear her talking softly to Ashley. He wanted to run out the door and never come back. But Brenda would have questions. Maybe he could keep one shred of trust and tell her what's been going on. He could only hope she would respect his honesty.

"She okay?" Nick asked, getting up from the bottom stair when Brenda came down. He tucked his hair behind his ear, looked at her.

"She's lying down. I think she just needs to rest. I've seen worse. What happened?" When Nick didn't answer, but looked at his boots. Brenda sensed a feeling for growing unease. "Maybe we should sit at the table." She suggested.

"I think that would be good."

Thirteen

"Are you sure you won't come?" Brenda asked. She'd asked almost every day that week. She had heard Ashley crying during the night. She felt relieved her daughter wasn't stone. "If you don't go, you'll regret it. Maybe not tomorrow, but in a year? You will."

"I'll take that chance." Ashley said slugging down her morning pills and brown bottle piss.

Brenda ground her teeth. "Fine. The service is at eleven. I don't know if I'll go to the cemetery or not. Depends on the rain." It was warm enough for Brenda to wear her spring jacket.

"Well, you know I won't be having sex while you're gone."

"Ash, that's not funny." Brenda looked at her. Ashley tried to hide it, but Brenda saw that hint of foggy pain far back in her eyes. "Do your homework." She said. Brenda set her coffee cup in the sink and went upstairs to shower. Ashley walked over and looked out the back window. She remembered the hidden tunnels, the secret door she thought was burrowed deep within the tree.

"Lucifer?" She asked softly. No one answered. She never felt so alone. She stopped by Brenda's purse hanging in the hallway. Brenda kept fifty dollars in emergency cash tucked inside her wallet. She wouldn't notice it was gone until it didn't matter anymore. Ashley plucked it out and slid it into her pocket.

She laid on the sofa pretending to read while Brenda rushed around looking for her black heels and the umbrella. "I'll have my mobile on if you need to call. If you change your mind, I'll turn around and come pick you up. Ash? Are you even hearing me? I want to get there early to talk to Nick's mom. She sounded horrible on the phone. Ash?"

"I heard you, Brenda. How could I not?"

Brenda had to leave because she didn't want to say something she'd regret. Ashley continued staring at the same page she'd been on for thirty minutes. *Just fucking leave.* Ashley stared harder at the stark page. Finally she saw a blur of Brenda move away from the door, heard her heels tapping on the wood floor. She pulled the heavy door closed behind her. Her car started and pulled out of the short driveway. Ashley could exhale. *Finally, alone.*

She had the entire process mapped out. She had looked at the bus schedule Brenda kept in the kitchen drawer. A bus that passed through Haggsville on its way up north left at 11:15. Ashley had to be on it.

Upstairs, she kicked off her sweatpants and pulled on the leather skirt Kristen had given her. It fit her like a second skin. It was smooth and cold. Ashley pulled on her ratty green cardigan over her thin white t-shirt. Her hair was stringy and unwashed. She shoved it back in a loose ponytail.

In the bathroom, she rounded her eyes with black and stared at herself. She looked older, old enough to get by. *How old are you?* If someone asked she couldn't hesitate. *Eighteen. Eighteen. I'm eighteen. Why?* She repeated over and over. *What's your name?* If they asked, *I don't have one. I'm an orphan. I'm nobody.*

Ashley shoved her money into a small bag and slung it across her middle. Brenda would be saying goodbye to Nick's body as Ashley rode north. The thought of his name made her want to fall forward and never stop crying. She'd see him soon. And this pain would be gone. He'd forgive her for not coming to his funeral.

Ashley walked the several blocks to the bus station and bought her ticket. The man behind the counter gave her a hard stare as he slid the ticket to her. "They're boarding now." he told her, pointing at the door to his left.

"Thanks." Ashley mumbled. She couldn't make eye contact. It felt like everyone knew what she was up to and would report her to Brenda. Everyone was noticing her. If the cops came through here asking if anyone had seen her, everyone would remember her. She tried to keep her head down. She wouldn't look at the driver. She sat near the back and looked out the window, her face turned away from the other passengers.

It drizzled. The bus smelled of wet rubber and damp clothing as it pulled away from the station heading north. Ashley watched the city fade, her heart beat madly in her chest. It was almost over. Either he'd take her, or reject her. Either way, he'd know her before everything was over.

The ride felt faster than it should have. Several hours and Ashley was standing at the bus stop on the empty main street. The rain stopped for the moment. But heavy clouds threatened its return. She jogged across the street to the Mad Monk art house. The lights were on. A bell over the door rang when she went inside. "Hello?" She called, looking around. It was mostly empty except for a makeshift bar in the corner, shelves stacked with paper and books. Records hung on the walls. Every appeared yellowed behind the grime of decades of cigarette smoke.

The same short fat man stuck his head out from the back. "Who's that?" he called coming out, dropping a box on the floor in front of him. Then he recognized her. More make-up and less clothing than last time, but it was the little blonde. He'd know those wide lost eyes anywhere. More like a doll than a girl. What was it about HH that drew all this young pussy to him like flies to honey? HH normally told them to get lost, but they kept showing up, wanting more.

"Stop with that shit. *No one.* I fucking mean it. I don't care how hot you think someone is. I don't want them in my face." HH had told him several times, when he came in bitching about more idiots hounding him about his work. "I don't want to fucking talk about it. Any of it. No more!" He slammed his hand against the desk. Jon always promised him he wouldn't tell anyone else, but damn once in a while a cute one came in. What could it hurt? What's HH going to do? Yell at him some more. He was a big guy, but Jon always figured he could take him if he wanted to fight about it.

"Hello there darling, what can I do for you?" Jon kicked the box aside.

Ashley wasn't sure where to begin. "You might not remember me, but I talked to you a few months ago, around Thanksgiving?"

She was funny, like he could forget. "I remember you. You were with that dead-looking vampire motherfucker, right? He with you now?"

Ashley cringed at the reference. "No, I'm alone. You said you would give me HH's address? Or, um, tell me where I could talk to him? I have some money." She said. The round tattooed man walked close to Ashley. She could smell his stale clothing. She wanted to gag when he put his thick fingers on her lower arm, stopping her from reaching inside her purse for the money.

"There's no need for any of that."

Ashley didn't believe him. "I know nothing is free."

Jon nodded, "That is true, unfortunately. But this is America. Why don't you come into my office? We can negotiate." This was the last thing she had to get through.

"Where?" She asked. He gestured to the doorway at the back of the shop. Ashley walked ahead, just wanting to get it over with. Jon locked the front door and turned around the "back in five minutes" sign. He wouldn't last long with this one.

Jon exhaled sharply and leaned against the wall in the back. He rearranged himself and zipped his pants back up. Ashley spit his cum out onto the floor, wiped her mouth with the back of her hand. "That's not very nice. Careful, darling, you might hurt my feelings." Ashley glared up at him.

"Got a mint or something?" Ashley pushed her hair out of her face. He had ripped it out of her ponytail.

Jon laughed, "No. But I got whiskey. On the house, considering." He went back out front, Ashley followed, leaving her bag and sweater on the floor of the office. He poured her a shot glass. He poured one for himself. "Cheers, beautiful." Jon said. Ashley slugged it down, hoping to cut the sour taste in her mouth.

"Well? The address?" She said while he picked up the glasses.

"You want another?" he asked her.

"No. I want what I paid for. His fucking address." She was tired of being jerked around. But Jon just laughed at her frustration.

"You don't need an address baby, he's right down the street."

Ashley looked towards the door. "What, where?"

"Few doors up across the road. The butcher shop. Tall dude, long hair. Serious face. Can't miss him." Ashley turned away from the grinning man and pulled at the door. Realizing it was locked, she turned the deadbolt over and tugged it open. Jon watched the whole thing with amusement.

"If he turns you away, you come back and see old Jon." The fat little man called after her. "I write poetry too!" He laughed. Ashley shuddered. She couldn't believe he was here all this time. She walked towards the butcher shop. Who she saw last time, that couldn't be him. He looked right at her and turned away like she was nothing. But now she knew she was. She was truly nothing to everyone and no one.

She wondered if Brenda would ever find her body. She hoped not. She wanted to just die in the woods like a sick animal, be eaten and dissolve back into the dirt. That's where she wanted to spend forever. But first she had to finish this. She had to know what he was like.

She sat on the bench across the street, looking into the shop window. A man came out. A woman went in. Ashley knew they would close soon, she could just go in there. But she was a coward, so she waited. She got up and forced herself across the street, and walked down a side alley. The little parking lot behind the buildings was a scattering of cars and trucks. She leaned against a brick wall, waiting. He had to drive one of these. The dented truck parked closest to the back door. She bet that was his.

The wind was picking up and whistling between the buildings. It didn't feel like February. Ashley realized she'd forgotten her sweater and bag at the Mad Monk. The back door groaned open and a man in navy work pants and a faded gray shirt came out. Earthy brown hair pulled back out of his face. When he stopped to look his eyes were cold and uncaring. As if he couldn't be bothered.

"You're Hog Head, aren't you?" She asked. He said nothing and walked towards his truck. Ashley couldn't just let him leave. Not after everything. She'd throw herself in front of his truck if she had to. "Please, I just want to talk to you. You don't know what your work means to me."

"Yeah, what's that?" His voice was deeper than she thought it would be.

"Huh?"

"What does it mean?"

"Everything. It means everything. I ran away from home. I just had to meet you before…" Ashley wasn't sure how much to tell him. She wanted to trust him as she thought she could. But she had trusted others- Brenda, Nick, Kristen, Wheeler and looked at what happened. She was sure this man was the answer to the mysteries that plagued her. But standing before him in the fading light, she wondered what the hell was she doing? He could give two shits about her.

She followed his gaze to the scars on her exposed arms. It was probably hopeful thinking, but he seemed to soften some. Like taking pity on a half dead dog. Maybe he'd take her home and shoot her. Save her the trouble of trying to do it herself. "Get in," he told her.

Ashley didn't wait for him to change his mind. She ran around the front of the truck and climbed into the passenger's side. She wanted to just gaze at him. He was so beautiful. Instead, she looked straight ahead, at her arms, anywhere but at him. She watched the buildings thin out as they went east out of town. The radio was off. He looked like he wanted to say something a few times, but didn't. Ashley just wanted to move things along before Brenda found out she was gone, called the police. She'd be locked up for good if they caught her now. Brenda wouldn't feel she was up for the job and send her back to the clinic or somewhere worse, somewhere with steel doors, and bars on the windows.

"I read about you, you know. I read about why you were in that hospital. I don't know if the other things are rumors or what... but..." She tried to indirectly look at him to see if her words upset him. He just shook his head slightly, acknowledging her words but not caring. "I'm not a virgin you know." She waited; he didn't speak, didn't even look at her. "I uh... I like the pain. It helps me forget about the voices."

Her voice sounded shy, not like the other's HH had encountered. There was something innocent about her. She was not like them. Not like him. Sweet, even damaged, more like his Judith was.

Ashley felt the truck slow. He turned into a yard that was more mud than grass. The house was grim, unloved. Dilapidated porch, ancient skeletal tree out front. No neighbors, just scrubby fields and bare forests. It felt right somehow. This was where she'd die.

HH turned off the engine to the truck. They sat

a moment listening to it cool. Rain hitting the windshield. Ashley struggled not to shake, not to show a sign of weakness. She was cold. She wondered once she went inside what he would do to her. He was so much bigger than she was. No one knew she was here. But what did she expect? Didn't she always know it would come to this?

HH was the first to move. The keys rattled in his hand. The door seemed to protest and grind when he swung it open. "Come on then," he told her she didn't move. Without a word, Ashley slipped out the other side and followed the man into the house. He unlocked the door and pushed it open. He gestured for Ashley to go in. She looked at him and passed by into the cold, dim house. She expected to see mutilated animal heads thrown around, mad writing scrawled in blood across the walls. Chains hanging from the ceiling, waiting to bind her.

The floorboards were bare, the sparse furniture old. Stacks of books carelessly piled on the coffee table, some tumbling to the floor. The house could have been deserted for all the charm it held. Ashley wrapped her arms around herself and walked further into the gloom. She looked out the back window at a bleak field. The dried bones of plants broken and battered by snow and rain. Beyond that, a thick brushy forest. In a few months all of this would be green, but she imagined she wouldn't be around to see it.

She heard HH finally come in and close the door. He flicked on a lamp, his heavy boots approached her, she waited for whatever he was to inflict upon her. Slit her open. He would only find mounds of dead flies, dust, her pockmarked bones. They had devoured every aspect of her humanity. She stood before him as nothing, just waiting. He didn't need to release the flies; they had never existed. She would never ascend. She'd fooled herself into believing she was a great being, that he was.

"Sit down." He told her. She turned and noticed he was not behind her, but in the kitchen. Ashley walked to the sofa and sat as instructed. He came over and dropped in the chair across from her. The table with books separated them. She finally got the courage to look up, look at Him. He who had dominated and wormed his way into her very mania. Even now, she felt her being wrapped around him. But Nick was right, he was just a man.

HH took a cigarette out of a half-empty pack on the table and lit it. He snapped the lid on the lighter shut and Ashley jumped. She saw him half smile, like he thought it was funny to see her scared. "So what am I going to do with you?" He asked, exhaling. "You smoke?" He offered her the cigarette, just out of her reach.

When Ashley got up to take it, he grabbed her wrist and looked her squarely in the eye. Ashley stared right back. Blank and cold. She took the cigarette from his hand; he released her, and she sat back down. HH got up and walked down the hallway. He came back with a black wool sweater. "Your hands are like ice.

Put this on." He told her.

Ashley gave him the cigarette in exchange for the garment. She pulled it on and tucked her legs underneath. The simple act of kindness unnerved her. HH sat back in the chair and continued to look at her, like he was trying to figure what to make of her. "So what's going on?" He finally asked. She shrugged, unsure what he meant. "Your arms. There's a story there." He could tell a few of the cuts required stitches, they were deep. Not cries for help, but pleas for death.

"I don't remember most of them. I..." She trailed off. Should she tell him she was like him? Or did he already know? "The guy who gave me your book said you're schizophrenic, is that true?"

HH had a deep, hollow laughter. "Is that what they say about me? Fucking shit, people, man. No, I'm not schizo. Why?" Ashley looked away, towards the front door. Her chin trembled. She was alone. Who was this man? HH realized his mistake by the look of sudden pain that splintered across her face.

"But I'm guessing you are, huh?" He felt like an asshole.

Ashley shoved her humanity aside, looked back at him. "So why were you locked up then?"

"Not important."

"Judith said she couldn't get pregnant for five years. That she had burns and scars from what you did to her. No normal sane person goes to the loony bin for the criminally insane."

"You spoke to Judith?"

Ashley caught a change in his demeanor right away. She felt a little more powerful. "Yeah, a few months ago. She told me all kinds of stuff. That you raped her. That you're dangerous. That you'll probably rape me too, or worse."

HH shook his head, "No, that's not... she wouldn't say that." He thought back to last week, when he saw her by chance in the shop. She had run away from him. He, who had been her lover, was now her monster. "She really said that, huh?"

Ashley wanted to take it back, but it was said. "She did right before she slammed the door in my face."

HH thought that sounded like Judith. "So why did you come then? After all these stories of rape and mutilation. If everyone thinks I'm fucking crazy why bother me? I've got nothing for you. Do you have a death wish?"

Ashley shrugged, "Maybe. My parents are gone. My best friend just killed himself. I've been raped. And I'll be *fucking crazy* until I die." Ashley said, throwing his own words back at him. She inhaled deep, she wanted to cry. She felt so stupid for coming here, what did she want? He wasn't a prophet. Nick had told her she wasn't like him. He was just some asshole with fucked up shit to say.

Brenda arrived home a little after two in the afternoon. She had gone to the cemetery. Besides some friends and Nick's mother, there weren't many people there. It rained the whole time. It was a dismal affair, Brenda couldn't wait to get home to Ashley. "Ash, I'm back. I've got something for you."

Nick's mother had given Brenda a letter Nick had written addressed to Ashley. Brenda hadn't opened it. It was too personal. Maybe she'd sit with Ashley while she read it to support her. She imagined whatever it said would be heartbreaking. "Ash?" Brenda called up the stairs again. Brenda hung up her coat and listened, no footsteps. Brenda noticed none of the lights were turned on, despite the darkness gathered outside the windows.

Ashley's door was wide open. "Ash?" Brenda's voice was gentle as she walked down the hall towards the emptiness she knew awaited her. *Please let her be okay.* Brenda had a horrible flash of Ashley hanging from the light fixture, laying bloody in a bathtub. Brenda looked around, everything was the same. Her bed was empty. Brenda rushed to the bathroom, empty.

"Ash!" She began turning on all the flights, calling the girl's name as she went. Upstairs, then downstairs, out to the backyard. Her daughter was gone. Her belongings, her medicine here. She called the police, told them everything. Called Timothy and cried into the phone. Brenda sat on the bottom step feeling helpless. Where could Ashley have gone? Was she okay? Was she scared or lost? Brenda didn't know.

She held Nick's envelope in her hands. Not knowing why, she felt the impulse to open it. It wasn't a note at all, but an address. *Holden Halsted 333 Old Theremin Highway, Haggsville.* Brenda read it again. Who was this? She recognized the town name. It was an hour's drive from the clinic. Nothing was there. She had been through it, one traffic light, a few stores, then nothing but farm fields and forest.

Brenda stared at the note, willed it to make sense. When it finally clicked, she sat back. Was this the man? The initials jumped out at her HH, short for Hog Head, but maybe an actual name? Brenda picked up the phone right away. Her hands trembled.

She knew it might be nothing, but she couldn't live with herself if she didn't know. She told the police about the note, the address. Her daughter could be there. They assured her they'd look into it. The village was in another county. It would take a little while to coordinate with the sheriff's department up there. They would call if they learned anything.

"So what's your name? You already know mine. You know where I live. Hell, you know my foster sister. Who are you?" He asked.

"I'm no one." She meant it. She felt like less than no one. A speck of dust spiraling in the air.

"I know I'm difficult to find. Usually only whores come around. Is that what you want?"

"No."

"Then why say those things, huh? Why say you're not a virgin?"

Ashley was curled up in the couch's corner. "Isn't that all that matters in life? At least to men, anyway. Your friend didn't even bother to ask me anything. But I figured you'd want to know. I don't know why."

HH knew what friend she was talking about, Jon that asshole. "How old are you really?" HH asked.

"I told you. I'm eighteen."

"You're lying. Again, How Old Are You?"

"I'm sixteen, okay?" That sounded better than fifteen. HH sat back and ran his hand through his hair, looking at her. "You need to leave. You shouldn't be here."

"What? Why?" He got up and walked over to her, taking her by the arm. "What are you doing? No, stop." She screamed and attempted to pull away from him.

"It was fucking stupid of me to bring you here. I doubt you're even sixteen. What the hell was I thinking?" HH looked at the ceiling. If anyone saw them, saw her, get into his truck he was fucked.

"I don't care. Just do whatever you want to me. Just don't throw me out. Please. I can't go home." Ashley fell on the floor and sobbed. She couldn't control herself. Her breathing came in chopped cries and gasps. HH couldn't let her die on his floor. Then he'd really be in it.

HH didn't even know her name. He crouched down on the floor beside her, "Take a breath, relax." He told the hysterical girl. He remembered Judith having attacks like this, where she couldn't stop crying, couldn't breathe. He gathered Ashley in his arms and rocked her back and forth like a child. Hell, she was a child.

"You're alright. Take a breath. Shh." Ashley felt his heavy arms pull her together when she thought she might crumble into dust on fall between the floorboards. She grieved for Nick and herself while he draped himself around her. "I'm here," he told her, repeating the same lines he used to with Judith. "I've got you."

Ashley clung to his arms and forced air into her lungs. Her tears soaked up by his cotton shirt. What was he doing? Why wouldn't he just strangle her and get it over with? They sat on the floor that way until the sun was down and the house was dark. A modest cast of light from the single lamp illuminated them, their long shadows smeared together across the floor.

She wondered how long he would hold her. It reminded her of Nick when he put his arm around her in the car when they were driving back. It seemed like ages ago, but was only a few months. She never thought she'd feel the weight of another's arms around her.

Her fingers wiggled free, crawled up HH's shirt, up his neck, to his face. Her hands were so thin and cold. HH just sat and let her touch him. He closed his eyes, remembering the last time, decades ago, he was with the only one he'd ever felt anything for. Ashley's lips scarcely touched him, came away, then returned. She was warm inside; he felt her. *Judith*. She was tender like his Judith.

But he knew it wasn't her. It was a girl. A sick, damaged girl. HH grabbed Ashley's arms below the shoulders and pulled her away from his body. She pushed forward, back to his mouth, but he held her tight in front of him. "No." He told her firmly.

She seemed to wilt in his grasp. "What then? Why am I here?" She asked desperately, needing for someone to tell her. He was all she had.

"I don't know, kid," He said.

"Ash, not kid." She told him her name. They looked, each searching for something in the other. A lost thing neither could ever offer.

"We need to call your parents." HH finally told her. Ashley leaned against him. He allowed this. It had been so long since he'd touched another person.

"I don't have any. I have Brenda, but she's killing me. I can't breathe around her." Ashley said into his shirt. She inhaled an organic musk that made her want to crawl beneath his clothes and immerse herself in it. "Let me stay. I can clean your house. You can do whatever you want to me. Everyone else does."

He sighed heavily. "What about your medication? I assume you're on something?"

"It's just poison meant to keep my blind to the fact that I don't really exist."

"Did they ever give you any of those little blue bastards?"

Ashley looked up at him, "Yeah, they didn't do much though. Now they mostly give me clozapine, well the liquid kind, Versacloz. It turns me into a fucking zombie."

"That's some serious shit." he said, knowing a few guys who had been given that when all else failed. It wasn't a light drug. "If they think you need that, you probably do. Do you have any with you?"

Ashley shook her head, "No, I don't need it. This is my last stop." It felt good to say it. "I thought..."

"What? That I was going to rape you with a pig head and strangle you to death?"

"I... I don't know what I thought. Maybe. I hoped. What's stopping you?"

HH chuckled at the girl's bleak outlook. "Maybe you're the first person I've come across in a while that makes me feel normal." Ashley tried to laugh, otherwise she was afraid of folding in on herself and never being able to claw her way back out.

HH held her small limp body, probably not over hundred pounds. He could crush her. Ashley longed for him to, like a spider under a shoe. But he didn't. They sat soundlessly, each wondering what to do with the other.

"I have to get off this floor." He finally said. The girl was still against him. He felt more like a piece of furniture than anything else. He grunted and attempted to stand. She clung to his neck in a sleepy haze. He was strong enough to carry her weight. He looked around, trying to decide what to do with her. If he was smart he'd leave her on the porch and lock the door. Turn off the lights. Pull the shades.

Her sleeves were pushed up. He looked at the layers of markings spanning her arms. A thick vertical line dominated them all. It was more pink than white, raised up off the skin. It was recent. The last month or two, he guessed. Tomorrow. Tomorrow she'd have to go. If the police found her here, he'd be in jail before the day was through. Most around here were familiar with some version of his history. But it was that, just history. He had a job, took his medication, and kept to himself. That didn't seem to matter much in a small town.

HH walked down the hall, careful not to bump the girl on the wall. He put her in bed and pulled up the crumbled blanket around her. She moaned and turned over, curling tighter around herself. With all the rumors and bullshit that seemed to circulate, she was the first one to see some truth. She may have had it backwards some, but she got something from his words. Maybe it took a sicker mind to recognize a sick mind.

If only he could keep her. How good would she feel against him? Kind and understanding. But she was fucking sixteen. There was no way. He put that idea completely out of his mind. It was wrong, even he could see that. He wasn't twenty anymore; she wasn't Judith. He leaned over her, watching her. What the fuck was he going to do?

The sound of tires pulling into his yard seemed to answer that for him. He stood up. The motion awakening Ashley. "What?" She propped herself up, surprised to find herself in his bed. Had he carried her here? Was he about to touch her?

"Quiet. Stay here." He told her. HH pulled the bedroom door shut behind him. Ashley didn't feel so tired anymore. She felt instantly tense. Had they somehow found her? No, she could not go back home. This was her last stop. She had planned it this way.

Ashley slid out of bed and crouched beside the door. She heard muffled talking. Men. "Yeah, she's here." Ashley heard HH say. *How could he?* Backing away from the door, she looked around for somewhere to hide. Saw a small bathroom through a side door and darted in, closing it behind her, turning the flimsy lock over.

The footsteps were moving through the house. Ashley opened his medicine cabinet. Her eye went directly to the old safety razor. With shaking hands, she unscrewed the bottom and removed the blade. She felt relief. *This was it.* The bedroom door opened. He said her name. But they were too late. Ashley shoved up her sleeves. She pulled the delicate silver rectangle down one arm, then the other. Then again, for good measure. The blood emerged, red and bright as ever.

The bathroom door rattled. "Come out of there, Ash. You need to go home."

"You're a fucking liar!" She screamed. "I trusted you. You were going to protect me."

More talk as several men asked what they should do? Break down the door? Was there a key? Did he have a screwdriver to remove the hinge? HH banged on the door, it rattled the walls. Ashley backed up until she hit the wall and slid down. The sweater he gave her soaking up the blood. Nothing had worked out the way it should have. He was supposed to love her, understand her like she did him. Now he was turning her over to the cops.

"Open the fucking door, Ash. You're not in trouble." HH pressed his shoulder against the door, once, twice, a third time, it gave away. HH and the two police officers looked down at the cowering little girl on the floor, crimson weeping from her arms.

She gasped, it was over. *Death take me now*. HH was the first to move; he scooped her up and took her out to the living room. He grabbed some gauze from the cabinet near the sink and wrapped it painfully tight around her arms. Ashley was lying on the couch under him, watching him try to save her. As if he cared. One policeman was calling for an ambulance. The other stood by, unsure what to do.

"Put your arms over your head like this," HH told her, guiding her hands back and resting them on the sofa. The blood was already soaking the bandages.

"I thought you'd love me." Ashley said. HH said something, but Ashley was far away now, and didn't hear it. She reflected on her last words, *love me*. At least she didn't die alone, she died where she was meant to, with *Him*. Even if he didn't understand her, she understood him. She guessed that was all that mattered. Maybe he'd feel a little less alone in the world, knowing she had existed briefly.

Fourteen

Ashley saw a familiar face when she opened her eyes. "You're dead?" She asked. Dr. Prendergast smiled, his teeth old and yellow, familiar. They used to frighten Ashley, the way the gum lines seemed to recede. It made his teeth look unnaturally long. Now it was comforting.

"You're alive?" He said, his humor as black as Ashley's. Ashley couldn't help but relax a little in his presence. She was mad at him for sending her away, but she liked his ghost. Or was she the ghost?

"Where am I? Why are you here?" She asked. She tried to sit up but found they buckled her thickly bandaged arms to the bed.

"Calm my dear, calm. They brought you up to the clinic. You were so close already. It was the nearest care facility. Did you miss us so much? You could have called, this seems a little dramatic, don't you think?" He joked, closing the file on his lap.

"Sorry, Pren. You know how teen girls love drama." Her head felt like it was floating several feet above her body. Even if she wanted to fight and run, her body wouldn't allow it. It kept her spirit held tightly within.

"Brenda is on her way."

Ashley nodded, "I figured." She felt the warm tears run down her cheeks, she couldn't stop them. She was so fucking sad. "I hate this." Dr. Prendergast set his hand over hers and gave her his grandfatherly look that said it would be alright. Ashley believed him. She inhaled deeply and tried to calm herself. But her heart ached. HH had turned her away. Nick was dead. Lucifer and friends vanished. Her own mother tried to kill her, and she couldn't even kill herself. She had never felt more trapped. She didn't know what was real anymore, what wasn't. Maybe Nick had never existed.

Brenda arrived by breakfast. She looked much older. She was still in her funeral dress and nice coat. But her makeup had worn off, her hair was wild around her face. She was determined not to throw herself on Ashley and hug her until Ashley begged her to stop. But that went out the window when she saw the white netting wrapped around the wounds. Thick yellow rubber buckles kept her arms at her sides.

"Ash," She whispered, pushing her motherly hysterics down into her guts. She heard that type of thing could manifest cancer, but she'd take that chance at the moment.

"Hey, Brenda, you found me." She said. She did still have one person. Why couldn't she be thankful for that?

Brend nodded and sat on the edge of the bed, grasping Ashley's hand. "I did." Brenda would always find her, no matter how dark. "Can I hug you?"

Ashley couldn't believe she asked. "Yeah." Brenda

covered her with a deep hug, kissed her on the cheek, muttered about how scared she was.

"I'm sorry." Ashley felt guilty. But Brenda told her to stop it.

"Don't apologize, it's over. You're okay. Thank God you're okay. That man did he...do anything else to you?"

"What? Who?"

Ashley looked at Brenda, confused. "That hog man."

"HH?"

"Whatever you want to call him. What did he do to you?"

"He didn't do anything. Brenda, what are you talking about? I did this, me, to myself. If anything, he saved me. The cops were just standing there, not doing shit. The last thing I remember was him wrapping up my arms, squeezing them to stop the bleeding."

"Honey? What about before that? What did he do before that? Something must have caused all this."

"Yeah, Brenda, it's called my life. He had nothing to do with this. I just wanted to meet him before I did it. But surprise, I failed again."

"So he didn't touch you?" Brenda asked, not sure if she should believe her or not. The cops had HH in a jail cell until they could talk to Ashley. All she had to do was say the word and he wouldn't be returning to his little house of perversion.

"No, never. It was nothing like. I hid when the police came. He tried to give me to them. I freaked out and found the razor in his bathroom. I did this. The only thing he did wrong was not leaving me in that parking lot. He probably fucking hates me. They didn't arrest him, did they?"

Brenda looked away, "Brenda? Did they?"

"It was just a procedure. He had an underage runaway in his house. And with his history, which they tell me is rather colorful, it was a precaution."

"That's bullshit! Tell them." Brenda sat unmoving, "Brenda? Tell them." Ashley's voice was calm and assertive. Brenda felt if something happened, she'd be a lot more hysterical, confused about the situation. The doctors examined her when she came in, found no evidence of anything except the self-inflicted red ribbons on her arms.

"Alright, alright. Just calm down. I have the sheriff's card, I'll go use the phone at the nurse's station."

Ashley sat back, resting her throbbing arms against the straps. She felt so helpless. Trying to see the truth of what happened in a stoned haze was something she was getting better at. Just months earlier she wouldn't have remembered what happened, She probably would have thrown herself through a glass window. Her decision this time was calm and planned. Nothing insane about it. She made a rational choice to end her life, only HH prevented it.

That was not something she had planned on. In his writings he was so indifferent to life and death. She expected him to stand by and watch, maybe rape her corpse and bury her out back when he was done with her. Did she really think he'd cut her open, and she'd emerge pure and reborn in his arms?

Ashley shook her head. She was fucking insane. She hoped they kept her here for life. If they ever let her out, she would just try again. Eventually she'd succeed, right? When her head was clear, it just made it that much easier for her to justify her decision. She'd never have any kind of proper life. She'd always need someone looking over her shoulder, silently directing her through any obstacle that might come up. What kind of life was that? No, she was better off bolted to this bed or rotting in the ground. There were no other choices.

Ashley sat on a bench in the clinic's small Zen garden. She'd been at the Oaks Clinic for almost three weeks. It was quiet here. A nurse Benedict told her Wheeler was taken to a secure unit after he assaulted a young nurse. He wouldn't be back. When they finally unbound her from the bed and let her put her sweatpants and t-shirt back on, she felt almost good. Human.

Brenda brushed her hair. "Did they keep the shirt?" Ashley asked, remembering it was HH's sweater. The only remnant she had that he had touched her. That he knew she existed. She had bloodied the sleeves. Her blood on his garment, that was as close as they'd ever come to being one.

"They cut it off you. Threw it away. Ashley, you don't want that." Ashley did want that. But agreed with Brenda.

"I want to stay here, Brenda. I don't want to go back to the city." Ashley had already discussed it with Dr. Prendergast. She had the option to be moved to a clinic for children, but she liked it here. She didn't like kids her age.

"Prendergast said as much. Is that what you really want? If that's your decision I'll pack up the house. Maybe I can still rent that little cottage we had before. We can move back there, you can come here during the day. Just like before."

"Brenda, you have a job and Timothy. An actual life. I don't need you caring for me. That's what you're paying these people to do."

"Ash, I'm your mother. Of course I'm moving back. Timothy will just have to understand."

"But he won't. It's always the boyfriend or the child."

"As if there was a choice. If that's how he feels then I don't need him. I'm not living so far away from you. That's my decision." Brenda said. She hugged the girl, Ashley put her head on her shoulder.

"I can respect that, Brenda." Brenda had something else she wanted to talk to Ashley about, but thought maybe she'd wait until they sorted the details out. She didn't want to get her hopes up. Even though Brenda was still on the fence about the idea, Dr. Prendergast thought it might be a good thing for Ashley.

Someday Ashley would need more than Brenda and medical staff as companions. Someone who could not only be a friend to her, but empathize with her.

Every Saturday without fail, HH drove the hour up to The Oaks Clinic. It was a nice place, set back in the forest against the county's nature preserve. He liked large windows, the greenery. They didn't even lock the doors during the day. It felt more like a spa than any hospital he'd ever been in. No razor wire or guard towers.

The nurse at the front desk greeted him and gave him a visitor's badge. "She's in the garden." she chirped and went back to her paperwork. Not giving him a second glance. The staff all knew him by now. He was hard to forget.

HH sat down onto the bench beside Ashley. She closed her sketchbook. "Happy birthday, kid." He said and handed her a brown bag. He liked to see the joy on her face whenever she opened the things he brought her.

"My birthday isn't for another week."

"Eighteen is big." Ashley unfolded the top of the bag and brought out a thin, vibrant white paperback. Hog Head's VI. He made a note to her inside.

She held it to her chest, "Thank you. Man, it's perfect. It really came out well, didn't it?" Her voice was so soft these days, as if she were hardly tethered to her body anymore. HH put his arm around her like a father. She leaned into his side. She was so small she fit perfectly. "I like that you put my sketches in it this time. That's amazing." She said flipping through the pages.

Her work beside his. Years ago, she thought his bloody shirt was the closest she'd come to him. Now they had merged as one in ink and paper for all times. Both sat unmoving on the bench, listening to the late summer insects singing in the trees.

About

Elizabeth Bedlam lives and writes from Michigan, USA

Also By

Hog Head

Judith drove two hours every week to see her foster brother at the state hospital. She had been doing this for the past five years. She was the only one who would. Their former foster mother couldn't even stand to look at him. She didn't get how Judith could.

Judith was his only family. She felt she had a responsibility to him. He was ill. Society was not kind to those suffering from mental illness. It wasn't like cancer, something you could scan, measure, and see. Something that could be cut out.

The institute sat back from the road behind a ten-foot chain-link fence decorated with razor wire. She had to have her ID checked before they allowed her to drive and park near B Unit. That was where they kept the functioning ones. HH referred to it as purgatory. They were treated with dignity, allowed to walk the grounds, visit the library, or play cards. Allowed in the art room or the shop room. It was better than being in Hell, which was C Unit, where he used to live when he first arrived. Heaven was the golden ticket- driving out the front door either in a passenger seat or a body bag. It was leaving. Period.

The staff inside the door checked out the paper sack Judith had brought her foster brother. The nurse recognized her and made small talk about how creative HH was. The nurse was new, had only been there a few months. Judith knew all the staff. She was one of the few frequent visitors. HH's doctors often told her how lucky HH was to have such a supportive sister.

Most patients didn't have anyone come to see them, let alone every week rain or shine. If Judith knew a snowstorm was coming, she'd arrive a day early to make sure she saw her foster brother. She couldn't stand the idea of him thinking she had abandoned him after everything.

The nurse rifled through Judith's paper bag. Judith brought HH the normal things he always asked for. Now that he had more freedom he could have soft graphite pencils and charcoal to draw and write with. Judith made him tapes of nature sounds to listen to. They weren't allowed to listen to anything aggressive or loud that might upset the other patients. HH only liked suicide metal, which naturally wasn't allowed. So instead of listening to "shit", as he called it, Judith made recordings of forest sounds, swamp sounds, rain, and wind. HH always liked the stretch of forest near their foster parent's farm. "Thanks, Judith." He told her when she brought him the first tapes a month after he'd arrived.

When Judith was let past the second entry point an orderly informed her HH was in the garden. The patients were getting upset because local wildlife kept eating their vegetables. They weren't allowed poisons or traps to stop them. So HH suggested a bag of blood meal to help keep the creatures at bay.

Judith watched him gently scooping the blood flakes out of the round plastic container and laying it around the rows of lettuce. She was glad he was here instead of in the ground, which is where he thought he belonged. When she saw him take a handful of blood meal and eat it, she walked towards him. Scolded him and told him to knock it off.

He licked his hand clean. "That's disgusting. You're going to get some sort of disease." HH shrugged. At least his death would be interesting. Death by blood meal. Sounded better than death by boredom. Judith pulled his hand away from his face. He wiped it on the front of his depressing gray uniform all the patients in his unit had to wear.

"Is it Thursday?" He asked. There was no point in him keeping track of days anymore. Time meant nothing here. The staff told him when to eat, when to line up and take pills, when to sleep. It didn't matter to him. It was one less thing he had to think about.

"Did you bring me my stuff?" He asked, gesturing for her to talk with him. They sat on a bench near the edge of the vegetable plot. Judith had the brown paper bag on her lap.

She handed him the sack. He casually looked through it. "New tapes?" He asked.

"We had a big storm Sunday. The wind was loud. I think you'll like it." She said. HH knew he would. The walls of the institution were so thick he could never hear nature outside, even if it rapped at his barred window full force. There was too much talk and white noise inside. He could hear nothing but people, buzzing like a hive day and night. "Your book sold out. The guy wants to make a second printing. I told him I'd ask you."

She had helped him print a hundred-page book filled with poetry, short essays, and charcoal drawings from the last five years. Anyone that followed his previous work was ecstatic. No one had heard anything from him since he was put away. The rest of the band was dead or in prison for one reason or another. No one even knew his actual name, so they just assumed he was probably dead too. But instead, he was here. Rumors were already circling that he had written the book from inside a mental institution for the criminally insane. How anyone found out, Judith wasn't sure.

No one knew how the book was printed and released if he was locked in the nuthouse. "He can't be that crazy if he's making books." Judith heard a guy comment in the bookstore. Judith was just a silent partner in all this. She secretly hoped someday HH would get out. Maybe he'd have a little money to live quietly off in a cabin somewhere. "Dr. Haltz said he might give me a small synthesizer," HH told her.

"I'm sure you'd like that." Judith wasn't sure she wanted her brother to make music of any kind anymore. She remembered him from before- lank brown hair to his waist, littered with signs of self-abuse. That stupid band, with its recordings, was one of the many of the reasons he was in here. That shit did nothing but fuel his sickness, push him farther towards the edge.

Judith felt her jaw tense when HH put a hand on her shoulder. HH glimpsed the ragged scar encircling her neck. She tried to keep it covered with scarves or high collars, but once in a while, it showed itself. HH felt his sister go ridged beside him. "Don't be like that. I'm doing better. I've been taking all the chemicals they've been giving me. Even when I don't want to, I do it. I do it because I know you would want me to."

"Good. That's good, HH." Judith felt if he was really doing better, he wouldn't make her call him that anymore. He had changed his name when he was twelve, shortly before he arrived at the foster home. He wouldn't let anyone call him anything else. He claimed it was the name of his true self. She was grateful he let her refer to him as HH instead of what it stood for, Hog Head.

"That's a fucking horrible name." She told him once when they were sixteen.

"Is it?" He said. She didn't press the subject further. She didn't know where the name came from. No one did except the social workers and the foster parents. They wouldn't talk about it, but let him call himself Hog Head.

"You released the book under Hog Head, right?" He double-checked with her several times, not wanting any other name on the book. She assured him she did just as he asked. This seemed to please him. He didn't want anyone to know who he was, where he was. All the staff knew him as HH. Anyone that knew his sister knew she had a foster brother called HH. No one knew Hog Head except for his foster family and in the local underground scene. He wanted to keep it that way. A faceless manifestation of his malady.

A bell rang overhead from the corner of the building. "Lunch," HH told her. That meant she had to go. "Can I hug you?" He asked knowing she hated him touching her, but was too nice to say no. He couldn't blame her, he was a disgusting human being. Back then and now, he was just foul.

"Of course," Judith said, not hesitating because he would have caught it. That pause. They stood up and he walked her to the front gate, the paper bag under one arm. At the exit, he set the bag down and gently hugged her with both arms. She was stiff in his embrace.

"Goodbye, sister." He was soft-spoken these days. His voice was less biting and harsh than when they were younger. She couldn't believe this was the same man. Institutional living softened him. The food and medication they fed him gave HH a moon face that hid the sharp points of his previous gaunt profile. His hair had remained, though. Judith wanted him to cut it, but he refused. The staff threatened to shave off his waist-length hair if he didn't start to wash it at least once a week.

"I'll see you next week, okay?" She always tried to

speak gently to him, as their foster mother had. One thing she knew about was that his mother, his birth mother, was not a gentlewoman. She had never spoken softly to him as a boy. Judith wanted to make up for that, but knew truthfully she never could. He was almost out of his twenties. He was who he was. He was made. Judith still had a hard time accepting this.

Before lights out, HH sat at a small table that was bolted to the floor of his room. He put in the tape of the storm Judith had recorded for him. How he missed the feel of wind and rain on his face. They wouldn't let patients outside during storms. He unfolded the paper inside the plastic case, Judith used to write him notes about how proud she was of him. How she missed him.

He felt the dry paper between his fingers, the crinkle sound as he unfolded it. She hadn't written him notes lately. He once asked her for a picture, but she had never enclosed one. "It's not a good idea." She told him. He knew it wasn't either, but still, he longed for one of her.

In bed, he stretched out and closed his eyes, remembering the feel of Judith underneath him. The first time he tried to fuck her, he couldn't. He wasn't a virgin, but she was. When she finally agreed to let him between her legs, he couldn't arouse himself.

"Did I do something wrong?" Judith asked, curled up at the head of the bed in her bra and panties. She felt ashamed immediately. She had been molested before she had come to the foster home. She had worked years to try to overcome it as best she could, to allow herself to be touched. She wanted HH to touch her. She trusted him. He claimed he was experienced. Yet now he couldn't or wouldn't fuck her.

"I don't know what's wrong." He laid down and brought her beside him. He touched her chest, moved his fingers into her panties. She was already so wet. HH wanted in his head to fuck her, but his body wouldn't cooperate. They felt each other up for almost an hour, but HH didn't defile her that night. He wouldn't have her until a few months later. And then over the course of two years, many times. Each time with increasing violence.

"Put it on." He told her the next time they were together. Judith didn't want to at first. "It's okay, just think of it as a mask." He told her. Judith was laid out across a bed of moldy straw in an old barn at the back of the property. HH had taken her clothes off.

"I'm cold." She told him, feeling the chilly spring wind on her pale bare legs.

"I'll warm you. Just let me..." He held up the severed hog head the band had used for a series of photos days before. "I thought you wanted this." He said as he stood over her. Judith had her arms crossed in front of her, covering her exposed breasts.

"HH I do... it's just I don't know about that." She nodded towards the head in his hands.

"I promise you'll like it," he told her. He got down on his knees and took one of her hands, pulling her to sit up. "Just like this." He smiled as he slipped the large ripe head over Judith's face. He gently pushed her back down into the mound of dirty straw. "There, now. Just lay there. Just like that." HH looked at the young naked girl, her face replaced with the grotesque shell of a pink swine. He could feel himself getting hard, pressing uncomfortably against his black jeans.

Judith whimpered when he finally stuck his fingers into her cunt and made her wet. When he touched her clit, she flinched. "Relax. Just enjoy it." His words were low and soothing. After he urged his cock into her, he did her slow and steady. He cupped her tits, stared down into the face of the pig that looked blankly up at him.

If Judith orgasmed he didn't know it. She was so quiet, only small sighs and gasps as he pushed in and out of her. He couldn't believe how snug she was. He had never fucked a girl before. His father had shown him... other things to do when a girl wasn't around. He wasn't supposed to talk about it. Judith felt better than any of those things.

He finished inside her. Left the wet juices seeping down her leg and onto the straw as he pulled out and rested. He put an arm over her. Breathing hard, he murmured things into her ear. Judith was still. "Judith?" He asked after a few minutes.

"Can I take it off now?" Her voice was far away. HH had all but forgotten she wore that pig face. He wished she would keep it on, but helped her pull it off. It left pink runs of blood in her fair hair.

"How do you feel?" He asked. Judith felt around pulling on her sad faded panties, her discolored yellow-white bra. She always thought her first time would be different. Not something out of a movie special, but just not this. Not like this.

"Fine. I'm fine." It worried her that her face would shatter if she forced a smile. HH was so euphoric he didn't even notice that she couldn't look at him. He sat up and stopped her from pulling on her jeans.

"Can I just kiss you?" He asked. He pushed her matted hair off her face. That was the only part Judith liked. She reveled in those moments when being with HH felt normal. When he was HH, not Hog Head. When sex didn't make her feel filthy. HH knew none of this. He didn't think too much about it. All that registered in his mind was that he liked it. He wanted to do it again. He wanted to do it with Judith.

The couple dressed and left the barn. They'd try several times to fuck without a pig head. But HH always ended up making her put it on. "I just fucking like it!" He screamed at her one time while she cried about *why? Why did she have to wear it!?*

"Fucking cunt." He walked out and slammed the bedroom door. But that was later when HH started hearing the voices. When his temper would roll in like a heavy crimson heat that he just didn't know what to do with. It made him feel like he was burning from the inside out. Like he was evolving into something else, more an animal than man. Nothing helped but blood and violence....

Made in the USA
Monee, IL
19 March 2021